THE LEGEND OF ILIA

BOOK ONE:
BEGINNINGS

The Legend of Ilia

BOOK ONE:
BEGINNINGS

Nicole Ashley Brown Segda

ELM HILL

**A Division of
HarperCollins Christian Publishing**

www.elmhillbooks.com

Book One: Beginnings
The Legend of Ilia

Published in Nashville, Tennessee, by Elm Hill, an imprint of Thomas Nelson. Elm Hill and Thomas Nelson are registered trademarks of HarperCollins Christian Publishing, Inc.

Elm Hill titles may be purchased in bulk for educational, business, fund-raising, or sales promotional use. For information, please e-mail SpecialMarkets@ ThomasNelson.com.

Library of Congress Cataloging-in-Publication Data

Library of Congress Control Number: 2018934475

ISBN 978-1-595545954 (Paperback)
ISBN 978-1-595547361 (Hardbound)
ISBN 978-1-595543066 (eBook)

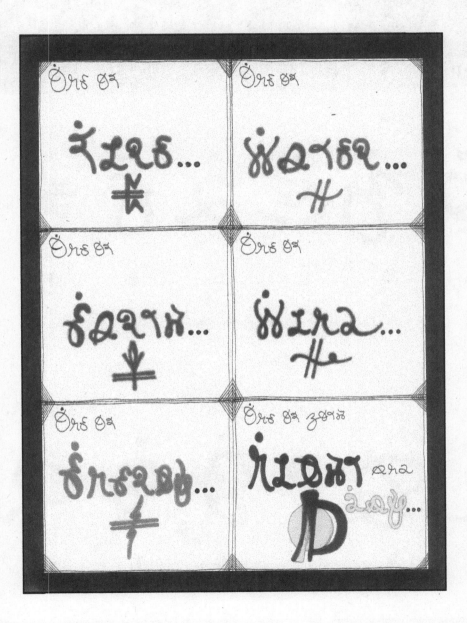

A B C D E F

N O P Q R S

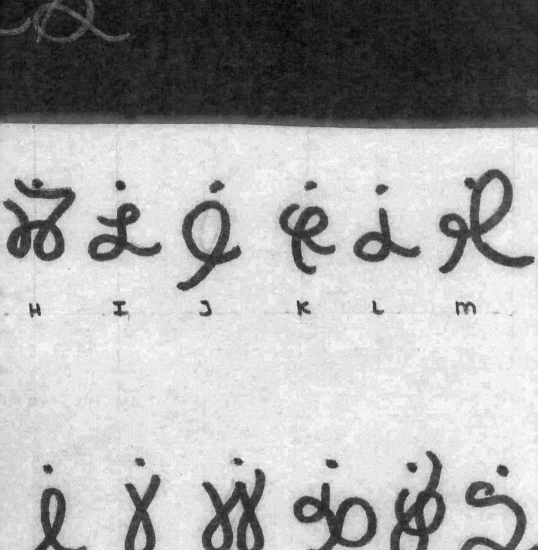

H   I   J   K   L   M

u   v   w   x   y   z

AENETIAN SEAS
Brecia castle
Aría
GAELITH
MOCCA SEAS
NESTHRA ISLANDS
CERULEAN SEAS
CAPE TERNIA
SENTRA
CYRIAN SEAS
Onyx Bay
Irsa

WATERS OF SHIVA

AENETIAN
SEAS

Aruria

ENTUS   •Lyssna

Mt.Voem

Tomb of
the Ancient
Kings

Ruby
Castle

BAY OF
CYLLUS

•Phyrre

Phoenix
Bay

Charyb
Bay

IGO
EAS

JEWEL

LARSONNE
SEAS

AENETIAN
SEAS

N
W   E
S

LAKE
FOREST
MOUNTAIN
WATERFALL
CASTLE
VOLCANO
CAVE

For my beautiful daughter Eleyna.
May you always let your light shine.
~Matthew 5:16~

TABLE OF CONTENTS

A centuries-old war finally ceased
But danger lurks in a mysterious region
Safeguarded from the threat are six
And they shall inherit the powers that be...

CHAPTER ONE

Chaos. Overturned carts. Guards shouting. Rush past raging confla-grations. Once quiet homes, now ashen memories. The billowing smoke suffocating those who dare save their livelihood. Ravenous rain extinguishing the fires, only to commence inundation. Cross the turgid river. Lifeless bodies floating. The lightning cracks, barely audible over the cries. Women wailing. Children screaming. Babies crying. Men dying. Agony. Run. Run across the blood-soaked earth. The earth trembling with the stampede of men. Battle the fierce wind. Her mighty gale encumbering those who flee. Fear arises in the dead of night. No one sleeps. Everyone runs. Faster.

"They must be spared."

A staircase...a boat...almost free. Some iniquity not too far behind.

A shadow appears at the top of the steps. An evil glare. A voice that pierces the dark like a thousand screams, "Seize them! They are getting away!"

A hurried admonition, "Don't separate." A kiss, and a song. Goodbye...

• •

Breathing restlessly and clinging to the side of the bed, Chase whispers, "A...a dream? Uncle Ashe, are you sure it was only a dream...'cause

1

it seemed awful real to me. There was fire, and it was storming, raining, thundering, and there was lightning too! It was really scary."

Ashe comes to the edge of the little wooden bed and sits down, "Now don't pout, Chase. Look around you. You're safe here in Uncle Ashe's house. Now give me a hug and get back to bed. Okay?"

Chase sighs, "Okay, Uncle Ashe. Love ya'. Oh! When will Auntie Lawa and Kae be home?"

"They'll be back from the market in Verdana tomorrow. Now, get some rest. Tomorrow is a big day."

Chase yawns. "Sure is. I turn five and I get to go to the fowist with Uncle Cole." He gestures with his arms, "Maybe we'll see a big, giant monster and get to fight it!"

Ashe laughs and rustles Chase's thick, black hair as he gives him a kiss on the forehead. He smiles warmly as he leaves the room. "Goodnight."

"Goodnight. Don't let the boop-boops bite."

Ashe's smile dissipates as he enters the hallway. His green eyes are overcast with remembrance of the grief that brought them here. When his parents died, Ashe was left to take care of the five orphans whom his family had rescued two years ago, not to mention his now three-year-old sister, Jessica. Cole is the same age as Ashe, twelve. Being the oldest, he and Cole have received the honorary title of uncle. Lara is the eldest girl at eleven years of age. Kaela is Lara's five-year-old sister. Joel is the youngest. He just turned three and is the brother of Chase and Cole.

Taking care of the kids was a major responsibility, especially being that Cole and Ashe are still kids themselves. The cottage they are living in has been in the Sylvan family for generations, and is sufficient for their needs. One long, broad, wood-floored hallway extending from a somewhat wider entrance foyer provides access to all of the rooms. The kitchen is through the first arch on the right and is large enough for all of them to congregate, which is more than can be said for the living room, however. The small living area that lies on the left of the corridor is cozy for four people but quickly becomes crowded with seven. The four midsize bedrooms are located in the back of the house and are shared amongst the children. Each bedroom is simply furnished with two beds, a dresser, and a shelf stacked with an assortment of books. A bathroom housing a washbasin, shower, and lavatory is in a little annex connected to the room for which it was built. Chase and Joel occupy one bedroom, Kae and Jessica inhabit another, Ashe and Cole split one, and Lara shares one with Maria. Maria is Ashe's and Jessica's twenty-five-year-old aunt who, thankfully, chose to raise the children as if they were her own. Taking care of the children became her priority and she was always concerned with giving them a proper education. Whenever she went into town, she would come back with books of various topics. In the morning, she taught them of the world and introduced them to areas of study like science, history, and language arts. Afternoons were often spent in the kitchen, drifting off into worlds of fantasy and adventure as Maria leafed through the pages of the cherished manuscripts.

Each child, however, showed a unique preference. Ashe would always listen intently when Maria talked about herbal lore, forestry, art, and architecture. He was hardly ever indoors. He could spend all day with the horses, either in the stables alongside the cottage, or out riding over the hills and valleys that mark the land. He would also make frequent excursions to the forest to find the plants discussed earlier in the day, bringing home his finds to share with the rest of the children. Lara became an avid reader of romance novels, sometimes blushing in the corner and often sighing to herself. At various times throughout the day she could be heard singing, lifting her voice in exultation. Kae would often accompany her, their voices harmonizing with each other in a song surely composed by angels. Joel would steal away to his room lugging a very old physics book, only coming out to impart the knowledge he had recently learned. Jessica was enraptured by the ancient mythos of Ilia, often daydreaming of living in such a time of mystery and adventure. And Chase, well, he liked everything. He could see the adventure that presented itself in each little bit of lore. He was eager to learn as much about the world as possible, sometimes forgetting the time and being reprimanded for it. Kae shared his interest as well, but more often found respite in stories of the sea and the mystical beasts of which the ocean is their domain. Cole was the exception. He would lurk in the shadows, watching. It was not that he did not enjoy the stories; he just didn't see the point. Getting lost in such idle fantasies was not going to change the harsh reality of their situation.

Despite Maria's presence, Lara has become the mother figure. Lara is the one who heals injuries with a simple kiss, and the one who always seems to know when something is wrong. She is the one who gently sings the children to sleep with her soft lullaby. Whether her words are spoken or sung, they ring with understanding and a tranquility that can calm the most violent of storms. And Ashe is the surrogate father. He is the mountain that provides strength and security. His advice is sound and certain, like the hum of the hearty Ash Tree when gently rapped upon. He provides shelter from the storm while it rages, awaiting the sweet song that will subdue it.

But even the mightiest mountains crumble. How can one stand against that which remains ambiguous? It puzzles him how so many great blessings could be borne from such a devastating night. What worries Ashe more than anything is that Chase has dreamt of this night. He has never had nightmares of such caliber before. But then again, it isn't exactly a nightmare. It is all real. Too real. He wishes he hadn't been old enough to remember what had happened. Never again does he want to experience that fateful night. He was hoping he could protect the others from that memory, but it's not like he could just take an eraser and remove that part of their childhood. The past is something they will have to live with for the rest of their lives. And no matter how far or how long they run, it will eventually catch up with them. Ashe heavily sighs as he plods down the dimly lit corridor to his room.

CHAPTER TWO

Kae bounds into Chase's bedroom, bringing the sunshine with her. Her lustrous brown hair flies behind her and her lilac eyes capture the few streaks of sunlight that pervade the room. She leaps onto Chase's bed and plants a kiss on his cheek. Quickly she runs away, giggling. "Get up, sleepy head. You have to go to the fowist with Uncle Cole, and when you come back there's gonna be a big party! I can't wait till you see what I gawt you for your burfday!"

Chase squints at her. He hates it when she kisses him. She is so annoying. She is like a little puppy, always on his heels and yapping away trying to get his attention. He doesn't know how she does it, but she always manages to spoil his fun. He yells after her, "It's my burfday today, so don't ruin it!"

Lara walks in. "Now, be nice. Just because it's your birthday doesn't mean you can be rude." She sits on the bed and opens her arms, "Come here. I want you to be careful in the forest today, okay? Stay with Uncle Cole."

"You don't hafta worry about me, Auntie Lawa. I'm a big boy now." Chase pouts, "But I still don't see why I have to be nice to her."

Lara laughs. "Because you have to be nice to everybody, and because I told you to. Now, get dressed. You don't want to be late."

Chase jumps out of bed and closes the door after Lara leaves. He quickly changes into his blazing red pants and matching shirt. He inspects his talisman, making sure that Kae hadn't somehow damaged his only memento of his parents. Satisfied with its condition, he places the silver charm in his pocket and pulls on his black boots. He sighs as he stares at himself in the mirror. Tousled black hair. Blue eyes. Copper-toned skin. A smile steals across his face as he ponders upon the significance of this day. He is officially five. He then bolts to the kitchen, where Ashe and Cole always are at seven o'clock in the morning.

The wooden shutters are open, allowing Ashe just enough light to read the morning paper. They are the only two in the room so the girls must still be getting ready. Joel is probably still sleeping, warm and cozy beneath his wool blankets. The mouthwatering smell of bacon and the subtler one of smoke from the now extinguished coals in the kitchen hearth is evidence that Maria is up but has already started with the daily chores.

Chase shouts as he passes beneath the arch leading to the kitchen, "Uncle Ashe! Uncle Cole!"

Cole rises from his chair, "Good morning, little lion. You all ready to go?"

Chase grabs some bacon from the plate on the counter and scarfs it down, "You betcha!" Chase grabs Cole's hand and drags him out of the kitchen and to the front door. He screams behind him, "Thanks for the bacon, Mawia. See ya later! Tell everybody I said bye!"

Chase and Cole are outside. The first rays of the sun are just beginning to peek through the forest. This continent—Ashe calls it Smithee—is covered with trees. Chase knows very little about the forest besides what he has read in books, because he was never able to explore it. He was confined to the fields and rivers that separate this little patch of land from the world around it. Ilia. Now, today, he can finally step past the tree line without fear of reprimand. He looks at this trek into the forest as his passage into a new stage of life. The age of five is certainly old enough to be a man. Well, at least a big boy. That brat Kae can no longer push him around and he will not fear whatever danger lies in the woods beyond. At least, he will not show that trepidation. The knowledge that Cole, Ashe, and Lara fear the forest enough to prohibit his entrance makes him uneasy. What lurks in the forest that makes them so worried?

They walk down the hill, the mystical forest coming closer with each step. The trees tower above them like giants, guardians to whatever rests inside. Their smoldering masses grow ever taller as they close the distance. The sound of the wet grass bending beneath their feet betrays their otherwise silent approach, alerting the ominous evergreen sentinels to their presence. One more step and Chase will travel into unknown territory, leaving behind the little cottage that, up until now, has been his entire world. He tightens his grasp on Cole's hand and takes a deep breath.

Cole looks down at his little brother. "Remember, I'll be with you always. Brothers forever...."

"We will always be brudders."

"Stay on the path that Ashe has marked out for us and we'll be fine. Did you remember to bring your talisman? Good. If you happen to stray from the path, this talisman will protect you."

Chase feels for his charm in his pocket and smiles when he finds it. "I can do this 'cause I'm a big boy now." He trudges off into the forest, Cole trailing behind.

The forest is a new world to Chase. His fears dissolve into deep veneration as the alluring ambiance of the woodlands invades his senses and renders him speechless. The dazzling sunlight filtering in through the canopy dances across the leaf-strewn path. Trees reach for the heavens and little animals scurry across the forest floor. Birds begin to chirp in the distance, their sweet song reverberating through the woods. Moss-covered trunks line the path, and dew hangs in the air like a curtain. All the forest seems to be alive and he can feel that life flowing through him.

Cole places his hand on Chase's shoulder. "Shhh. Look. What do you see?"

Chase looks but he doesn't see anything. Ahead there are only trees, their branches swaying with the breeze. Yet the appendages seem to be moving of their own volition. He takes a closer look. He can make out a figure. The slender body of a female seems to be intertwined with the thick trunk of the oversized oak. The woman gingerly steps from her wooden base, unaware of the presence of the two boys. "A dryad?"

Chase's eyes widen. He takes a closer look at the other trees, and he can now see the dryad that protects each one. He refrains from running his hands along the bark of the trees. He recalls from his reading that dryads are very sensitive when it comes to humans, for who knows what their intentions might be.

They continue along the path. Each sight is new and refreshing. He takes pleasure in them as Cole moves on ahead of him. Ants hurry from behind rocks. Bees flit from flower to flower. Creepers hang from the canopy, twisting around tree trunks as if they too are alive with the spirit of the forest. Chase is lost in the splendor of his surroundings. He breathes in his environment, trying to capture as much of the forest as possible. His feet are barely able to keep up with the curiosity that continues to grow with each resplendent spectacle.

He looks ahead and Cole is nowhere to be found. The path has disappeared. Everywhere he turns, trees fill his view. Their menacing branches thriving with old, gnarled growth soar above him and block out the warm radiance of the sun. Shivers run down his spine as the overwhelming reality rages over him and all of a sudden the forest seems to be a dangerous place.

• •

Silence. The sound of the birds has faded. Everything is still and lifeless and the once glorious forest now seems adverse. The brush is thick and nettles sting his bare arms. Fear. Darkness drives away any hope of being found. Malignant roots spring from the ground, tripping him as he wanders aimlessly through the dense woodland. Snakes hiss and slither around his feet. The eerie collective scream of boop-boops is unmistakable in the distance. The original name of these merciless plant monsters was replaced and forgotten centuries ago with this far less formidable one. An earlier culture's obvious attempt to assuage the ferocity of such ravenous beasts by changing its name was to no avail.

Chase calls for rescue, but the echo of his voice is chilling. No one answers. No one. Alone. Frightened. Lost. Chase falls to his knees and weeps. He tries to wipe away his tears but it is useless. He wonders what Kae would think, him boasting about being a big boy only to cry when he gets a little lost. No. He would not let her have this victory. He reaches into his pocket and pulls out his charm. Standing up, he shouts, "I am not afraid. I am a big boy, so you can't hurt me!"

A rumbling noise comes from deep within the forest. It is low and primitive.

Chase takes an involuntary step back. Clutching his talisman ever tighter, he acknowledges the growl, "Hello? Cole?"

Another growl. Closer. Fiercer. A creature charges from the shadows. A mass of golden fur and jagged claws. Chase is frozen in terror. The monster rages ever closer, its bitter eyes transfixed on its prey. Chase watches the mighty lion as it leaps through the air. A power surges through Chase. A light surrounds the beast. Almost blinding. Chase turns away, waiting for those razorlike claws to tear through his willing flesh. A body slumps to the ground. The force of the fall shakes the forest, as if a giant has awakened. Chase waits. His heart frantically pounds within his heaving chest. Nothing happens. He slowly opens his eyes and faces his predator. The lion lies dead, the carcass nothing but blackened bones. The golden mane is no more. Smoke curls from the brittle remains. He looks around, for he has an uneasy feeling that he is being watched ... but he sees no one else there. Chase stares at his hands.

A familiar voice breaks through the darkness, "Chase! Where are you? Chase!"

Relief fills him at the welcome sound of Cole's voice. Chase rushes through the forest in the direction from which his brother's voice had come. His heart is beating rapidly. His young mind struggles to figure out what has happened. Before he has much time to ponder the recent events, his feet carry him to a path. The untamed brush no longer holds him captive and the forest seems to welcome him again. Chase can see Cole up ahead.

"Cole! Here I am! Cole!"

Cole turns around and rushes towards his brother. The worry recedes from his ebony eyes and is instantly replaced with relief. Cole hugs Chase and warns him to never go off by himself again.

"I was so worried. What happened to you? Are you okay? You feel a little warm. I'm glad you're okay. Don't do that again, you hear?"

Chase just stands there looking up at his brother. He doesn't know what to say. How can he answer the questions when he doesn't have the answers himself? Whatever happened back there he will never forget, but it is something that he will probably never understand. He just wants to go home.

"I've had enough of the fowist for today, Cole. Can we go home now?"

"Of course."

They follow the path to the edge of the forest and head home. It is late in the afternoon and the sun shines in all its glory when they step into the familiar clearing in view of the familiar house on top of the familiar hill. Chase is somewhat disheartened that his journey is over but he is glad to be home. How he longs to curl up in under the blankets of his bed and sleep, hoping that when he wakes up it will all just be one strange dream. He looks up into the sky. There is not a single cloud. It is the perfect day to celebrate a birthday, but Chase doesn't feel much like celebrating. There is a huge party, just like Kae had promised. There is cake and ice cream. Presents are piled on the table. Kae doesn't try to give Chase any more kisses, not that he had noticed. Her present is a silver chain for his charm. She had to spend all of her allowance in order to buy it. Kae watches excitedly as Chase opens up the little jewelry box. Chase stares at it for a minute and then puts it aside. He isn't in the mood for a party. He doesn't care that the girls had spent all week preparing for this day. He just wants to be alone, "Why can't you all leave me alone? I just want to be alone!" He darts to his room and slams the door.

The others sitting around the picnic table are silent, surprised by Chase's unexpected reaction. Kae stares at the little box. She takes it in her hands and dejectedly looks down. With trembling lips, she says quietly, "I'm sorry. I didn't mean to ruin Chase's burfday."

CHAPTER THREE

Kae kneels beside a lake. "So how's the water today, Twiggy? Crystal-clear as always?" Her eyes follow the little stream that quietly flows from the lake and past the familiar cottage. The river meanders off into the mysterious distance, flanked by the trees of the forbidden forest. The lazy waters amble around a bend and she can only imagine where the path may lead. She sighs, "I wish I were a fish so I could just swim away from this place."

Chase sneaks up behind her. "Who are you talking to?"

Kae turns in surprise. "Oh! You haven't met Twiggy?"

A baffled, somewhat worried, look crosses his face. "Who's Twiggy?"

Kae laughs as she averts her gaze back to the water. "He's a fish, silly!"

"You're thirteen and talking to a fish? I don't get you."

Kae turns around to look at him. "I don't get you either. You just disappear and don't come home until after dinner. Where do you go?"

Chase just glances at her and shrugs. "Bye. Have fun with your fish."

Kae watches Chase as he walks off and she conspiratorially whispers to Twiggy, "I'm gonna follow him."

• •

Jessica leans out the door of the cottage, "Hey, Joel! Mrs. Maria told me to tell ya' that she is making soup for lunch."

Joel bolts up, his short black hair mimicking his reaction. "The one with the red beans and tomatoes!"

Jessica laughs. "It's not lunchtime yet, Joel. We just had breakfast an hour ago. You're silly."

"Am not! You ... you have germs!"

"Nuh-unhh." She runs towards where Joel is and grabs his hand, "Come on, Joel. Let's try to find a datrymia!"

He looks confused. "What's a datrymia?"

Jessica releases his hand as she gesticulates, "Uncle Ashe told me all about them. They're a rare bird that lives in the forest. Not even Uncle Ashe has seen one!"

"They live in the forest? We're not supposed to go in there alone."

Jessica's golden hair flashes in the sunlight as she turns and gestures for him to follow her. A wry grin matches the mischief dancing in her lavender eyes. "We're not alone. There's two of us, isn't there?"

Joel sits back down. "I don't know, Jessy. What if we get in trouble?"

She sighs, "Maybe Uncle Ashe will come with us. I'll go ask him. You just stay right here and wait for me." She runs back into the house, eager to start the day's adventure.

Joel watches as she enters the house. "One of these days she is going to get me in a lot of trouble."

• •

Ashe is in the kitchen reading the <u>Ilia World Herald</u>, as usual. Wisps of brown hair shadow his emerald green eyes. Lara is sitting across from Ashe perusing a romance novel. She closes the book and sighs, "How romantic. Do you think that love like that really exists?"

Ashe puts down his newspaper, "Like what?"

Lara smiles and leans closer to Ashe, "They never realized they were in love until he was taken prisoner by an evil sorceress. But they couldn't be together because she had no idea where he was held captive. She would have given her life to save him." Tears fall from her golden eyes as she struggles to conclude her story, "When she thought he had died she grew desperate and was ready to sacrifice herself to the raging sea, but then she heard his voice ... calling her. And they finally found each other and could live their lives together...."

Ashe bites his lip. "Interesting." He returns to his newspaper.

Lara stands up and throws the book at him, "How can you be so nonchalant?"

Jessica peeks in, "Uhh. Excuse me. Joel and I were ... wondering ... when the soup will be ... ready."

Maria walks in behind her, brushing an auburn strand of hair away from her caring brown eyes, "I haven't even started the fire for the oven yet, dear. Go on out and play. I promise I will call you when lunch is ready."

Jessica leaves. She smiles when she sees Joel still sitting where she had left him. "Perhaps we'll hunt for the datrymia another day. I have a better idea."

Joel stands up and crosses his arms. "As long as we don't get in trouble. Whatcha' wanna do?"

Jessica leans in towards Joel and smirks. "We're gonna get Uncle Ashe and Aunt Lara together."

Ashe smiles as he walks outside, his newspaper folded underneath his arm. He revels in the warmth of the sun and Lara is not too far behind him. She spies Joel and Jessica with their heads bent in conspiracy and she clears her throat. "And what might you two be up to?"

Jessica looks up in surprise but quickly regains her composure. "We were just talking about how beautiful Uncle Ashe's paintings are and we were about to ask him if he could paint another one."

Ashe proudly consents, "What would you like me to paint?"

Joel can barely control his enthusiasm when he jumps up to tell his idea, "Paint Aunt Lara!"

Jessica giggles when Joel nearly loses his balance due to the vehemence of his suggestion. Unable to resist the temptation, she gently nudges him and he falls to the ground. He glares up at her and pulls her down with him.

Ashe and Lara laugh at this spectacle, both making futile attempts to suppress their mirth. Amidst the laughter, they catch each other's glance. Lara averts her gaze as the mirthful sensation leaves her and is replaced by something newer. Something more powerful and much deeper than anything she has ever felt before.

Ashe clears his throat, "Shall I, Lara? May I paint your portrait?"

Lara shakes her head at the two children lying on the ground, still laughing and laughing harder as a knot forms in their stomachs. She lets out a breath. "Only if you keep it."

Ashe suspiciously stares at her. "Okay ... but I'll have to ask what *you* are up to."

Lara flips her hair as she turns. "I'm going to see if lunch is ready." She quickly runs into the house, not daring to look behind her.

Ashe crosses his arms as he watches Lara leave. Her brown tresses wave to him as if more of an invitation than a goodbye. A hint of a smile spreads across his face.

• •

Chase looks around. He doesn't see anyone so he quickly slips into the forest. Kae moves out from behind a rock and slowly proceeds towards the woods. She hesitates at the forest's edge but decides to continue trailing him. She has never been in the forest before. She had always been afraid of it. She could never forget that day eight years ago when Chase had gone to the forest for the first time. When he came back, he had somehow changed. He had always kept to himself, but after that day he became even more isolated. More distant. Perhaps something had happened while he was in the forest that she was unaware of, but the notion that she had in some way triggered this alteration unremittingly troubled her. Her thoughts settle into a faint whisper as the melodious tune of the forest begins ringing in her ears. The essence of the woodland is one of harmony. The serenity washes over Kae like a gentle wave.

A song fills the air, lifting her spirit and luring her deeper into the forest. The voice is sweet and pure. Her senses recede into the background, forgotten, as the harmonious string of notes becomes all that exists. The shifting world around her loses its substance as the sound materializes and solidifies. Trancelike she follows the music to the base of a mountain. She begins to climb, higher and higher. The melody amplifies and quickens as she ascends. Her heart races to match the deathly pace. She has to discover the source of the stunning voice. At the apex of the mountain rests a woman. A sheer gown cascades around her slender figure, accentuating her ample features. Rosy-red hair falls around her like a veil. Her bronze skin sparkles with the light of the sun. Her voice beckons Kae. Kae is completely enraptured by the celestial sound. Her hands reach for the creature. She feels as if she were flying. Floating on a soft cloud.

"Kae!" Chase's anxious voice awakens Kae from her trance.

Her body is tumbling toward the earth. She is falling, plummeting ever faster to her death. Her muscles tense in panic. Brilliant flashes of light dance in front of her dilated pupils. She closes her eyes and screams. The crisp air pierces her lungs, leaving her breathless. Her eyes are welded shut by her stinging tears. A forced shriek steals from her dry throat as the muscles in her stomach constrict with queasiness.

Arms close around her body. Her heart jumps. Her body uncontrollably shivers from the strain induced by her overpowering fear. A fear of falling. Forever falling into a black nothingness to never again see the light of day. Tears fill her eyes as the realization that she is still alive washes over her. She can see a blurred Chase gazing down at her, the sun shining brightly overhead.

A warm hand smooths the hair away from her face. Her spent body is protectively cradled in Chase's muscular arms. A gentle whisper, "Shhh. You're okay. I'm here... I'm here."

CHAPTER FOUR

Joel burst into the kitchen, "Look what the nice mailman brought us!" Ashe motions for the mail. Among the assortment of papers are two crisp white envelopes sealed with the stamp of melted green wax. Ashe recognizes it to be the seal of the Emerald Royal Guard. They are addressed to Cole and himself. He hands one to Cole and opens the other one.

Everyone crowds around. "What does it say?"

Cole skims through one of the letters and his face tightens. "We've been drafted. We're to help the Nesthra Islands in their fight for freedom from Sentra rule."

Everyone is quiet. They remain motionless but the tension in their bodies is evident. War. An unspoken word in the Sylvan household. Of course, everyone knew what it was. It was something that tore families apart and splintered mighty nations. It was why they were all here, in this house. It was why they never knew who their parents were. The reason why they never will know.

Now, the two people who had held this mismatched family together and who they look to for advice and guidance are leaving. With one letter their entire lives are thrown to the wind. Scattered and broken, more now than ever they yearned for the answer to a question that haunts them: Who am I?

Lara is unable to manage her composure as the implications of the letter take hold of her and leave her breathless. She faints and falls to the floor. Ashe instantly goes to her aid, catching her before her head hits the floor. He gently kisses her on her forehead and brings her unconscious body into the fold of his arms. Her eyes flutter open and she tightens her grasp on him.

"Ashe, don't leave me."

Ashe helps her to her feet and leads her outside. The morning air is crisp and the verdant plain is wet with dew. They come to rest at an outdoor table overlooking the forest. The lush meadow comes alive with the caressing touch of the light breeze. Lara closes her eyes and lets the wind carry away her uneasiness. A little rabbit passes by, it's button nose and gray ears twitching. Ashe watches quietly as it bounds off into the woods.

Lara takes a deep breath. "I wish you didn't have to go. I mean ... war ... people ... they die in wars. Do you remember the last war?"

Ashe looks down. "The Lion Wars. Yes. But I wish that I didn't. There was so much pain. It ripped this world in twain for so many centuries. Then one night it all ended. The kingdoms of Laentus and Jewel put aside their differences to fight for a common cause."

"Chase still has nightmares," Lara whispers as she frowns and furrows her brow.

Ashe looks up at her with concern. "Is he the only one?"

Lara sighs, "No, Jessica has the same dreams. I don't understand it. She wasn't there. And she's so young. It's too early...." She looks up at him in earnest. "Should we tell them ... before you leave?"

Ashe shakes his head. "Now is not the time. They must find out for themselves."

A contemplative silence. A figure looms in the background. His eyes are intent on Lara and what she will say next. Is she only worried for Ashe? Why not call *his* name? Cole....

Lara crosses her arms. "How long do we have?"

"I've estimated that it will take at least fifteen days to reach the military base, and that's taking the shortcut through the Southern Woods."

Ashe puts his head in his hands, "I have to catch the transport to the Nesthra Islands in a month."

Lara whispers, "A week. But that's not enough time. It's not fair. What if we never see each other again?"

Ashe stands up. "Don't say that. You're not going to lose me. I'll be with you always. Please don't make it any harder than it already is. I feel as if my life is being ripped from me!"

Lara rises. "Do you have any idea what this is doing to me? God help me, but I love you!"

Ashe whips around. "What did you say?"

Through tear-filled eyes she gazes at Ashe. "I love you, Ashe Sylvan."

Ashe falls to the ground as if the wind had been knocked out of him. He had no idea she felt this way. Those glances. The talks. He thought he had dreamt them. He thought so many things to be true except that which he wanted to hear ... to say. He knew she was waiting for a response, but what should he say? How should he say it? He tears at his hair. Hadn't he rehearsed this? Something about the moon and the stars....

Lara sits down beside him and holds his hand. "You don't have to say anything. Just stay close to me." She rests her head on his shoulders. Her delicate hand on his heaving chest.

Ashe strokes her hair. The smooth silky strands always send shivers through him. And her eyes. Oh! How he loves her eyes. He can get lost in them forever, losing all else save this one being that he cherishes the most. Her eyes shine with the brilliance of the stars to match the radiating warmth of her smile. And her melodic voice sweeps him away into a world of which dreams are made of. Their dreams. Their world. He brings her tear-stained face to his. A kiss. Sweet. Soft. Their lips have met before but never with such emotion. Such earnest. All their dreams focused on this one moment. In all his twenty-three years he had never felt more complete. More certain that no matter how long or how far he searched he would never find anyone as right for him as she was. Never had anything seemed more right. So perfect.

Ashe gazes into Lara's bright golden eyes. "I love you, too."

Chase rises from his seat at the kitchen table. His eyes reflect the resolution that he has formed in his mind. He gently grabs Kae's arm and pulls her from the kitchen into the hallway. He lowers his mouth to her ear and excitedly whispers, "I want to show you something."

He guides her from the house to a discreet little path. The path lies some ways from the cottage and beyond the lake that had been a sort of boundary for Kae. She has never ventured past the far side of the water save that one time she followed Chase into the woods three years ago. Her excitement builds as they follow the familiar stream of which Kae has traveled only in her mind. The trail matches the course of the river, deeper into the mystical forest. Kae freezes when she sees where it leads.

Chase releases her arm and looks back at her. "What's wrong?"

Her voice is low. "I can't go in there. What if... the Siren is still in there?"

Chase looks around impatiently and sighs, "I won't let anything harm you."

Kae searches his expression. "Promise."

Chase puts his hand on his heart, "I, Chase Blader, promise that no harm will come to Kaela Lee while she is under my protection. Happy?"

Kae blushes and hesitantly follows Chase into the woods. She has forgotten how beautiful it is. The atmosphere is exhilarating. She takes a deep breath. The smell of fresh pine fills her nostrils and her head swims with reminiscence. She restrains her enthusiasm, keeping in mind that the magic of the forest is potent and deadly. She is careful to not be lured in by the sheer beauty of it all.

The path continues across a bridge and on into dense foliage. Chase and Kae come to a halt midway across the bridge, reveling in the freshness of the air and innocence of the unscathed environment. The river roars wildly under them. The warm sun rises high above them. They are surrounded by a world of wonder. Regretfully, they proceed across the bridge. They reach solid ground and Chase furtively moves behind Kae.

He places his hands over her eyes. Warm hands. Her breath quickens. "Where are you taking me?"

He whispers in her ear, "It's a surprise."

Chills run through her body. She is intensely aware of the closeness of Chase's body and of the deep stirrings deep within herself. She can barely think. What is this she is feeling?

He slowly lifts his hands. "Don't peek." He takes her hands and leads her down a slope. The mossy rocks are slippery and she nearly loses her balance, but Chase steadies her with his strong grip. She can feel the muscles tense in his warm hands as he continues to safely guide her down the pebbly grade. Her breath quickens as that strange feeling once again surges through her. She can hear the river, almost at her feet. A mist engulfs her. She can feel the soft droplets of water come to rest on her skin. All her cares are washed away.

Chase's warm voice breaks through her reverie, renewing the strange sensations that she has been feeling whenever he is near. "Okay. Open your eyes."

A magnificent waterfall rises above her, stretching forever upward. A splash of color. A rush of spirit. Freedom. A carefree smile crosses her glowing face. She turns to Chase. Her eyes sparkle with tears of happiness. A wide smile appears across his face as he takes pleasure in her reaction. This place is his place, and he wants to share it with her. He had a feeling she would be attracted to the marvelous waterfall, but his attraction to Kae at this moment comes as a surprise to him. Her dancing eyes seem to reach inside him and touch some unfamiliar emotion. His hands become clammy as if she could melt him with her compelling smile. Chase lets out the breath he hasn't realized he has been holding. Her power over him somewhat dissipates as she turns away. Kae merrily laughs as she watches little fish try to swim up the cascading falls. Fighting a losing battle. War. Cole. Ashe. Her smile is quickly gone.

Chase rests on the rocks. "I come up here to escape. Just forget my worries. I was hoping it would do the same for you...."

Kae sits down beside him. "Thank you … it's just that something I saw brought me back to reality. It really is great here."

The desolate look on her face isn't what he is expecting to see. The consoling tone in her voice only irritates him. Chase stands up. "I can tell that you don't want to be here. Come on. We can get home by nightfall."

"Don't be like that. Really, let's stay a little longer."

"I hate it when you do that! Why can't you just do what you want to do instead of trying to appease everybody else?"

Kae gets up. "You're the one that brought me to your little secret hiding place! I never asked you to take me here!"

Chase rages. "Fine. See if I ever try to be nice to you again! I know you have a thing for water so I figured you'd enjoy this!"

"You shouldn't assume things then! Take me home."

"Now you want to go home? You know what? Find your own way home. I'm outta here." Chase walks off into the forest, leaving Kae alone on the rocks.

She screams after him, "The nerve! When I get my hands on you, Chase Blader…!"

• •

Joel and Jessica are reclining outside on the grass. The afternoon sun beats down on them, but they don't feel it. They don't feel anything. Empty.

"Jessica, what's going to happen to us?"

Jessica shrugs. "I don't know, Joel. I don't know. But whatever happens, it was fun while it lasted."

Joel sits up. "Yeah. I don't want them to go. Ashe said that there has been talk of a possible uprising in Nesthra. But according to the newspaper, it wasn't that serious. Why now? There have been problems in that region for decades. And of course, every government has its flaws. Why them? Why is Smithee being dragged into this civil war anyways?

Nesthra gained independence from this continent a long time ago." The frustration is evident in his voice.

"I just know that I want to make the most of the time we have left. Things are gonna change, Joel."

Joel looks up at her. "Let's go. I'm tired of waiting for permission. Datrymias live in the forest, right?" Joel walks on towards the woods. "What are you waiting for?"

Jessica blinks and then chases after him. "Are you sure?"

No answer. He treads steadily down the hill and charges into the forest. He has only one goal in mind: find that stupid bird. He no longer cares what *they* think. It's not like they're going to be around to notice anyways.

Jessica stumbles along behind him. "Slow down. What's up with you? Hello, Ilia to Joel."

He turns sharply. "What? Isn't this what you've been urging me to do for the past three years?"

"Yeah. But we've never been here before. We don't know where to go and you're obviously angry."

"Why should you care? Nobody else does! They're all leaving me! Pretty soon you'll all leave and I'll be alone. The youngest cast aside like a piece of garbage! I always get left out. Cole never took *me* to the forest! And I'm just supposed to *understand*? No! I'm not gonna be bullied anymore, especially by the likes of you!"

A tear rolls down Jessica's cheek, but her voice is steady. "Fine. If that's the way you feel … just know, Joel, that you were the one that pushed me away." She runs back towards home.

Joel screams. "See! I told you you'd all leave me, sooner or later…." He slumps to the ground and cries tears of anger.

A creature scurries across the path in front of him. Annoyed by its lively chattering, he takes his hand and brutally sweeps it away. The small animal flies through the air, its body landing in a clump of grass alongside the trail. Joel rises, instantly remorseful of his action. The creature hadn't done anything to him. He was too caught up in his own self-pity to consider the consequences of his actions. Stupid. How could he have been so stupid? No wonder why no one wants to be around him. He quickly runs towards the injured squirrel, its broken body motionless. He kneels solemnly beside the animal. A faint pounding reverberates through his head. He leans in closer and can sense the dwindling beat of the squirrel's heart. Joel carefully picks up the squirrel and nestles it in his arms. He closes his eyes and prays. Something stirs within him. He can feel the life of the little squirrel returning as he concentrates on his prayer, himself feeling somewhat drained.

When Joel opens his eyes, two black beady eyes are staring back up at him. He can almost read the thoughts of the little squirrel. Expressing its gratitude and understanding of the situation. Joel laughs at the thought that the little creature could possible fathom in its little mind what has just happened, much less why. The squirrel continues to stare up at him, as if expecting some sort of *You're welcome*.

Joel places the creature on the path in front of him and motions for it to scurry off. Instead of bounding into the woods, it stands on its back legs, its hands in front of it as if begging for something. Joel sits down cross-legged and puts his hand on his chin. He carefully observes the squirrel and sighs, "What are you waiting for? Go on now." The creature goes to all fours and slowly proceeds towards Joel. Joel nervously looks around and then back at the squirrel. "You want to come home with me?" The squirrel bounds into Joel's lap and scampers up and around his arm to his shoulder. Joel laughs despite his reservations. "I take that as a yes." He turns his head to look at the furry creature. "Well, if you're gonna be my pet, you have to have a name." Joel contemplates for a moment. The squirrel races around Joel's body, its little feet tickling him in the process. "You're an energetic little bugger, aren't you?" He smiles as an idea comes to him. "I think I'll call you Sparky." Sparky chatters wildly as if in agreement. Joel nods his head. "Sparky it is then."

Joel brushes off his clothes as he stands, Sparky sitting contently on his shoulder. He whistles merrily as he treads the path back towards home. He hasn't forgotten what brought him to the forest in the first place, but he has realized that wallowing in self-pity is not going to make things any better. And it's certainly not going to change things. He will no longer let circumstances affect his attitude. What's the use of complaining about things that cannot be changed?

• •

Kae scoots to the edge of the river, letting the cool current flow over her bare feet. The tranquility of the water quickly washes away her anger. Why do they always end up fighting?

Kae sighs, "Perhaps, Chase is right." Did she just say that? When was the last time she thought about what she wanted? Why couldn't she be more optimistic? "Why do I always have to ruin everything?"

Oh, cheer up, my dear. You musn't be too hard on yerself.

Kae jumps up. "Who's there?"

A spirited laugh. The sound seems to be of the river itself, flowing endlessly over the cobblestone. The mystical voice seems to echo through her mind.

Kae can sense the being. Close. Hidden. She surveys the forest. Nothing. She turns back towards the river as another laugh spills through her mind. She focuses her attention on the water. It flows casually around unseen barriers. In the mist, she can make out the rough outline of a creature. All she can surmise is that the being is tall and serpentine. Color begins to fill the void. A rich shade of deep blue reminds Kae of the deep recesses of the ocean. The comparison confuses her. She has never been past the forest, much less even seen the ocean. Her eyes catch the glint of the shimmering scales that outline the body. The sea monster soars above her. The fins that adorn the head act as a sort of crown. Majestic. It speaks telepathically: *It's been ages since I've encountered someone with your abilities. I knew there was something special about you when I first heard you talking to Twiggy.*

Kae is speechless. This had to be a figment of her imagination. "Am I going crazy?"

Another laugh: *No, my dear. You're unique. Yes! The spirit of the sea beckons to you.*

Kae slowly approaches the beast and reaches out. Her fingers glide across the smooth scales. "You're real?"

I better be. Centuries spent looking, waiting for you couldn't have been all for nothing.

Kae could hardly breathe. "Me? Centuries?"

The creature brings her head down to look squarely into Kae's lilac eyes: *Yep. You're the one.* The sea monster scrutinizes Kae's demeanor: *Oh, dear… you don't know, do you? Tsk. Tsk. Well, first things first. What will you call me?*

Kae looks puzzled.

Give me a name. You know, that thing you call someone when you want to get his or her attention. Hmmm. You're awfully quiet for someone who was just talking to herself a minute ago.

Kae raises her eyebrows. "How does Nikoi sound?"

Nikoi smiles, and then vanishes back into the mist. Kae is standing in the middle of the river, drenched in mist. She looks around her. The creature is gone.

She hears a rustle in the woods. A figure appears from behind some foliage. His hands are in his pockets and he shrugs as if he has a burden needed lifting. He walks down to the water's edge and rests on the bank. He rests his chin upon his hands and Kae notices the silver talisman dangling from his neck. It pleases Kae that he has finally worn the chain she had given him eleven years ago. Kae wades towards him. He watches her as she comes nearer. Time seems to pass slowly. Breathing is heavy. She finally reaches the boy and kneels beside him. No words. A mutual understanding. The war was taking its toll on everyone.

CHAPTER FIVE

"Joel, wake up."

Joel yawns. "Cole? What time is it? Are you leaving already?

Cole crouches on the floor. "Yes, but I wanted to talk to you. Jessica told me what happened... in the forest."

Joel sits up. "I didn't mean it, Cole, honestly!"

"Shhh. I should have taken you to the forest, but the truth is I was scared. I didn't want to risk losing you like I almost lost Chase.... Why didn't you tell me you were feeling this way? I will always be by your side. That's what brothers are for. We even have a tendency to be overprotective sometimes." He smiles and then sighs, "Joel, just because I'm going to war doesn't mean I'm leaving you. Besides, Chase will still be here. So will Jessica, Kae, Lara...."

Joel still looks worried. "But what if... you don't come back?"

Cole rises. "Come with me."

Joel follows him outside. The moon rises high in the night sky. Illuminating dreams. Ruling her kingdom with all her glories in silent submission.

Cole stands behind Joel, his hands on his younger brother's shoulders. "Look at the sky. It stretches all across Ilia. Each night, before you sleep, look at the sky and know that I will be looking at the same stars, the same moon. Wherever you go, I'll be with you."

26

Chase steps out of the little house and walks towards his brothers. "I had a feeling you two would be out here. Is everything all right?"

Joel turns to look at Chase and Cole. "Yeah. Brothers forever...."

In unison, "We'll always be brothers."

Chase sighs, "It seems that every night we would come out here, stand in this very same spot, and just look up at the stars. Envisioning the world through their eyes as they look down upon us. In some ways, it seems that they are guiding us but we being unable to follow. Now you and Ashe have this rare chance to walk the path they have long ago taken and marked for future travelers. Just promise me that you will find your way back home."

Cole turns to Chase and smiles. "I wouldn't have it any other way."

Chase nods. "Well, I guess it's time you are headed on your way. The others are waiting in the kitchen." At this announcement, they all silently head back towards the house. As they leave the outdoors, the brilliance of the stars fade. Clouds overcome the pristine night. The air is heavy and moist. A storm is brewing.

• •

Ashe and Lara are standing in the kitchen. Their fingers intertwined and heads bowed in silence. Jessica helps Maria prepare a snack for the boys' journey to supplement the food they will have to forage on their way through the Southern Woods to the military base. Kae dejectedly leans against the counter. No one makes a sound. So many thoughts running rampant through their heads but no words to express them.

Everyone looks up as Joel, Chase, and Cole walk somberly into the kitchen. Then they look back down. Joel and Cole take seats at the table. Chase remains standing in the doorway.

Cole is the first to speak. "So, this is it." Lara hugs Ashe and begins to cry. She opens her eyes and stares at Cole. Sorrow once again fills her eyes. She feels as if she is also losing a brother. He dares not look at her for fear of what she would see in his eyes. Perhaps, if he had come to her first, things would be different. She would be hugging him, not Ashe. He rises from his chair and walks outside. He's already said his goodbyes. Why prolong the pain?

Ashe gives Lara a final kiss and breaks the embrace. He grabs his duffel bag and slings it over his shoulder. He walks towards the front door, then turns. One by one Ashe looks at the children whom he spent his childhood raising. No regrets. He walks out the door and follows Cole into the vast new world.

• •

Lara retreats to her room and cries herself to sleep. After cleaning up the kitchen, Jessica and Maria retire as well. Joel lingers but eventually finds enough strength to stumble down the hallway to his room and crawl into bed. The past week has been an uphill battle. No one was prepared for their lives to be shattered like a piece of glass.

The storm clouds burst open. Lightning cracks in the distance. The rhythmic drumming of the heavy rain upon the house echoes the beating of their hearts.

Kae and Chase are still in the kitchen. Restless. Chase moves from the doorway towards the counter where Kae is sitting. "You should get some rest."

Kae looks up at him. "So should you."

Chase walks toward the window and watches as the rain pounds against the glass. "I'm leaving."

Kae's body tightens. "What do you mean?"

"I'm tired of this place. The forest." He turns around to look at Kae. "There's an entire world I have yet to explore. I want adventure. I want a life."

"But what about Joel?"

Chase strides towards her and grabs her arms. He pleads. "Kae. I want to know who I am. Do you seriously think I can find the answers to my questions here?" He pulls his necklace out of his shirt. "See this charm? My parents gave it to me. It's the only connection I have to my past."

Kae tries to hold back her passion. "You're going to give up your life here for some wild goose chase? You can't live in the past, Chase, otherwise you'll never experience your future. And why do you have to leave now? You have responsibilities here, Chase. People that love you…. How do you think Joel will feel if he wakes up in the morning and discovers that you're gone too?"

Chase walks towards the door. "Why can't you understand? I have to find the answers to my past before I can even consider my future."

Kae jumps off the counter. "Do you hear yourself? Do you know how unreasonable you sound?"

"I don't care how I sound! I know how I feel and I can't stay here any longer!" He runs out the door into the pouring rain.

Kae runs after him. "Chase! Don't make the biggest mistake of your life. Don't you think that I haven't thought about leaving too? But I don't because my place is here."

"Stop lying to yourself. If you weren't so afraid, you'd be leaving with me. Now go inside, I don't want you to catch a cold." He finds the path Ashe and Cole had taken just under an hour ago, heading north instead. His form dwindles as he walks away until, eventually, it disappears altogether.

Kae stands on the muddy ground as the rain pours down on her. Her shivering body is frozen with despair. She forlornly stares off into the darkness. Grief-stricken, she sinks to the ground and cries. "I'm not afraid…."

A dim yellow light casts its hollow luminescence on her as the door to the house opens. Joel is standing in the threshold. "Kae?"

Kae slowly gets up. "Go back to bed, Joel."

"I heard voices. Where's Chase?"

Kae makes her way towards Joel. "He's gone."

Joel stares at Kae. Her drenched hair. Her muddy clothes. Her face. He can see the pain in her eyes and can hear the somberness in her voice.

He lets her pass him in order to enter the house. The door creaks shut. Something inside him wrenches. He looks at the puddle slowly forming as Kae stands motionless before him in her soaking wet bedclothes. Even the little pool of water seems desolate. Kae looks at Joel, her somber gaze matching his own. She slowly walks towards him. Her strength leaves her and she falls to her knees. Joel joins her in her grief, the impact of the loss draining his energy as well. She cradles him in her arms. Pain. Tears.

CHAPTER SIX

Smithee is larger than he thought. Miles of forest, and beyond that—more forest. When will it end? He had his fill of nature. If only he could get off this silly continent with its stupid trees. There aren't even any roads. Sure, he had started off well enough. But he let his curiosity get the better of him. For all he knows he could be traveling in circles. Perhaps his departure two weeks ago was somewhat premature. He hadn't even taken any food along with him. He is grateful for his knowledge of forestry that he had acquired through Maria's lessons and Ashe's explorations, but living off nuts and berries was hardly something he had in mind when he first decided to take this journey. If only he could find Verdana. It has to be around here somewhere. No worries. He's been lost in the forest before. Not that he is admitting he is lost now. He knows exactly where he is. He's here. In the forest. On Smithee. The only problem is figuring out exactly where here is.

A voice startles him. "Ya lost, stranger?"

Chase turns around. A heavyset man with reddish-brown hair stands before him. His torn clothes are caked with mud and his long gray beard is in desperate need of a trim. He is probably in his mid-fifties, but the layers of filth that cling to his sordid skin make him look much older. The rancid stench emanating from the man supports Chase's conclusion that he probably lives in this forest and doesn't get many chances to wash himself.

The man chuckles. "That cat got yer tongue, ain't he? Don't let me looks scare ya. I'm not no noble if that's what ya was thinkin'." He wipes his callused hand on his mud-caked overalls and extends it. "Name's John."

Chase keeps his hands in his pockets. "Chase. And I'm not lost, I just don't know how to get out of this forest."

John shakes his head. "Certainly. As far as getting out of this here forest, leave that to me. I know these here woods like I know the back of me hand. If ya don't mind mah askin', whatcha runnin' from?"

"I'm not running from anything."

John shrugs. "Suit yerself. Ya don't have to tell Old John here ya problems if ya don't wanna. Makes no difference to me." He lumbers off into the forest, motioning for Chase to follow him. "How'd ya end up in this here forest, eh? I reckon ya be from these parts considering the direction ya was coming. Come to think of it, I betcha yer from that little cottage there setting nice and purdy between the Southern Woods and the Northern Woods, which ya are in now." John looks back at Chase, still a reasonable distance away, when he does not hear a response.

Chase smiles wanly and mumbles a "Yah."

John makes his way through the forest, seemingly following a path that only he can see. He continues with his small talk. "Any ideer where ya headed?"

Chase rolls his eyes. "No. Any direction away from Smithee is fine with me."

"An honest answer. I like that. It seems that nowadays everybody that be headed on a journey has a destination in mind but they just saying that so they don't sound like some idiot." John shakes his head and chuckles. "That bravado don't fool me none so when they says that, they do sounds like idiots without them knowing it."

Chase can't help but laugh. "You're all right."

"Of course I am. It's them idiots you have to watch out for." John stops and turns, an amused look on his face. "And some of 'em idiots are rude too. Ya won't believe what they said to me." His eyes widen. "Can you believe they said that I smell like garbage too rotten for a hog to roll in?"

Avoiding the question, Chase instead replies, "Thanks for the warning. I'll definitely watch out for flagrant idiots."

John slaps Chase on the shoulder. "Atta boy, I knew that there head on yer shoulders be a good one." He continues winding his way through the forest, still engaging Chase in idle banter. Shortly, they come upon a path. "Here we are." John stops and points to the right. "About fifteen miles thatta way is the Emerald castle and after that's the commercial town of Verdana. Five miles beyond that's the shore. That's the quickest way out of this here forest. Talk to Tom and he'll give ya a boat if ya mention me. He be somewhere in Verdana, I reckon."

"Thanks for your help. I wish there was something I could do to repay your kindness. Where can I find you if I ever come back this way?"

John chuckles. "That I cannot help ya with. I go wherever there is work. And sometimes I have no work. And sometimes I have the privilege to work for the king hisself. Yep, yer lookin' at the man who has mopped the floors walked by royalty. Go to any one of them kingdoms and I'll betcha me britches they've heard of Old John."

Chase shakes his head and walks off in the direction John had pointed. The accent is new to him. Although quirky, John seems friendly enough. He only wonders whether the people of Verdana will be as helpful. He eventually comes upon a castle, just like John said he would. At first it just seems to be a hill. There are no distinctive features save a green flag bearing the golden outline of a bear. No guards are visible but he can hear a marked rustling coming from the bushes. The simplistic design of the castle intrigues him. Its appearance and form is not typical of other castles he has read about, but he can see the ingenuity of it. Being hidden in a hill and surrounded by trees is fortification in its own right. Perhaps the forest is its walls. And perhaps something unseen protects this humble fortress. Rumors have reached even their little cottage atop the hill that there are things in the real world that cannot be explained by science. He believes those rumors wholeheartedly. That encounter with the lion eleven years ago is ingrained in the back of his mind. An act of God? Something inside of him? Or both?

He walks on past the castle. The dense forest gradually thins to become nothing more than a copse of newly sprouted saplings. Ahead of him, ruddy stones form a perimeter around a rather large city. An iron gate is lowered, restricting passage through the twenty-foot tall threshold of the city. Sentries pace the high-walled structure, their golden armor gleaming in the afternoon sunlight. A guard calls down to Chase, his voice barking with command. "What business do you have in Verdana, stranger?"

A subtle wind sweeps around Chase, bearing a hint of salty air. The ocean is not far. He could bypass the city, but there is that little matter of a lack of transportation. Chase opens his arms in a gesture of friendliness and answers the guard. "I am a traveler, sir. I seek food and rest."

"From what parts do you hail?"

Chase clears his throat. "Between the Northern Woods and the Southern Woods is the cottage where I have spent all but three years of my childhood, sir."

The guard harrumphs. "The only people that have come from that direction are three women. Unless my eyes and ears deceive me, you are male."

Chase sighs but manages to keep the irritation out of his voice. "Please, sir, I mean no harm. I only seek refuge for the night."

"From what do you seek refuge?"

An edge laces Chase's words. "I am not running from anything, sir. I am on a journey."

The guard consults with one of his companions and then coughs. "We cannot let you enter."

Chase closes his eyes and clenches his fist. Why does everything have to be so complicated? All he wants is a place to sleep, something to eat, and a boat. Does he appear to be that much of a threat? He's not even armed. What's he gonna do, hit them with a stick? Well, if it came to that ... Chase shakes his head and keeps his voice controlled. "I am sorry to have troubled you, it's just that Old John said...."

The guard's voice once again bellows from above him. "What name did you just say?"

The anger bubbling inside Chase is ready to explode. He is now trying to leave and the guard is still pestering him with questions. Chase glares up at the guard and retorts. "Old John." Chase turns to walk down the path from which he had just come, but the sound of clanking iron stops him. The metal gate is being raised. The guard announces from his post atop the wall, "Why didn't you just say that in the first place?"

Chase walks through the entrance, not bothering to answer the guard. He is peeved at the moment, and why does everybody think he is running from something? He tightens his jaw in frustration. But his anger is gone as quickly as it had come, replaced by his innate curiosity of new things. A little town bustles with life. Children run through the streets; their laughter warms his heart. Dogs bark and chase their tails. People sell their wares. Their voices ring through the streets that are lined with booths and some more permanent structures constructed of wood. The two-story buildings serve as both places of business and the homes of those who own them. As Chase traverses the wide lane, he notes that signs are posted above each door, indicating the purpose of the dwelling.

Chase enters through a doorway marked "The Green Tavern." Bars tend to be good sources of information. He strides towards the bartender who is diligently wiping clean some mugs. The bartender raises an eye when Chase enters, but continues on with his business. Chase clears his throat. "Excuse me, I am looking for a man who goes by the name of Tom. Do you know where I can find him?"

The bartender ignores him but one of the customers speaks up. "What business do ya 'ave wit' 'im, aye matey?"

Chase turns to look at the man who has spoken. Red stubble adorns his chin, and his skin is weathered from many years spent at sea. He seems to be in his forties, and the distant look in his blue eyes foretells the wisdom he has gained from experience. Chase answers, "I need a boat, sir."

The man laughs. "An' what makes ya think that e'll give one to ya?"

"Old John said that if I needed a boat, Tom will be the person to talk to, sir."

The man slowly rises from his seat at the counter and walks towards Chase. He stops inches from Chase's nose and glares down at him. "How'd ya know Old John?"

Without flinching, Chase replies, "I met him in the Northern Woods while on my way here, to Verdana."

"Did he warn ya about me?"

Chase can see a glimmer in his eyes, instantly relaxing. "Unless you're a flagrant idiot, no."

A hearty roar bellows from deep within the man's belly. "Hey, Pete, get my friend ... whad'ya say yer name was?"

"I didn't, but the name's Chase."

The man laughs again. "Pete, get my friend Chase here a bite to eat, will ya? He looks famished."

The bartender looks up and nods to a girl waiting in a corner for his instructions. The girl bustles through a door off to the side of the bar. The bartender returns to wiping down the mugs but directs an occasional glance towards Chase.

The man speaks the thoughts of the bartender. "It isn't often we get strangers in these parts. Everyone has been a little wary lately, especially with the war and everything." He extends his hand. "I'm sure you've probably assumed as much, but I be Tom."

Chase shakes his hand. Tom's firm grip is callused and belies many years of grueling work, but his smile is friendly. He motions for Chase to sit down at one of the five tables and then takes a seat himself. He leans back in his chair and sighs, "We'll leave in the morning. Until then, why don't ya go look around? I'll get a room for ya at the Emerald Inn while yer at it."

The girl returns from the back room with a tray of cold stew and a piece of bread. Chase smiles up at her as she carefully places the items on the table in front of him. Her eyes do not avert from the task at hand, but a tinge of red begins to paint her cheeks. She briskly turns, thankful that this handsome boy with his dazzling blue eyes is too hungry to notice her blush. She retreats to the back room, only to be reprimanded for not serving the guest his drink. She grabs a clean mug from the counter and prepares to pour the ale when Chase calls to her. "Just water, please. I don't drink." Pete looks up from his work but his expression is unreadable. The girl fills up the mug with water and brings it over to the table.

Tom heartily laughs as Chase inhales his food and empties the glass. The girl recedes to her corner, stifling a giggle and casting wary glances at her boss. Pete seems oblivious just cleaning the mugs, but she knows better.

Chase nods and rises from his chair. He walks out the door, no longer hungry and relieved that he will be able to continue on his journey.

CHAPTER SEVEN

"We're making good progress. At this rate, we'll be at the base a few days earlier than we expected."

Cole sighs, "I don't see why you're so eager to get there. I think that three years of our life given to play mercenary in this war that is not even ours is long enough."

Ashe looks over to him and smiles. "If you look at it that way, it will seem like a lot more than three years."

Cole rolls his eyes. "So how do you propose I look at it?"

"Well, I see it as an opportunity to help those in need. They wouldn't have called us into this war if it wasn't...."

Cole puts his hand on Ashe's shoulder. "Do you feel that?"

Ashe cautiously looks around. He doesn't see or hear anything, but he certainly can *feel* something. He closes his eyes and tries to pinpoint the source of the disturbance. His breathing slows as he focuses upon the strange aura unfamiliar to the forest. His mind rules out the signatures of him, Cole, and the animals around them. A sudden coldness fills him and he is abruptly taken back to the present place and time. His eyes open with a quickness. "We're being watched."

Cole's body tightens with awareness. "I do not recognize the presence, but I feel as if I should."

Ashe shakes off the uneasiness. "Let's keep going."

Cole removes his hand from Ashe's shoulder and nods.

• •

Joel enters the kitchen and pulls up a chair beside Jessica. He rubs his eyes and yawns.

"Good afternoon, sleepy head." She smiles.

Joel looks around. "Where's everybody?"

"Kae and Lara were going to Verdana today to pick up some supplies, remember?"

Joel lowers his head in defeat. "They've left already, haven't they?"

"At the crack of dawn. They should be in Verdana by now."

Joel agitatedly taps his finger and pouts. He was going to complain but he thinks better of it. If he hasn't learned his lesson by now, he never will. He sighs, "Where do you think Chase is?"

Jessica shrugs. "I'd laugh if he is still on Smithee."

Joel does laugh. "Yeah."

A scream pierces through the house. Moments later Maria comes barging into the hallway from Joel's bedroom. "Joel!!"

Jessica looks at Joel from across the table and smirks. "What have you done now?"

Joel rises from his chair and shrugs. He walks into the hallway, Jessica not too far behind.

The look of absolute disgust mirrors the revulsion in Maria's voice. "What is a rat doing in your laundry?"

Jessica giggles but then swallows her outburst when Maria casts a warning glance at her.

Joel's brow furrows. "If you're talking about Sparky, he's not a rat. He's a squirrel."

Maria blows the disheveled red hair away from her face and points to the front door. "Just get that *thing* out of my house."

Joel sighs as he enters his room. When he comes out, the squirrel is standing on his shoulder. Maria turns away in disgust, but Jessica eagerly edges forward. She follows the duo outside and closes the

39

door behind her. Her eyes are filled with wonder. "How long have you had...uh...Sparky?"

"About three weeks."

Jessica contemplates the time-frame and correlates it with Joel's tantrum. "I see."

Joel stares at her. "What's wrong?"

"Nothing." She rubs her arms. "It's a little chilly out here. I think I'm going to go back inside."

Joel gently grabs her arm. "Jessica, if it's about what I said...I'm sorry."

She smiles at him but it does not hold its usual warmth. She turns and enters the house.

Joel sighs. He regrets so many things that happened that day. He had accused his brother of loving Chase more than he loves him. He threw away his friendship with Jessica, all because he was feeling sorry for himself. He had been selfish, not realizing that he wasn't the only one losing a brother. He nearly killed this small creature that had become such a dear companion. He turns to the little squirrel that is quietly watching him with his beady black eyes. "If I ever start to do something foolish, stop me before it's too late. I don't care what you have to do—bite me if that's what it takes. Anything is better than having to live with this remorse." Sparky rubs his nose with both of his hands and chatters softly as if in compliance.

Joel places his hand on the doorknob but then remembers what Maria had said about Sparky. "I guess I have to find a better hiding place for you, huh?" He places his hands on his hips and taps his foot. He looks over at Sparky and crosses his arms. "How do you feel about the living room?" The little squirrel cocks his head and then bounds into Joel's shirt. Joel smiles and then enters the house, the little stowaway remaining quiet and motionless while Joel stealthily makes his way to the unused living room. Sparky's little head appears as Joel whispers "Okay." The little squirrel jumps out and finds himself a new hiding place underneath one of the old dusty armchairs. Maria enters the hallway just as Joel walks back through the arch. She looks at him suspiciously. Joel puts his hands behind his back and smiles.

• •

Lara slides off her horse and takes a deep breath. "The air is so fresh. And it is humming with the welcome tune of everyday life. Isn't this exhilarating?"

Kae ties the mare's halter to a hitching post and runs her hands through the coarse mane. She slaps the horse on her flanks and then stares at the dusty lane that runs through the center of Verdana. Little booths with chubby men selling their wares behind them line the street. Cliques of various age groups and gender congregate under colorful pavilions, their joyous laughter competing with the ring of the vender's voice. Kae's attention is averted upward as someone calls out in warning. The youths alongside the street disperse as a woman at a second story balcony beats a dusty old rug against the side of the building. A dingy cloud of dirt is thrown into the air and then gently floats down to the street below. The cloud dissipates and the group returns to their normal hangout below the balcony. A mirthful scream returns her eyes to the street. A little girl giggles wildly as she runs around, trying to escape from the boy who is chasing her. Other groups of rambunctious children play, ignorant of the harshness of this world. Normally a venture into town would be the highlight of the month, but with everything that has been going on, even the city has lost its appeal. She sighs, "I'll ask Pete if he has some extra barley so we can have bread for tomorrow."

Lara's concern for her sister is expressed upon her face but she only nods. "I'll get the material for our clothes and perhaps I'll pick out some choice nuts for Joel. He seems to have taken to them in the past couple of weeks. I'll meet you at the tavern in say three hours or so?"

Kae manages a smile. "Sounds like a plan." She watches Lara leave to go shopping and then silently walks towards the Green Tavern without paying attention to where she is going. She bumps into a man who is leaving the bar the same time she is entering it. She rubs her arm and walks through the door without bothering to look back. Her thoughts are far from her present situation. Troubled as they may be, though, she always found time for her manners. She mumbles an apology. If the person had said sorry, she hadn't heard it.

Chase rubs his arm and briskly turns around to face the person who he had just run into. His heart jumps into his throat as he recognizes the wavy brown hair and slender form. His breath quickens as he considers whether he should speak to her or hide. He hadn't expected to see her so soon after he left on his journey; what will she think to discover that he is still hanging around Verdana? So much for his bravado. Her seeing him here now only proves that she had been right. He has no doubt in his mind that leaving was the right thing to do, but his timing could not have been worse. She seems to have had no problem in finding her way here. He could have left three weeks later and, with Kae's navigational skills, been exactly where he is now. Perhaps, he should have waited until she was ready to leave as well. As much as she annoys him, it would be nice to have someone to talk to. They used to fight all the time when they were younger. But it seems that ever since that day in the forest, they've fought less. He'd always known how much that incident when he was five had changed him, but she seemed altered as well. The last kiss she gave him was on the morning of his fifth birthday. He involuntarily frowns. He clenches his teeth when he realizes that actually bothers him. There is something about her that intrigues him. He knows everything about her. The way her delicate voice, full of some mysterious influence, can wield him powerless. Her radiant smile that can drive away the wildest of storms. The way her laughter seems to flow around him and through him, and wash away his doubts. How he could get lost in her profoundly lilac eyes forever, not caring whether he will ever return to the path down which he was walking. And she remains a mystery. One he is willing to solve. But first he must find the answer to the question that asks who he is. And only then will he pursue the puzzle that is Kaela Lee. He nods his head in resolve. Yes. This is something he has to do for himself. With one last look at Kae, he turns and walks away.

• •

Pete looks up from his work and smiles when he sees Kae enter. "Ah. Good day, Miss Kaela."

Kae nods. "Life been treating you well?"

Pete chuckles. "It 'as since you walked in."

Kae takes a seat at the bar and smiles. "You're too kind."

Pete points towards the door. "I don't think that customer oo just left would agree with ya."

Kae involuntarily looks back at the threshold. No one is there. She turns back to the bartender and sighs, "You can't please everyone."

"Some'in wrong, Miss Kaela?"

"I'm just tired, that's all."

Pete puts down his rag and crosses his arms. "Now, 'ow long 'ave I known ya?"

"Eleven years. I've been coming to Verdana since I was five."

Pete rests his elbows on the counter. "An' ya still don't trust me wit' yer troubles. An' besides, listening ta others is in my job description."

Kae looks up at him. "No offense, but you're a bartender."

Pete looks straight into her eyes. "An' to oo do ya think people tell all their troubles? Ya wouldn't believe the number of people oo come in 'ere trying to escape from their problems, only creating a much larger one." He shakes his head. "I've only seen a 'an'ful of people oo 'aven't taken to drinking. Myself being one of 'em. I commend those who actually try to deal wit' their problems instead of trying to escape from 'em."

"Then why do you continue to serve alcohol?"

Pete cautiously looks around and then leans in closer to Kae. "Oo said I serve alcohol?"

Kae opens her mouth in surprise and then whispers, "Then what do you serve?"

"It's my own special concoction. I call it ... Root Beer."

She laughs. "You are a sly one. But if you don't make beer, why do you purchase barley?"

A radiant grin stretches across his face. "Why else? So I can see your lovely face every month."

Kae bubbles with laughter. It is contagious and Pete begins to laugh as well. After a few moments of hilarity, the laughter subdues and Pete returns to his work. He grabs a mug and tops it off with the foamy brown liquid dubbed Root Beer and hands it to Kae. "For you, Miss Kaela." Kae stifles another outburst and smiles instead. She downs the drink and wipes away the foam from her mouth, Pete shaking his head as she does so. She rises from the stool and puts her hands together. "Now that that's done, let's get down to business."

Pete throws the towel over his shoulder and motions for Kae to follow him into the back room where the barley is stored.

• •

Chase strolls down the wide avenue, eagerly inspecting the items laid out upon the vending tables. Fresh fruits and vegetables are piled high in wooden crates. Huge salmon hang from a line, the butcher behind them slicing some choice fish into bite-sized morsels. The sharp clank of a hammer hitting metal emanates from an open room nestled beneath the second story of a building. Chase watches with interest as the blacksmith aptly forges a weapon, the sizzling orange sparks flying off the hard stone as he strikes the hot iron.

Next to the blacksmith's workshop lies a discreet little hut. It is somewhat larger than the others that he has seen and it is curtained off by golden drapes. Settled in the shadows, he wouldn't have noticed it if it hadn't been for its proximity to the metal shop. Curiosity takes over and Chase proceeds towards the tent. He draws aside the curtains and enters. A clear flap in the roof, along with two tall candlesticks, allows light into the otherwise drab pavilion. A young woman—probably no older than

Lara—sits behind a counter. Her light red-brown hair is pulled up into a neat bun and she daintily places loose strands of it behind her ears as she reads. She looks up from her book as Chase enters and smiles. "May I help you, sir?"

Chase looks around the room and notes the various trinkets and baubles that are placed in glass cases. Precious stones of various cuts and colors twinkle with the amber light. Even to him they are beautiful, and each piece seems to have their own story to tell. Their own mystery. He walks over to one of the cases and his mouth opens in awe.

"These are fabulous. The craftsmanship is remarkable. I wonder if Kae has seen this...." He turns to the jeweler, nearly blushing. "Are these your works?"

The jeweler stands and grins, obviously delighted by the compliment. "I wish that they were. But no, they were designed and crafted by my father." She walks over to Chase. "He passed away two years ago. Shortly after his death, I opened up this shop to display his works. I've tried my hand at working these precious stones but I don't think that I will ever achieve his level of mastery." She sighs and returns to her stool behind the counter.

Chase turns towards the shopkeeper. "He sounds like a great man. I would have liked to have met him."

The jeweler smiles. "You are very kind." She cocks her head. "You are not from these parts, are you?"

"I grew up around here, but as far as being born here, no. Or at least, I think not."

She places her hands over her mouth and shakes her head. "Silly me. There I go again, talking the customer's head off. Well, uh, is there anything here that you would like to buy, for yourself or for someone else ... I heard you mention a 'Kae' earlier...."

Chase blushes. "I don't have any money." Chase remembers his talisman and adds. "I was actually looking for some information."

Her brown eyes lose some of its fire at the lost prospect of selling something but her smile remains. "If it concerns jewelry, then you've definitely come to the right place. However, any other matter and I'm not sure if I'll be of much help...."

Chase nods his head in understanding. He removes his talisman from around his neck and carefully hands it to the shopkeeper. "What can you tell me about this piece?"

She expertly inspects it. Her lips slightly part and she looks up at Chase with amazement. "Where did you get this?"

Chase searches her eyes for an explanation and, finding none, he answers, "My mother gave it to me. Is there a problem?"

The woman breathes heavily. She opens her mouth to speak but shakes her head instead. Her eyes dart from Chase to the necklace, and then back to Chase. She clears her throat. "How old are you?"

The question takes Chase by surprise, so he stutters, "Sixteen."

She lets out a deep breath. "Thirteen years ago, my father was employed by your mother."

Chase nods his head. "The Lion Wars...."

"Yes. While he was working on this project I wasn't allowed to watch, but he told me about it later; much later, right before he died." She closes her eyes and continues, "They were forged from the same stone, the stone being taken from deep within a cavern that is hidden in the mountains that separates Laentus from Jewel...."

Chase interrupts her. "They? I don't understand...."

"There are two. Each bears a symbol from the Ancient Ilian language, spoken by the ancient peoples of these lands."

A chill runs through his body. "I thought that was a myth...."

She smiles. "You'd be surprised what is real. The ancient peoples did exist, *do* exist. Go to Gaelith and see for yourself."

Chase shakes his head in disbelief. "You said they are symbols. They have to mean something, right?"

She slowly nods. "Yes. More than you know. I can translate the symbol, but I cannot tell you what significance this talisman bears."

Chase bites his lips in anticipation. "Please, tell me. You have no idea how long I've waited...."

She closes her eyes and traces the engraved symbol with her index finger. Her eyes dart open, revealing her awesome fear. Without a word, she places the talisman in Chase's hands and curls his fingers over the stone.

His hand grows warm, as if he holds a flame in his palm. Chase closes his eyes and lets the warmth spill over him, embracing the power emanating from his necklace. The power surges through him and fills him with visions of things long past and of things yet to come:

A blazing red light dances upon the sharp edge of a sword and then expands to fill his vision. The crimson wave washes over him, through him, and then recedes into an abysmal blackness. The heat intensifies as the black void is eaten away by a shimmering shade of blue. The blue radiance swims across his vision, desperately searching for the scarlet glow....

The jeweler cups his hand in hers and her voice is but a whisper, "What do you see?"

Chase opens his eyes. "Fire." With that one word, it seems that the pattern of his entire life up to this point has begun to form. It is yet unclear, but its presence is definite. God has a purpose for him, as He does all His children. But his burden just somehow seems more. He feels that there will be much hardship along his path, but he will never be without recourse.

The jeweler's voice releases him from his reverie. "Yes. You are the one. You must continue on your journey." She tightens her grip on his hand and then releases it. "Keep it safe."

Chase nods and places the talisman around his neck. The slightly warm stone rests against his chest, giving him assurance. He lifts the curtain but he freezes. He whips around, the drapery falling back to its closed position as he strides back towards the counter like a madman. "The other one. The other talisman. What does it say?"

She smiles but her eyes seem troubled. "I am sorry. I may have already said too much."

Chase clenches his teeth in frustration; not with the jeweler, but with the situation. He nods once more. "Thank you."

The woman smiles dimly and watches him leave. The golden curtain falls back into place and she sighs, "Godspeed."

CHAPTER EIGHT

"Ah, Miss Lara, good even to ya," Pete says and nods his head as Lara enters the tavern. "Miss Kaela is in the storeroom. I guess she found something of interest, but I 'ave no clue as to what that might be."

Lara smiles back at him as she pulls up a chair from one of the tables. "A good evening it is, Master Pete, and how do you fare?"

Pete shrugs. "I've got no reason to complain. So, I reckon you two'll be leavin' in the morning, eh?"

"Actually, we are heading back to the cottage tonight. Maria needs the entire day to bake the bread for tomorrow's supper," she cocks her head, "and it will not do to arrive at midday, I suppose."

Pete furrows his brow and stares at her. "You and the missus be careful, ya 'ear?" He smiles but his eyes are awash with doubt. "The woods aren't as safe as they used ta be."

"I appreciate your concern, Pete, but Kae and I can take care of ourselves. Besides, we are always careful to not stray from the path so as to not entice some creature's bestial tendencies."

He leans across the counter. "It's not the creatures of the forest that I'm worried about, Miss Lara. The war has brought to Verdana men who might as well be monsters. I wonder which is worse, the demons that Queen Mala conjures up or the savage men that occupy Sentran ranks."

"What are Sentran soldiers doing in Verdana?"

"I don't know. They just come—and when they leave, it's as if they take wit' dem a part of our 'umanity." He points to the door. "I shiver every time one of dem black-cad warriors steps tru dat door. It's like seeing some ominous pillar just come to life, the darkness interrupted only by the white harpy design on their breastplates and the white plumes of their helmets. Even that splash of white is menacing. Misplaced." His body trembles slightly at the thought.

Lara mimics his reaction but manages to smile. "They are just men. They have chosen to fight for Sentra and that does not make them any less so."

Pete drives away his thoughts and chuckles. "Sorry, Miss Lara, I didn't mean to worry ya. Just flapping my trap, dat's all." He sighs, "Well, I guess I won't 'ave ta worry about it for too much longer now, will I?"

"I don't understand."

He puts his hands on his waist and lets out a deep sigh. "I've been in Verdana all my life. I think it's time for a change of scenery. From what I 'ear, there's a nice town on Jewel—Phyrre's the name—where me and the little lady can retire."

Lara smiles. "Well, I wish you the best of luck, Pete." She crosses her arms. "And where is my sister?"

Kae retreats from the back room with a sack of barley and some corn. "I'm coming. I'm coming." She dumps the grains onto the floor and dusts off her hands. "There. Now let's get these goods home. My mouth is already watering from the thought of tomorrow night's dinner."

Lara sniffs. "What's gotten into you? When I left you a couple of hours ago you were, well, you weren't so ... happy."

Kae smiles at Pete and shrugs. "I've just decided that I'm going to rejoice in what I do have, instead of whining about what I don't. There are just some things that I can't change, but that's not going to stop me from changing the things that I can." She stretches and then, bending her knees, lifts the two sacks of grain onto her shoulders. She blows a stray hair out of her face. "Let's get this load on the horse while I still have enough strength to carry it." She strides out the door into the declining bustle of patrons and venders, signaling the passage of the day into the night. Lara waves to Pete and then follows her sister.

• •

Lightning streaks across the sky, the ensuing thunder accentuating the desperate cries. Blinding flashes of light temporarily divide the abysmal blackness of the night, the ruddy residue sizzling with uninhibited power. Three cloaked figures stumble through a maze of lifeless bodies, the bloody remains strewn across the rain-beaten path. Fires consume all that has been utterly untouched by the bite of deathly steel. Horrific wails escape the sore throats of those being burned alive. Their charcoaled remains depicting the utter destruction of humanity in the wake of a vengeful ruler and her chaotic wrath. Black-armored soldiers ransack the streets, the pale moonlight shining on their blood-soaked swords. And the three hooded guardians continue to run: one clings to the sleeping bundle nestled within its arms, another carries the half-awake child, and the other leads the eldest boy. They cross the raging river and hurry down a stony flight of stairs....

"Seize them! They are getting away." The woman remains featureless, but malice permeates through her words. She stands tall at the top of the stairs, barking orders to her men. Her finger points to the half-awake boy, as if trying to enchant him with this simple gesture. And perhaps the enchantment would have worked had he seen her face.

They are at the water's edge, a boat awaits. The tormented waves crash against the creaking hull, swelling over the sides. The salty water stings the tender skin of their tear-soaked faces. The figure carrying the half-awake child places something around his neck and then hugs him tightly before delivering him into the hands of those onboard the vessel. Immediately, the boat breaks free from the harbor, those on board silently watching as their lives are being ripped from them. There are other children huddled along the decks of the vessel, all orphans. Each is as equally frightened and confused as the three children who just boarded, their cloaks pulled about them as if finding reassurance in the damp fabric. There are adults as well, but the half-awake child keeps his eyes on the shore. The three figures climb into another much smaller boat. One stands arm outstretched. The older boy standing next to him calls out, but his words are swallowed by the pounding of the waves.

The roaring wind and raging sea seem to quiet just long enough for the half-awake boy to hear the words of the figure who had carried him to safety. "Don't separate." She sings goodbye. The wind takes hold of her hood but then the scene fades. Mother. Mother....

"Mother!" Chase sits up in the bed. The torrential rain pelts the windows, pouring down from the heavens as the sweat beads across his warm skin.

Tom stirs in the bed next to Chase's. He rubs his eyes and yawns. "Whatcha screamin' an' hollerin' 'bout, huh?" He rises and stretches his arms over his head.

Chase wipes off the sweat from his forehead and swings his legs over the side of the bed. "I had a nightmare."

Tom sniffs and lays his head back down on his pillow. "Well, why don't ya have them a little quieter next time, eh?"

Chase leans over and places his chin in his hands. "Only, I think it's more than that. I think it means something."

Tom props himself up on his elbows. "Look, that's fine and dandy and all, but if ya want ta leave come morning, I suggest you get some sleep." He once again lowers his head back onto the pillow.

Chase sighs and gets back under the covers. After a few moments of staring up at the exposed beams of the ceiling, he once again sighs. He turns over, trying to find a comfortable position. He closes his eyes but they open just as quickly. He listens to the rain falling down upon the roof. The hiatus between the pitter-patter of the individual droplets lengthens until the rain stops altogether. He sighs. He impatiently drums his fingers against the mattress. He rolls over in bed again.

Tom reluctantly peels open his eyes and purses his lips. After much futile labor in trying to ignore Chase's insomnia, he finally sits up. He sighs and drops his shoulders. "So ya want ta talk about it?"

Chase rises and crosses his legs. "Do you know who your parents are, Tom?"

"Yes. And they are both dead, God rest their souls."

"I never knew mine. But I have dreams about them. But they are hooded. I can never see their faces. In the dreams, we are running from something, someone. And there is someone else, a woman I think. And there is a man that I feel I should know, like his image is right in front of me but it is unclear as well. And we escape, but throughout all my life I think that I have continued running."

Tom nods. "The question is: will ya ever stop—running, that is?"

Chase looks up at Tom. Even in the dim light he can see the sincerity on Tom's face. He sighs, "I don't know if I can."

"To stop, turn, and face yer opponent is a conscious choice only ya can make. Just keep in mind that this thing, whatever it is, will continue to chase ya 'til ya confront it."

Chase looks down at his hands. "And then what? Just wait for this thing to come out of the shadows with a white flag and an open hand? It's not as simple as it sounds."

"Perhaps not, but how long do ya think ya can endure the race? We are only human, with human limitations. What happens when ya become exhausted an' this thing catches up with ya, ya being barely able to resist the pull of gravity to topple over where ya stand? To have run yer entire life, to eventually lose the fight that ya wasn't ready for. Why not set yer own terms?" Tom sighs, "Look, Chase, I've only just met ya, but I've met many people like ya, mahself included. Perhaps, whatcha are running from is yerself."

Chase stares at Tom surprised at the depth of his words, but he isn't about to insult this man just because his first impression deviated from what he now thinks of him. He had also made a similar assumption about Old John, which has also proved to be quite the opposite. Due to their rugged appearances, he had thought that it also reflected a somewhat feebleness of mind. And hard to admit, he had also been somewhat scared of them. He laughs inwardly at the thought. There is no doubt that they can hold their own in a fight, but the kindness they have shown him proves his senses to be wrong, again. Chase can feel a knot in his chest that can only be shame. If he was so quick to judge others based on their appearances, how is he any better than those flagrant idiots that Old John is so wary of? Up to this point, he has never been able to fully express his feelings, not even with Kae, but he feels as if he can trust this stranger. Without realizing it, he has already told this man things that he wasn't even aware that he felt. He has already revealed that much, and he sees no point in holding back now.

He runs his hand through his hair, the black strands glistening in the moonlight. "Perhaps, I am. Perhaps, I'm not. Either way, I feel … trapped. That no matter how fast and how far I run, I'll just end up back where I started. Which just makes the running pointless, but I'd rather do that than do nothing."

Tom nods. "Is where ya started from really all that bad?"

Chase puts his hands behind his head. "No, it's just that I keep on thinking that there is something more. There should be something more."

"Not everything is as it seems, and perhaps whatcha are looking for has been right in front of ya all along." Tom scratches his head. "Ya came from the south, right?"

Chase furrows his brow. "What? Yes. What does that have to do with anything?"

"Well then, ya must have seen the Emerald Castle, or not, rather if ya haven't realized it."

Understanding sweeps across his face. "Yes … the hill that is not a hill."

Tom chuckles. "Exactly. When I was a young lad like yerself, my first assignment as a sailor in the Assyrian Royal Navy—this was back when the kingdoms were united mind ya—was to be part of the unit that would escort King Avram and Queen Alysia to the Emerald Castle. Not one of us sailors has been on Smithee before, and all we knew of castles was the kind made out of stone, mind ya. We were told that if we went into the forest, we have gone too far—why we didn't have someone with us to point out the hill slash castle I do not know—so we reach the forest and have to retrace our steps. So we traipse around this hill for hours, in the hot sun, sweating like hogs in the meat market. And then, finally, we notice the door."

Chase laughs. "You'd think that King... the king and queen would know where their own home is."

"What do ya mean? Oh, no no no no. King Avram and Queen Alysia rule Laentus. The rulers of Smithee are King Albert and Queen Emalee." Tom cocks his head. "Ya don't know much about politics, do ya?"

"I don't know anything about politics."

Tom crawls underneath the covers and yawns. "Let's make a deal. I will tell ya all I know...."

"About politics?"

"About anything. I will tell ya all I know if ya promise to go to bed and not bother me until morning. Deal?"

Chase lays his head on the pillow and yawns as well. "Deal."

CHAPTER NINE

The morning sun filters into the hotel room through the gauzy curtains as tiny dust particles gently dance in the warm glow. The light spills across the wooden beams of the floor, the shadows receding under the trundle beds and hiding in dim corners. The song of the birds welcomes the bright new day after a prolonged series of rainstorms and thickening clouds had served to dampen the usual happiness consistent with the onset of spring. This season of rebirth has been present for two months and there have only been a handful of days graced by the sun. But even those days were darkened by circumstance. Along with the arrival of verdant fields, came the birth of a war that sought to once again threaten the security of the Ilian peoples. Families were torn apart, emotions were running high, and mistakes were made. But he has to make do with what he has and live with what he has done. He must continue.

Both Tom and Chase have been up since the crack of dawn and are now making the final preparations for their journey. Chase looks up from pulling on his boots and puts his introspections aside when Tom whistles to get his attention. Tom throws him an extra pack. "Here. Blanket, water jug, rope, and switchblade—all the provisions required for a journey in a handy little backpack."

Chase catches it and slings it across his shoulders. Both men make final adjustments on their gear, and with a silent nod they head out the door and embark on their adventure.

The metal gate lowers behind them, the raucous holding a tone that seems to say, *Thanks for visiting, now get out.* Tom slaps Chase on the back and laughs. "Well, boy, let's head out, shall we?"

Chase nods and follows Tom around the walled city in a path directed north towards the Indigo Sea. Tom turns his head. "Well, ya held up yer end of the bargain, an' I'm a man of mah word." He gathers his thoughts and continues, "Now, first things first." He clears his throat. "Sorry to deceive you, but the common tongue of these parts leaves my throat sore if I exercise it for extended amounts of time. My apologies for having now to revert to my native language of Laentian."

Chase looks nervously around him. To employ the common language of Smithee as if it were his own, Tom hinted at truths of which he could not completely grasp but could at least understand the implications of. Without pretense, he questions, "Are you a spy?"

Tom shrugs nonchalantly. "In a sense, but in these times of war, who isn't? And as to your next question of who I really am—I am Tom. I make a living as a merchant seaman of sorts, but I live for the adventure. Some consider us pirates, but who else has enough command of the sea to withstand the black hordes of Sentra? You may counter that the Assyrian Royal Navy patrols the waters, but their glory faded along with the power of the kingdom, stalwartly waiting in the mists for their legendary savior who will never come. I had been a member of this fleet operating on borrowed glory but soon became disillusioned by the hypocrisy of it all. I set out on my own, finding work where I could and surviving on sheer force of will. I currently act as a messenger, and of this matter I will speak no more. Last night we made a bargain, so let's get on with it."

Chase sighs as he weighs his options. He can enlist the aid of this deceptive man who has all but outright admitted to being a brigand engaged in clandestine activities, or he can wash his hands of him and continue on by himself. Given the intrinsic peril of such a tentative relationship and his own inherent lack of direction, neither prospect seems rather appealing. Tom, however, has a boat and is willing to guide Chase in his quest, perhaps too willing, but Chase is not presently concerned with Tom's reasons for doing so. There awaits the possibility of locating another eager boatman, but frankly he doesn't want to take the time to look. As far as he is concerned, the sooner he gets off Smithee the better. Otherwise, he would change his mind and never leave. He gathers his courage to confront the heart of his worries. "Should I expect to find a knife in my back?"

Tom turns, allowing Chase to see the truth evident in his eyes. "I will not lie to you. Should you betray me, my vengeance will be swift. I do not take you on lightly. My mission grows ever urgent as this war presses on, but there is something about you that piques my interest."

Chase involuntarily clutches his talisman. Not exactly the answer he was looking for, but it will have to do. Adjusting his pack, he nods. "The day shortens. Let's be on our way for I am eager to be off this continent. I have much to learn, so if you are still game, please introduce me to the world."

"Before we can delve into cold hard politics, a little history lesson is required." He makes sure that Chase is listening and then he turns forward and clears his throat.

"At one time, centuries ago but after the Great Flood, all the kingdoms—Laentus, Jewel, Gaelith, and Smithee—were united under one sovereign, Lord Donovan of Ilia. His wife was Lady Gwendolyn of Ilia. Sentra was not a barren wasteland as we know it today, but a thriving seat from which Lord Donovan ruled. There was, of course, never absolute peace, but there were times more peaceful than others. The Lord and Lady had four sons, all of whom died in various skirmishes around the world. So when Lord Donovan died and with Lady Gwendolyn passing away soon after him, there was no one to legitimately receive the throne. His two brothers, King David of Jewel and King Lanacan of Laentus, however, survived the deceased high king. They fought over who should rightfully take the crown and become the high king of Ilia, thus beginning the Lion Wars."

"I've read about that, but I didn't know that they were brothers."

Tom clears his throat. "Yes, well, they ended up dead within a few short months of the commencement of the war. Well, technically King David disappeared and his body was never found, but I do not doubt that after three thousand years he is dead."

"No, neither do I." Chase's brow is furrowed. "How come the war didn't end with the death of the two kings?"

"The Lion Wars became a family legacy really. Son after son after son took up their swords against each other. Warfare became a sort of tradition for the two kingdoms."

Chase cocks his head. "So the kingdoms of Laentus and Jewel are tied by blood? Is that what the Dragon Treaty was based upon?"

Tom furiously shakes his head. "Let me clarify. The current line of succession for Jewel does trace back to King David, but the Laentian nobility does not. Have you heard of the Massacre of Neptune?"

Chase nods slowly. "Yes, I remember now. About fifteen hundred years ago, the Laentian castle was raided and the entire royal family was murdered." He shivers at the thought. "The assassin was captured and beheaded. Despite the gruesome end of the family's reign, the coronation of the new king was rather peaceful. Following the rules of ascension, the crown was passed down to the Duke of Assyria."

Tom smiles back at Chase. "Well done. But alas, those rules of ascension of which you spoke are obsolete now. As a result of the war and the ensuing conquest, the major houses expanded until all the dukedoms were integrated into one entity, hence the substituted and now universally accepted nomenclature of Assyria. Just imagine the havoc that would result if there were a repeat of the Massacre of Neptune. With no clear line of succession, the kingdom would dissolve."

"Have the kings not realized this?" Chase regrets the words as soon as they come out of his mouth. He wishes he had phrased his question better.

Tom raises an eyebrow. "No offense, but despite your book knowledge, you are rather naïve."

Chase crosses his arms and answers his own question. "I know. Of course they realize this, but they cannot fathom giving up any portion of their power, despite the fact that this greed is a detriment to the well-being of the people and the kingdom for that matter. And I know that I shouldn't be surprised in this, but that in itself worries me." Another thought comes to mind. "With the death of the royal family, any claim on the crown of the high king that Laentus had was dissolved. So, what was the point in continuing the war?"

"Over time, the reason for the war was reshaped from a quest for power to a fight for land. Instead of blood, war ran through their veins. The ancient kings thrived on it. For all intents and purposes, with Laentus' connection to Lord Donovan obliterated, the king of Jewel was the rightful heir to the throne but he wasn't recognized as such then and he isn't known as such now."

Chase considers this but is still troubled. "Last night you said that you were a sailor back when the kingdoms were still united. Is it safe to assume that there was a short period within the last thirty years when a High King was recognized?"

Tom nods. "Ah. You're not as naïve as I thought. Still I wouldn't say that assumptions would be safe, but you are correct in this reasoning. For a time, a very short time mind you, King James of Jewel was considered the High King but he abdicated in lieu of a threatening regeneration of the animosity between the kingdoms of Laentus and Jewel. His reign was during an abnormally long period of peace, and the people of Ilia sought out someone to lead them. The logical choice was King James, and we Ilians are logical people. Most of the time. Anyways, old habits die hard and war was beginning to rear its ugly head once again. Seeing to the needs of the people for once, the two war hawks put aside their weapons and instead shook hands. It is believed that his highness' abdication is a condition as stated by the Dragon Treaty, but no one can be for sure. Now, all that remains of a once glorious united land is a dwindling confederacy, each kingdom having to handle this new threat from Sentra virtually by themselves." Tom sniffs and shakes his head. "It's ironic if you think about it. This new threat arising from where the problems that ignited the Lion Wars began."

Chase's pace slackens as he processes this information. "The Dragon Treaty ended the Lion Wars...."

Tom nudges Chase forward and continues, "Yes, but much suspicion surrounds what occurred on that fateful night that saw the conclusion of the Lion Wars. I'm not even sure of it myself, and I was there." He involuntarily rubs his arms and shivers as a memory flashes before his eyes. "Those poor children. So many families were torn apart. It should have never come to that. Don't get me wrong. I have the utmost respect for the kings and queens of Ilia, but they have a tendency to let the power go to their heads. And this time, the stakes were just too high. With great power comes great responsibility, and great sacrifice." Tom contemplates for a moment and then continues, "But sometimes it's not the power that drives a king, or a man for that matter, but fear."

Chase stares at Tom, who consciously keeps his eyes on the trail ahead of them. Chase walks half a step behind him, himself drawn into silence by his own fears. They continue along the path, neither one saying a word. What could be said? The distant yet undeniable ring of truth amplifies the portent of the statement. Images from his previous night's dream dance in front of him, in particular a man—the man who was in the boat awaiting their arrival. Chase sighs but his exhalation is broken by a bewildered gasp. He grabs Tom's arm, forcing the sailor to face him. "What did you say?"

Tom glares back at Chase as if staring into the eyes of a madman. "Sometimes a man ... is driven by fear."

Chase tightens his grip on Tom's arm. "No! Before that ... that night ... you were there ... you helped us escape!"

• •

Lara lies on the soaked green grass of the hill on which the Sylvan cottage is situated. She stares up at the clouds that float overhead in the brilliant blue sky and smiles.

"It feels so good to be home."

She turns her head to look at Kae who is quietly sitting on the grass beside her. Lara's smile dissipates as she sees the solemn look on her sister's face. She sighs and supports herself on her elbows.

"If I hadn't known better, I would say that perhaps you should get some rest, but being that you haven't slept well since Chase left, I doubt that you would take that advice."

Kae continues to stare out across the field but her expression becomes more rigid. "If I hadn't known better, I would say that you were inferring that what Chase has or has not done matters to me."

Lara sits up and wraps her arms around her knees. "Does it?"

Kae turns to face Lara, the look on her face vicious yet helpless at the same time. "Of course not." She closes her eyes and sets her jaw. "I just thought that…things…would be different." She opens her eyes and stares out at the mountains in the horizon again. "It doesn't matter anymore."

Lara wraps an arm around Kae's shoulder and draws her into her embrace. She caresses her hair and whispers, "I know. I know. I miss them, too." A single tear rolls down Kae's face.

Lara releases her embrace and she gingerly stands up. For a moment the wind seems to pick up speed, swirling around her in welcome. The moment ends but leaves her with a smile upon her face. She runs the rest of the way up the hill, stopping and turning for only a second in order to call to her sister. "Come on. Let's go for a ride."

Kae looks up, drawn away from her reverie. She chases Lara to the stables, but she has already mounted a horse by the time Kae reaches them. She leans against the flank of one of the horses, trying to catch her breath. Lara darts off upon the horse, leaving Kae in a fit of carefree laughter. Kae swings her leg over the brown mare with ease, and then sets out to pursue her sister who is already halfway across the field.

Lara leans forward clutching the gray mane of the white stallion, using shifts in her body position to guide the horse. She races across the plain, the hooves reverberating upon the lush land and the wind rushing past her, creating a playful rhythm of earth and sky and giving her a sense of freedom. She leans forward farther and the stallion understands this signal to run faster. Lara laughs in delight as the combined songs of the earth and the sky blend into one luxurious harmony. She rises up to a near sitting position, slowing the stallion to a brisk canter. The horse circles around, rearing its head and snorting as if in mimic of Lara's laughter. Staring across the plain, she sees Kae coming and waves a hand.

Kae smiles and lets her horse come to a stop beside Lara's mount. She gracefully dismounts and strokes the black mane of the mare. The two horses take this opportunity to graze, their perked up ears the only indication that they are aware of their surroundings.

Lara closes her eyes and lifts her arms in exultation. She inhales deeply and then lets out one long cry, the wind wrapping itself around her voice and carrying it across the land. The horses twitch their ears, but are otherwise unaffected by this display that they have become accustomed to whenever the woman with golden eyes takes them for a ride. With a sigh, she lets the cry die and then looks earnestly at her sister.

Kae matches Lara's gaze and fervently shakes her head. "Un-uhnn. I have no mind to be screaming my problems to the world."

Lara furrows her brow in mock consternation, the smile evident in her glowing golden eyes. "What do you mean?"

Kae laughs. "You know perfectly well what I mean, Lara."

A mischievous grin creeps across Lara's face. "I am swifter on foot and faster on a horse, as well. I guess that when things go by so quickly, focusing on the details instead of the panoramic view in front of me tends to slow me down. I still see them but in the long run, they just aren't as important." She jumps off the horse onto the ground. "Experience should not shape our attitude. It only serves as a lesson, and we must learn from it lest we forget what is most important in life."

Kae crosses her arms in contemplation. "And what would that be?"

Lara's eyes dance with a fire that Kae has never seen before. "To live it."

Kae laughs. "Perhaps, but I don't see the point in...."

"Exactly. There is no point. It just serves as a way to release pent-up emotion."

Kae looks around and sighs, "You won't tell anyone, will you?"

Lara's hands fly to her chest, feigning apprehension. "And admit that I do the very same thing? Of course not."

Kae closes her eyes and turns so that she is facing the wind. She opens her mouth, but then closes it again. She turns to her sister as if looking for some kind of assurance but is only met with the calm stare of her black mare. A white flash is darting towards the horizon. She hadn't even heard the hoofbeats of the horse as it galloped away, as if the mare had flown the distance. Kae smiles, appreciating the solitude that Lara had given her. Gathering her courage, she takes a deep breath and then expels it in one melodious burst. Her voice grows, sound flowing from deep within her on a rising current of emotion. The tumultuous waves washing away her pain, a pain that she had not even realized had been there in the first place. The waves recede, disappearing into a sea of tranquility.

With her eyes still closed and mouth still open, sound no longer coming from it, she begins to twirl. Dancing to some tune that only she can hear. The sweetness of it restores her and she feels at peace, but the moment is shattered by an overwhelming sense of doom. The sweet song has changed to a baleful cry, getting fainter as she strains to hear it. With urgency, she mounts her horse and races back towards the Sylvan cottage.

• •

Ashe folds up the tent in which they had taken shelter during the previous night's rainstorm and secures it with a length of sinew. He sets the bundle down next to the rest of their belongings and then paces towards the river to replenish the dwindling supply of water in his jug. He takes a seat next to Cole who is slowly turning the spit from which hangs a wild boar that Ashe had flushed from the forest earlier that morning. The hot coals nestled in a cooking pit burn red despite the fact that the fire has long since died down. Ashe takes a drink from his water jug and wipes his mouth. "Some storm last night, huh? I'm glad that we found those stones," he pats the log on which they sit, "because the wood around here is far too wet to even produce tendrils of smoke."

Cole turns the stones, using a branch as a poker. He stares at the coals and sighs, "Yeah."

Ashe leans forward and puts his hands together. "What's wrong?"

"It is just unnerving to know that we are being watched. This entire situation just seems wrong. I have an uneasy feeling about this war." He puts down the poker and looks at Ashe. "I am not sure that we should go to Nesthra."

Ashe sighs, "To tell you the truth neither am I, but we really don't have a choice. This may not be our war at the moment, but if we don't finish this in Nesthra, it will eventually consume all of Ilia."

Cole snorts. "You talk as if our involvement in this war will really change its outcome."

Ashe rises and douses the coals with water. "I don't claim to know the future; it's just that trying to help makes more difference than doing nothing." He removes the pig from the spit and carefully slices it. He sets out a portion for Cole and for himself and then places the remainder of the meat in a waterproof pouch. They eat their breakfast in silence and then continue on their way towards the rendezvous point in Cape Terna.

Cole stops suddenly, turning his head to survey the surrounding forest.

Noting Cole's abrupt pause, Ashe examines each shadow cast by the thick patches of undergrowth, seeing nothing. He turns to Cole to urge him ahead but finds the man's gaze intent on a certain area behind some silver-specked foliage. Upon closer evaluation, Ashe realizes that what he had thought to be some sort of flower are two yellow eyes. The rest of the body begins to fill in, a shaggy silver coat replacing what he had thought to be leaves. The wolf makes no move towards either man save to step from the shadows that had been its hiding place.

Ashe's voice cracks with wariness. "Seems we have found our stalker."

Cole tightens his jaw. "Then why do I still feel as if we are walking into a trap?"

• •

Jessica paces down the hallway and shudders as if an imagined wind has just swept through the house. She runs her hands up and down her arms and shakes her head as if dispelling some chilling notion. Instead of joining Maria and Joel in the kitchen, she returns to her room and crawls into bed. She shivers once more and pulls the blankets closer around her body. Her breathing becomes shallow and her head begins to pound as startling images dance before her eyes. The view of her room begins to swirl into a blinding mass of spiraling color, until the room is gone altogether. She feels her body being pulled into the void and a pain races through her as if every nerve in her body is tingling with sensation. A light appears at the end of what had at first appeared to be a tunnel into oblivion. Its gravitational force becomes stronger as she nears it. She can feel her entire body wrenching, as if the very atoms of her entire being are struggling to separate and to leave her as some forgotten amorphous entity. She reaches the end of the tunnel. The searing heat and blinding light rend her body rigid. The light flashes and it is over.

She is back in her room, her body writhing and her fingers clutching the sides of her bed. Her eyes are wide open but unseeing for the moment. Her body ceases convulsing but she lies still, frozen with fear. A sense of deep foreboding haunts her thoughts but her sobbing eventually recedes into a series of hiccups. When her vision clears, she sees the worried faces of Joel and Maria peering down at her. She tries to sit up but her strength fails her. She feebly reaches out and Joel cups her hand between his. He kneels beside her as Maria moves to the other side of the bed and begins dabbing Jessica's sweat-beaded brow with a damp cloth. Jessica opens her mouth to speak but finds her throat to be dry and useless.

Joel rises and sits on the edge of the bed. He lifts Jessica's weary body and cradles her in his arms. He caresses her back and gently kisses the top of her head. Closing her eyes, Jessica weeps.

Maria partially closes the door as she leaves the room, giving Jessica and Joel some privacy. She finds Lara and Kae in the hallway staring at her, frightened.

Lara is the first to speak. "We heard screaming...."

Kae continues, "Is everything all right?"

Maria's face is flustered, unsure of the answer to the question. She and Joel had been in the kitchen when they heard moaning coming from Jessica's room. Without a word they were out of their chairs and making a mad dash towards the room that Kae shares with Jessica. They found Jessica on her bed, her face contorted in unimaginable pain and her chest heaving erratically. Seeing her like that, inexpressible fear seized her heart, paralyzing her. And then she began to scream, a blood-curdling cry that shattered her already dwindling resolve. And all she could do was stand there, frozen in fear.

Then Joel took charge rushing to Jessica's side, securing her thrashing body and raising his voice in a desperate effort to reach her. Maria watched as a light filled the room and began to grow, her mouth gaping open as she saw Joel to be its source. His eyes were closed and he seemed unaware of the power that was emanating from his body. Both he and Jessica cried out and the light spilled across the room, the energy rushing through Maria and leaving her breathless. She closed her hazel eyes and waited for the sizzling warmth to be gone, praying that the light will not take her with it. The sensation passed and she opened her eyes. Joel was standing over Jessica, drained but determined to appear strong when she would finally awake. She crossed over to the bed, the claws of fear still clutching her heart. A breath of relief had escaped her mouth when Jessica came around. Thank God that Jessica is alive, but she could just as easily have been dead. So is everything all right? She looks back at the room from whence she came and then turns to face Lara and Kae.

"I don't understand it, so how can I possibly determine whether or not everything is all right? One moment she is fine, then on her deathbed the next. She is alive but shaken, and I can't help but feel that this is not the last time that something like this will happen." She covers her face with her hands, the red tresses of her hair falling forward like a crimson wave of despair. "And I have no idea of how to stop it."

The door to the room opens and Joel steps out. He pulls the door shut and looks at the three women in the hall. He wipes his brow and puts his hands behind his neck, bringing his elbows together before him. "She's resting, now." He leans against the door and slides down to the floor. "I think she'll be fine, but I'll remain close just in case."

Lara smiles. "Seems that you are her own personal protector now."

Joel looks up at her and returns her smile. "I wouldn't have it any other way."

CHAPTER TEN

Tom stares into Chase's troubled blue eyes, his own sapphire irises filled with suspicion and a seriousness that counteracts his normally casual countenance. The skin of his arm beneath Chase's grip gradually grows warmer with each breath, the warmth of his body seeming to flow towards that one spot. A chill passes over him, only surpassed by the intense heat of Chase's hands threatening to draw his very essence from this corporeal cage of blood and bones. Slowly Chase removes his hand, taking the burning sensation away with it. Tom takes a breath as his body temperature returns to normal, all the while keeping his gaze fixed on Chase.

A moment passes before anyone speaks. The sounds of the forest around them seemingly dulled as in acquiescence to some tacit request for silence. Tom speaks with a slow firmness.

"Control your temper, lest it gets the better of you. You have great passion, great power, but you lack the control necessary to harness these gifts without destroying yourself and those around you. Without control, the gift becomes a curse."

Chase tries to look away, but Tom's stern gaze holds his attention. Abashed, yet terrified at the same time, he struggles to regain his composure only to find himself paralyzed by Tom's magnetic stare, barely able to breathe, much less blink. He opens his mouth to speak, only an indiscernible mumble allowed to escape from his dry throat. The wrinkles in Tom's forehead soften as the intense fire in his eyes dwindles to a dying spark. Then the gravity is gone, overtaken by an overwhelming sympathy. With the release of tension, Chase feels freed from the invisible bonds that had held him in stasis.

Once again Tom speaks, but his tone is gentler, if not empathetic. "Yes, I was there. But you must understand there are many painful memories associated with that night. Memories which I have tried to forget, only to see them more clearly. I know your pain, the pain of loss. Please do not force me to relive it." He turns away and hurriedly rids his face of all signs of his sadness.

Chase moves to put a comforting hand on Tom's shoulder but is interrupted by the sound of a horn that pierces the still forest with its shrill call. The call is answered with a chorus of men's voices, raised in anticipation for battle. The bugle blares twice more in rapid succession and is once again drowned out by the return of shouts. Voices screaming what could only mean "Charge."

Without a word, both Tom and Chase head for the direction from whence the sounds of battle came. Both eager to learn what battle is possibly being fought on the shores of Smithee, and against whom. Neither one inclined to voice their fears that the war in Sentra is spreading, that the dark power is growing.

Tom places a hand on Chase's shoulder as he urges him to take cover behind a stand of bushes. "Wait."

Chase looks back at him with indignation but follows his instruction. Breathing heavily with the anticipation for battle, he gasps. "What's wrong?" He looks impatiently towards the direction from which the battle is being fought and then turns his gaze upon Tom. "Why have we stopped?"

Tom lowers to his haunches and pulls Chase down with him. He wipes away the sweat condensing on his furrowed brow and stares resolutely into Chase's blue eyes, demanding his attention. His voice is kept to a whisper but holds authority, "What do you hope to gain by charging into battle not even knowing which side to fight for, much less what you are fighting against?"

Chase, frustrated, wipes his clammy hands on his trousers. "What do you mean?" He points towards the battle. "People are dying while we rest here doing nothing! I do not have time for these games!"

Tom puts his hands on Chase's shoulders. "Listen to me. If you go out there, you will die. This is not some game. This is war. You cannot be strutting about like some chicken with its head chopped off!" Chase starts to rise but Tom tightens his grip, pushing him back down. "I know you only want to help, but your corpse will not be of much use to anybody save to serve as food for the crows." Chase stops struggling so Tom removes his hands. "I know how you feel, but you must understand that any action you take in this will be rash—it will be your death."

Chase fidgets as he looks away. "You cannot expect me to wait out this battle when I can hear the screams of the men as they die not even a quarter of a mile away!"

Tom stands. "I expect no such thing. I am a veteran of war, you are but a novice. We will do this my way."

Chase looks up at him with reverent shock as he falters to stand. He straightens as his body becomes rigid with resolve. "Tell me what must be done."

• •

The earth itself seems to stand still in accordance with the paralysis that has overtaken the two men, watching, waiting for the lone wolf to either attack or flee. Ashe's vigilant eyes shine like two emerald flames, desperately searching the amber windows to the soul of the beast for any indication of its intentions. Yet the eyes hold no secret, only serving as a device through which the creature sees.

Cole is more focused on the wolf as a whole, seeing the creature as less of a threat and more of an obstacle. The creature stands on the path that leads toward Cape Terna, wherein lies the intended transport vessel that will take them to the Nesthran Islands and deep into the heart of battle. Cole finds this to be rather amusing, as if this wolf would intentionally block their passage in warning of what is to come should they continue. He laughs, realizing that his mind has manipulated the situation to coincide with his fears of going to Nesthra.

Ashe breaks his gaze upon the wolf to momentarily look upon his friend who seems to be going out of his mind. "What's so funny?" His gaze returns to the wolf before he can completely get the question out.

Cole lowers to the ground, balancing himself on the balls of his feet with his elbows resting on his knees. "Would you think me crazy if I told you that I thought this wolf is guiding us, warning us?"

The wolf yawns and stretches its front legs before circling around in search of a good resting spot and finally lying down once it finds one. Its yellow eyes stare up at Cole for a few seconds, and then disappear as the wolf closes its eyes to sleep.

Ashe keeps an eye on the wolf as he thwarts Cole's question. "Guide or not, it is still a wild animal. I think it best that we leave now before it wakes from its slumber."

Cole rises and laughs. "And here I took you for the ultimate authority in animals."

"What is that supposed to mean?"

Cole sighs, "She is not sleeping."

Ashe raises an eyebrow. "She? How do you know for certain that this wolf is female and that it is not asleep?"

"I just do."

Ashe clutches his pack as he maneuvers around the wolf. "Well then, yes."

Cole looks tenderly upon the silver mass of fur lying in the center of the road and then follows Ashe's lead. He stops for a moment to ponder Ashe's remark. "Yes to what?"

Ashe answers over his shoulder. "I do think you are crazy." He laughs. "But then again I must be as well, for I believe you."

Cole eagerly takes this opening. "Then, in light of this warning, why do we continue? Why risk our lives to rescue this territory from oppression, opening up an opportunity for some other power-hungry government to replace it in the meanwhile? It's a never-ending cycle. It's pointless. It's futile."

Ashe turns and takes a deep breath. "The warning serves as a reminder to take caution, not to retreat. If you backed down every time an obstacle was thrown in your path, you would never get anywhere. You would accomplish nothing. You need to learn to take risks, because life is full of them. Fighting this war may very well be the last things we do, but I would rather die in battle for the life of another and for the peace of mind of an entire nation, creating a world where the child can go to sleep at night and have his father be there to tuck him in, than to idly sit at home as if the world is free of problems and waste away to dust, having done nothing. Life is not a spectator sport, for if it were, we wouldn't truly be living it. *That* is pointless." He pauses to take another deep breath and calm himself down. "Feel free to return home, but know that that journey I do not plan to make until I have accomplished what is required of me in this war. Go home. I hope you can live with yourself for doing so."

Cole looks down in embarrassment, his face red with shame. "No." He looks up, his jaw set with determination as he stares at Ashe. "I couldn't live with myself. Especially if anything should happen to you. I made a promise to myself that I would look out for you, Ashe, for Lara's sake."

Ashe studies Cole's face and nods his head in understanding. "I can't say that I am sorry. Perhaps that is selfish of me, but I love her, too." He deliberately turns and walks down the path.

Cole sighs and then ambles after him, unsure of his thoughts, his feelings. He shouldn't be ashamed of his feelings; after all, he has no control over them, so why does he? He shivers involuntarily, his mind wary of where his heart is taking him and in what his uninhibited yet unrequited love could result. And the worst of it is that Ashe knows. Cole has no fear that he will tell Lara, but he knows. Ashe knows. And he will be watching him like a hawk, restricting him from indulging in fantasy, restricting him from even a single unwarranted look. All of a sudden the world seems to have gotten smaller. The cramped space is dizzying and he falls to the ground, unconscious.

CHAPTER ELEVEN

Maria quietly sips a cup of tea, her eyes staring past the two women sitting across the kitchen table from her. The cup in her hand rattles ever so slightly, her nerves still shaky from that morning's events. With a sigh she returns to the present. Seeing the worried faces of Lara and Kae, she smiles to help relieve the tension. Finishing the last of her tea, Maria gingerly gets up and places the cup in the sink. For a moment her hands grip the edge of the countertop as a fit of hysteria seizes her. Lara and Kae rush up to support her as tears uncontrollably fall from her eyes. Maria is helped back to her seat, and once seated she breaks the mournful silence.

"I have failed my brother. I promised to protect her, but when she needed me most, I too was helpless." She futilely attempts to wipe away her tears. "Oh, Albert, I am sorry that I was not strong enough. I can only pray that she has the strength to do what I could not. Please, Lord, protect her and watch over her. Please, Lord, forgive me."

Lara kneels down and hugs this woman upon whom was placed a great burden, herself understanding of its import.

"Maria, let me bear this load with you. Albert never expected you to do this alone, yet you have taken it upon yourself to do so. I commend you for your sacrifice. You have not failed—we are all alive and well. That is all that matters."

Maria bites her lip. "But I should have given more of myself."

Kae puts her hand on Maria's shoulder. "You have already given more than enough. Maria, you mustn't worry so; through your efforts we have seen your unerring love not only for Jessica but for all of us. But someday we must learn to fight our own battles. And in doing so, we gain the confidence that we will succeed and the determination to not only succeed, but to surpass."

Maria stands and walks towards the window, the bright sun illuminating her tear-streaked face as she observes Jessica and Joel resting outside atop the hill. Despite all the hardship they had faced, being orphans, never knowing the past or what the future will require of them, the secrets that have been kept, they are still innocent. Joel has a way about him in which he can discern the truth of the beauty in all things, tirelessly seeking knowledge but in the process also gaining a wisdom well beyond his years. Jessica sees the world through new eyes, delighting in the wonders it has to offer but ever fearful of embracing them, much in the same way that Kae deals with whatever life hands to her. And Chase, she knew him to be the most afraid of all. He pursues his past but fears confrontation, and he discounts the future but inadvertently acknowledges it with the continuation of his journey. Maria sighs.

"I guess that all that I can do now is pray. Pray and hope that we will survive this."

Kae looks questioningly at Lara. "Survive?"

Lara only nods, staring out at the world as if searching for some sign. A foundation for which to believe that they have a chance, however slim it may be.

• •

Joel supports himself on one elbow as he looks over at Jessica. "How are you feeling?"

Jessica wraps her arms around her knees and shrugs. "I'm scared, Joel. I am really scared. I have this nagging feeling that something is going to happen. Something that will change all our lives forever. But it is strange, as if this something has already taken place. And it is just waiting to strike. It has been waiting for a long time, but soon its waiting will end." She involuntarily shivers. "And I also feel that we have some role to play in all this. What happened this morning was not an accident." She looks at Joel, trying to hold back her tears. "If you hadn't been there, I don't know what would have … I might have…."

Joel takes her in his arms. "You don't have to worry. If this thing ever comes back, I'll be right here next to you. We'll beat this. You can count on it or my name isn't Joel Blader." He smiles down at her. "But you know, you have the worst timing. I was about to eat breakfast, which I still haven't done yet by the way."

Jessica punches him in the stomach and laughs. "That's not fair. I am trying to wallow in grief here and here you are making me laugh."

"No," Joel pushes her to the ground and tickles her, his hysterical laughter matching hers, "this is making you laugh."

Jessica wiggles free of Joel's hands and clumsily stands up, holding her hands up to ward him off. In broken speech riddled with hiccups and giggles, she gasps. "That is not helping. I am trying to be serious." She manages to maintain a stern face.

Joel crosses his legs and folds his hands together. "Okay, I am listening."

She eyes him suspiciously and then takes a seat on the ground next to him. With a heavy sigh she continues, "I think I had a vision."

"A vision? Do you mean like a premonition or something?" Joel taps his finger to his lips.

Her chest heaves in frustration as she pleads, "I don't know exactly. All I know is that what I saw I don't ever want to see again." She pauses as she gathers her thoughts. "I saw a man completely dressed in black. He was … he killed someone, a woman I think. There was blood all over his hands and he was laughing, the laugh of a madman. And then it was as if I was the man hearing his thoughts, seeing through his eyes. *I have won. At last, this world is mine. The very elements which have sought to destroy me are now at my disposal.* I saw a world destroyed in fire and countless bodies strewn upon the ground, as if there had been some great battle. And kneeling before me was...." She closes her eyes and clears her dry throat, unable to continue.

Joel puts his hand on her shoulder. "Who was kneeling before you?"

Jessica looks up at Joel. "It was Chase."

• •

A pungent wetness trickles down his face. Cole moves to wipe the moisture from his brow but finds himself unable to do so. His entire body lies motionless, paralyzed. He desperately tries to move his muscles, even a finger would suffice, but his efforts are to no avail. Darkness surrounds him, though he can feel the warmth of the sun beating down on his body. No, not darkness. His eyes are closed. He seethes with frustration at the idea that he lacks the strength to even open his eyes. The slow rhythm of his heartbeat pounds through his ears, his head throbbing with the undulating tone. He can hear voices, low voices. If only he could reach them, he might be able to escape from this prison. Panic seizes him. A prison? Where are the bars? Where are the guards? What is going on? If he could breathe at this moment, he knew that his breath would be sporadic. Panic grips him again. He cannot breathe. Is he dead? No, he couldn't be. He hears his heart ... heard his heartbeat. Where has the pounding gone to? His mind races. The low voices he had heard before are but a distant whisper. Ever fading into the surrounding darkness that threatens to devour his very essence. He can feel himself being sucked into the void, helpless to pull himself free from the swirling abyss.

Sinister laughter resounds through his head, beckoning for him to let go of his inhibitions. The taunting laughter grows in strength as he is pulled farther into oblivion, now being accompanied by a voice. "Fighting this inevitability is futile. I promise you, my child, you will die."

As quickly as the void and the voice had come, they are gone. Perhaps they had been sucked into the swirling darkness that had threatened to take him as well. His lungs swell as he takes a deep breath. He coughs and rolls over, his muscles constricting and expanding rapidly with the shock of being able to function once more. Something laboriously beats against his chest, gaining strength with each breath that he takes. The pain of it is almost unbearable, the agony of being given new life. He rests his head on the inside of his arm, unwilling to move for fear of the pain that it would bring. His entire body seems thin, as if stretched and pulled in all directions. His insides heave viciously as the bile rises quickly from his stomach and into his throat. He vomits, the action draining any ounce of energy he may have had left. His breathing normalizes, each breath expelling the pain that had accompanied his revival. He rolls onto his back and, for the first time, he opens his eyes. His smoky gray pupils take in the sight of a smiling Ashe looking down at him. Something warm and wet brushes the side of his face. He turns his head to see the wolf that they had encountered before. She ceases licking him and looks up to stare at him with her deep yellow eyes. Cole looks past the wolf to a man whom he has never seen before. The stranger balances himself on the balls of his feet and rests his elbows on his knees. His leathery face is rugged yet kindly. The man smiles at him. "Ya all right, stranger? Yer friends here were mighty worried 'bout ya. I guess it be a good thing that I came along, eh?" He extends his hand.

Cole takes it and is helped to a sitting position. He looks around, his gaze resting once again upon the stranger. He clears his throat. "What … happened?"

Ashe speaks. "I was walking down the road and then I heard a desperate howling. I turned around and you were gone. I knew then that something was wrong. I ran back the way I had come and found you lying on the ground. The wolf was by your side with her muzzle lifted toward the heavens as if in supplication." He pauses. "As soon as I saw your motionless body, I knew that if I didn't act quickly you would be dead. I checked for some type of wound, but found none." He nodded towards the stranger. "Then he came along. Without a word he began removing various items from his pack, only looking up once from his task to ask me your name." Ashe sits on the ground next to Cole, the serious expression on his face drawing his features taut. "It was the strangest thing. He just leaned back and told me to begin. Somehow I understood what I needed to do in order to bring you back, knew what potions to use and to what extent. I felt as if I had done this sort of thing countless times before. And when it was done, I knew that you would return to us, to the world of the living."

The stranger intercedes. "Perhaps next time ya will not need the aid of the potions. I am a mere woods guide, but I know talent when I see it. What ya 'ave just accomplished on yer very first attempt shows yer potential." He scratches the fur under the wolf's chin. "Perhaps ya didn't even need me potions, ya certainly didn't need me guidance." He looks up at them and smiles. "Seems that Old John here has found some very rare people indeed." The wolf howls, making Old John laugh. "So, does this beautiful lady have a name?"

Cole recalls how they had first come upon the creature hiding amongst the shadows of the forest. "Her name is Shadow."

Ashe looks questioningly at Cole but then directs his smile to the stranger. He puts his hand on Cole's shoulder, turning to face him. "There was no doubt in my mind. None, whatsoever." He removes his hand and sighs, "Something very powerful is at work here. I could not feel its presence until I began to draw your life back into your body. I cannot feel it now, but I believe that you can. You are somehow attuned to this malevolence. I fear that the danger has not yet passed."

Cole stands and looks out at the forest road before him, dappled with shadow and sunshine, forever leading him toward some unforeseen destination. Cape Terna is their indicated rendezvous, but what lies in wait for him beyond that? Memories of events long past dance before his eyes, as well as memories of people long gone but not forgotten. Sixteen years ago they were rescued from the clutches of death brought on by war, only to be willingly returning to that from which they fled. There was no escaping the inevitable truth of it all. There was no use in trying to hide from their own destiny. He sighs heavily, "And so it begins."

Old John chuckles as he labors to stand. He places his left hand on his hip and his right hand over his eyes. Staring up at the sun, he remarks. "Life, it be a cycle. Where one journey ends, another begins. Just as the sun heralds the coming of day and the waning of night, the moon is the messenger of the darkness that drives away the light." He sighs and looks upon the two men before him, his eyes twinkling with some unspoken thought.

Ashe clears his throat. "Are you suggesting that this war is a mere battle in the history of the world?"

Old John's mouth frowns for a moment before relaxing into a smile. "Ya should nae put too much credit to me words. I am an old man and have the tendency to talk of things of which I have no knowledge about."

Cole crosses his arms as he stares at the stranger, trying to discern his intentions. "It brings suspicion when one as you discredits their own words. Now tell me true, old man, why are you really here?"

Ashe places his hand on Cole's shoulder in tacit warning that he is bordering wariness with rudeness.

Old John waves his hand in surrender. "Then the truth it is. Ya see, young man, I was sent."

Ashe and Cole instinctively take a defensive stance, but only Ashe is able to speak in spite of his dry throat. "Explain yourself."

Old John sighs, "I am a messenger. I was sent by someone from your past to provide aid to you in your fight for the future."

Cole's voice is ice. "Then deliver your message."

"Beware of flagrant idiots."

Ashe nearly chokes. "What? What is that supposed to mean?"

Old John asserts himself. "It means exactly what it states. Beware of flagrant idiots. Note that plural is used. One is of no consequence, but when there are two, there is possibility offspring. Flagrant idiot parents beget flagrant idiot children."

Cole licks his lips. "So, what you are actually saying is to be wary of flagrant idiot children. And how are we to identify these abominations?"

Old John stares at Cole, his demeanor void of expression. "Well, you're one."

CHAPTER TWELVE

They continue running, a desperate race in what Chase has determined to be the wrong direction. They are parallel to the sounds of battle. He looks towards the cries of dying men and he nearly stumbles into Tom who has for no apparent reason stopped. Chase puts his hands on his knees as he leans forward to catch his breath. When he finally looks up, he is startled by what he sees. The forest has given way to a small clearing in which stands the ashen remains of a campfire and beyond that a shack of dried timber and forest detritus. Tom motions towards the shed.

"Welcome to my humble abode."

With that, he makes for the house and opens the door, gesturing for Chase to come inside.

If the hut had looked small on the outside, it seemed even more cramped once in it. It was relatively dry but that was the only luxury afforded it. The putrid smell is overwhelming and the disheveled papers that litter the floor leaves little imagination as to what they cover. A little nook stood out of place, housing a fireplace and presenting a fairly clean if not comfortable living area. Chase makes his way for this partitioned area and carefully sits down on one of the hand-carved chairs, perplexed on how this space could possibly fit in the square of a building that he had seen from the outside. It is as if he has stepped into a completely different world, things not always being as they seemed.

He focuses his attention on Tom who is across the room retrieving some obviously precious parcel. When Tom once again faces him he can see that he holds in two hands before him a long package wrapped in white linen. For a moment Tom stands there watching him, as if trying to decide something. He sighs and walks into the clutter-free space, still contemplative. He carefully takes a seat and deftly holds the bundle in his lap. Tom slowly unwraps the bundle, his eyes intent on his work. He looks up and for the briefest of moments his stare seems to peer into Chase's very mind, discerning his thoughts and intentions.

Chase shakes his head, disregarding his soaring imagination, and focuses on the object revealed before him. His mouth opens in awe at the shining blade, the glow of the fire dancing off the deadly edge. He gasps with the realization that it was not the reflection that he saw, but real flames licking up the sides of the sword. He is drawn to the artifact, something from deep within him fights to escape. He releases his inhibitions, allowing the sensation to surge through him and surround him with exuberant bliss. He reaches out for the flame sword, and then it is gone. The dream fades away like a distant memory....

Chase's deep breathing slowly returns to normal as he groggily opens his eyes. Panic seizes him as he tries to gather his wits. The comfortable nook with the cozy fireplace is gone. A chill creeps in through the cracks in the walls and he is painfully aware of a sore bottom obtained from sitting on the rock-hard dirt floor. He nearly falls backwards when he sees Tom's hawklike gaze intent on him. Those blue eyes are like daggers, piercing the depths of his very being. Chase starts to rise but finds himself unable to do so. "What have you done to me?"

Tom folds his hands across his lap and nods towards a white bundle that rests on the floor between them. "See for yourself."

Chase growls. "But it's wrapped."

"Then unwrap it."

"But I cannot move."

Tom cocks his head. "Are you sure about that?"

Chase tries to squirm but he makes no progress. "Yes. What is this? What is going on?"

Tom frowns. "If I told you, then that would defeat the purpose." He reaches over and unwraps the bundle. He lays the object atop the white linen square.

Chase nearly laughs with the nonsense of it all.

"It's a stick."

"But it's not just any stick."

Chase sighs exasperatedly, "It's a stick."

Tom lifts a finger. "Ah, but did you not believe it to be a weapon?"

Somewhat unnerved by how Tom could have possibly known his dreams, Chase answers incredulously, "But that was before you unwrapped it."

Tom smiles. "So you admit that this stick had the potential to be a deadly weapon?"

"Anything could have been wrapped up in that cloth."

Tom claps his hands together. "My point exactly. You see, Chase, anything is possible."

Chase rages. "What does this have to do with anything? While we sit here chatting our heads off, people are dying. Couldn't this little demonstration of yours have waited?"

"It has to do with everything. You are wrong about that. No."

Chase stands. "How can I possibly be wrong about that? I can hear their cries as if they are in this very room!"

Tom laughs. "You're standing."

"What?"

"Earlier you said that you couldn't move, but now you are standing."

Frustration crosses Chase's face. "Well, since I can move now, I am leaving. You said that you were going to help but so far you have done nothing but play your little games. I am tired of being some puppet. I have my own life. I am not here by choice but I make my choice now. I choose to quit this tiring charade and help those men." He makes for the door but some invisible force stops him. His progress stopped, he reverses direction and makes towards Tom, his ire evident in his icy blue eyes. He stops short of strangling the old man but is not past glowering down at him. "Release me from this prison. Now."

Chase is surprised to see empathy in the man's eyes. Tom sighs, "Only you have the key. These walls you see around you are your own construct. I have no power here. I am but a guide."

Color drains from Chase's face. "Are you implying that this is all in my head? You are just a figment of my imagination?"

"Yes and Yes. But you are not crazy, and I am but a breath in the wind. Even still, if you do not find a solution to this problem you will be trapped here."

Chase pondered that for a moment. "What if the problem is impossible to solve?"

"Like I said before, anything is possible." He motions at the stick in the middle of the floor. "And as you have seen, things are not always what they seem."

Chase takes a seat on the floor as he mulls over the problem. Men are dying, but Tom had said he had been wrong about that. Perhaps they were all trapped in illusion as well, and the screams he heard were of their own frightful nightmares. If there was indeed a battle going on, for who knows how long this illusion could have been going on. This had all started with the sound of the bugle. Yes. The bugle. It hadn't been a signal to charge but heralded the initiation of the dream. And if there was a battle currently being fought, perhaps the Sentran ranks wielded this vile magic before even having set foot on the shore. That reality would soon change, though, and it would be a slaughter. He shakes his head. He is approaching this in the wrong way. He has to think of the solution. He jumps up. "The stick."

Tom cocks his head. "What about the stick?"

"If it can be a weapon, why can't it be a key?"

"But it's a stick."

Chase's eyes are alit with determination. "Anything is possible." He runs and snatches up the stick.

Tom concedes. "Well, now that you have the key, where is the lock?"

Chase immediately advances for the door, managing to insert the key-stick into the lock. He hears a click but his passage is still blocked by some unseen force. Noting this, he reassesses the situation. "There must be more than one lock." He runs his hands through his hair. "For being an illusion, it all seems so real."

Rubbing his chin, Tom offers. "All of it?"

"Well, no, the lavish room with the fireplace and the chair that I was sitting on just seem to have vanished... and yet...," he begins stabbing at the nonexistent chair and the fireplace in the cozy room that wasn't there. He closes his eyes as he maneuvers through the desolate room as if avoiding unseen obstacles, wildly jabbing and twisting the weapon-stick at air.

Opening his eyes, he now sees the reality before him, no longer trapped in the illusion. He can hear the cries of men, not a quarter a mile away but all around him, converting from abject horror to blinding wrath as they each are simultaneously released from their illusions. Opening one lock had started a chain reaction that unlocked the rest. These men were well-trained and spared no time in meeting the onslaught of the black forces creeping onto the northern banks. In his hands he is holding a stick covered in the green mucus that is the monsters' blood. The sandy ground around him is littered with smoldering black bodies. Chase drops the stick, somewhat confused but mostly mortified by the death that seems to beleaguer him. Chaos surrounds him. Man and monster. Steel and fang. He watches as with deft efficiency the soldiers hew down their enemy.

Then he sees Tom, slashing and maneuvering his way through the carnage to where Chase stands, dispelling the enemy with a surety that belies his expertise in the matter. He gives Chase a nod and throws to him a bloodied sword, glistening bright red in the sunlight. "May this give you better luck than its previous owner."

Putting a death grip on the green and gilt hilt, Chase prepares himself for any battle that he may be drawn into. A gurgling screech behind him warns him of an attacker. With lightning speed he plunges his sword through the creature's body, twisting the weapon as he retrieves it from the smoldering mass. He turns in time to thwart another attack, and another. With a quick survey of his surroundings he sees the monsters dropping like flies, some having been engaged in brutal battle and some even in surprise as a steel point penetrates their back. Turning swiftly, his sword arcs up and around, splitting a monster in two. The bloody battle had reached a turning point, the Emerald Army finally being able to hew down their deceptive enemy.

The last monster falls and a cry of victory issues forth from the mouths of bloody, tired, and sweaty men. Breathing heavily, Chase drops to the ground and lets his sword fall from his hand. He looks up as a shadow stands before him. The man gives him a hand and steadily pulls Chase up onto his feet. The man is dressed in the green and gold livery of an Emerald Army officer, but if the dress had not given away the man's import, his bearing would have. The man claps a hand on Chase's shoulder and smiles.

"That was some pretty fancy fighting you did back there. I don't know who you are, but thanks." The man looks at the remains of the battle behind him and then turns to once again look at Chase. "My men and I, we owe you our lives." The man leaves, shaking his head in amusement, grumbling underneath his breath something about a stick.

Tom steps forward and, wiping his brow, he smirks. "If I hadn't known better, I would say that you have done this before."

Chase shrugs slightly but remains silent.

Tom sighs, "Well, you've earned yourself an audience with the king."

At this, Chase finally speaks. "The king? King Albert of Smithee, I am going to meet him?"

Tom laughs at Chase's apparent uneasiness. "Do not worry. You'll do fine."

Grabbing Chase's arm, he leads him through the forest along the trail that is being taken by the soldiers back to the Emerald Castle. Looking back at the battle site one last time, Chase shudders to think that he could have died this day. If the invading force had not been stopped here, how long would they have gone unchecked? Who could have possibly survived? Chase gulps as his thoughts turn to Kae. To his friends. In more ways than one, this had been a landmark battle. His thoughts are interrupted by Tom's insistent tugging. With a heavy sigh he resigns to being dragged back into the heart of the continent which only hours ago he had been preparing to leave.

CHAPTER THIRTEEN

The woman holds her cloak tightly around her body to ward off the chill of the night. Normally, living behind these massive walls of the city and with the Emerald Guard patrolling the streets, security was something that she had taken for granted. All her years of awaiting the day had not prepared her for the reality of it all. She remembered those blue eyes of his but they had belonged to another man, and how could she forget the talisman? She regrets having lied to the boy about her knowledge of it, but her part in all of it was really of no consequence. It was true that her father had been assigned to the task, but due to his deteriorating health the job was left to her. She had been twelve at the time, but had been working with stone ever since she was four and, of course, she had learned from the best. But, as she has noted before, her part in all of it was really of no consequence. The real importance lies in the fact the talisman was forged. But alas, the real hope lies not in the dim memory of the past but in the glimpse of a future that she hopefully had managed to perpetuate.

At least, at first she had felt hope, but as the moon cast light and shadow through her tent window, all she could feel was an overwhelming dread. During the day her fear had somewhat dissipated, but now walking through these desolate streets, running past dark alleys, and looking back over her shoulder, her anxiety has manifested into sheer terror. She takes a deep breath as she rounds the corner that will take her onto her street of residence. The porch light is a welcome beacon.

And then her fears are realized. A deep voice resounds from the depths of the shadows, a somewhat jaunting, self-righteous tone. "Mistress Cara."

Cara stops in her tracks as she hears her name, sounding vile due to the nature of the disembodied voice. Despite the trembling of her body, her voice sounds rather clear and maybe even a little confident. "You don't belong here."

A jilting laughter causes her to cringe but her distaste transforms into panic as the shadows surrounding her seem to swirl and coalesce into the form of a man. She cannot see the man's face, if it indeed is a man, but she gets the strange sensation that he is smiling at her. Chills run up and down her body and any shred of confidence she had had before is gone, leaving her with the feeling of being bare and whimpering for all the world to judge. The man laughs again.

"So, are you, of all people, banishing me to the fiery depths from whence I came?" He scoffs. "I think not."

Cara clenches her fists, gathering her courage. "Whatever you are selling, I am not buying."

"Ooh, I'm offended. A downright refusal before you even hear what I have to offer? Now, where is the business sense in that? Come, come, my dear, surely your opinion of me isn't so low as to deny me a chance."

"First of all, I already know your proposal, and second of all, I am not your 'dear.' If you think for one second that I will to you give the time of day, you are seriously mistaken. You have come to the wrong person. Now go. You may think my threats to be empty, but so are yours."

The man crosses his arms and throws back his head in amusement. "You're a feisty one. I like that in my women, but I am here purely on business. If I can't convince you to join with me, then just as a sign of my sincerity on the matter, I will share with you one little tidbit of information." He pauses for a moment and then continues, "You, my dear, have been betrayed."

Cara's heart clenches, immediately recognizing the implications of the statement. "By who?"

The man raises a finger. "Ahh-ahh-ahh, I have divulged my one bit of information and, unless you've changed your mind, I will take my leave."

Cara can barely control her rage. "I will never join you."

The man shrugs. "Have it your way."

Now that she is alone, she tears down her barricades and weeps. Having allowed herself this one act of selfishness, she can now focus on the task before her, resolving to identify the betrayer before it is too late; before all that they had worked for crumbles into the ashes of despair and depravity. She looks cautiously around her and then slips into the comforting recesses of the building that she had gotten used to calling home. Closing the door behind her she sighs heavily, having resigned to the idea that on the morrow she will have to leave these walls that had sheltered her for most of her life. She unties her cloak, letting it drop to the planked floor. She observes silently as the moonlight filters in through the window, casting itself across the completely utilitarian furniture that fills the little space she calls her home. Her hand clutches the crystal hanging on a chain around her neck, sending a prayer and a message. Without bothering to change into her bedclothes, she crawls beneath the woolen blanket on her bed and drifts into a tormented sleep.

• •

Chase reclines on the grass with his hands behind his head. Staring up at the stars shining brightly above him, he remembers things of the past. He recalls standing not too long ago on the top of a hill on a night much like this. Promises had been made, and broken. *Brothers forever, we will always be brothers.* Nothing will ever change that, but the memory is clouded by another. *I, Chase Blader, promise that no harm shall come to Kaela Lee while she is under my protection.* By leaving the way he did, he had hurt her more than anything else could ever have. And then, at the waterfall, if only he could have controlled his temper and not stormed off.... If only he could find the courage to make things right.... If only it didn't have to be this way ... if. Kae had told him that he could not live in the past, but the past haunts him wherever he goes. It is a foundation which must not be ignored, otherwise the future would be meaningless. From the past do we learn, and with learning comes understanding.

Chase looks over as Tom returns from his venture into the woods. His gaze falls upon the stars once again. "There's something in the air tonight."

Tom sits down and crosses his legs. "What makes you say that?"

"It reeks of memory and purpose." Chase sighs, "I feel anxious, like something momentous is about to happen ... or already has."

Tom shrugs inconsequentially. "Or perhaps both are correct."

Chase laughs. "Or I could just be going crazy."

Tom cocks his head and purses his lips. "Well then, I guess it's a good thing the royal family was away, lest you infect them with the bug of insanity."

Giving him a sidelong glance, Chase continues, "I'm telling you. It's in the air. Even the king and queen seek a lighter breeze. The air here hangs heavy, further oppressing me the longer I stay here."

Raising his brow and rubbing his chin, Tom queries. "You wouldn't happen to be Gaelithian, would you?"

Chase rises to stare squarely at Tom, his expression grave and earnest. "Why do you ask? What does it mean to be Gaelithian?"

Tom rubs his hands voraciously. "I wasn't being serious ... but there are rumors that the old legends are still prevalent in parts of this world. In ancient Ilian history, there were supposed races that could ... command the elements: Fire, Water, Earth, and Wind. There are others, but they are more obscure." He gauges Chase's reaction to this and then continues, "From your unaffected expression, I guess that you have heard of this. Anyways, Gaelithians are said to be descendants of the People of the Skies who, as their name implies, commanded the winds. This, however, is just conjecture and I was only correlating it to the statement you made about there being something in the air."

Chase is in deep contemplation. After a few moments, he laughs. "I don't suppose I am Gaelithian, but I would like to see this place sometime." He remembers something. "You know, a lady I met the other day said something about Gaelith. Perhaps I will be able to find some answers there."

Tom nods. "Well, before we set off there is something that has been brought to my attention that I need to take care of immediately." He studies Chase for a moment before speaking again. "I will be going to the Sylvan cottage. You can either come with me or find another guide."

A question arises in Chase's eyes but he leaves it unsaid. Instead, he spreads his hands before him in acquiescence. "Does anyone else have a boat?"

Tom shakes his head. "No."

"Then I guess I have no choice. But I am not ready to face them." He puts his head down in shame and then looks off into the distance. "I will stay in the forest ... I know of a place."

Tom slaps his hands to his knees and rises. "Very well. We leave in the morning."

Chase huffs. "You have no retort as to my cowardice."

"Being that you honored my discretion in this matter, I will do the same."

Chase rises to stand beside Tom. "Hey, Tom, I want to thank you. Not only for the boat and everything, but you've helped me in more ways than you know. In some ways, I feel that you have been guiding me or helping me all along, as if our pasts are somehow connected."

"Don't you go getting all sentimental on me now." He shivers. "I can't stand for tears. But you're welcome. Besides, I enjoy the company."

Chase sighs, "I seriously hope you were only joking about the tears, especially after today."

Tom replies wryly. "Today? Oh, right, I nearly forgot you single-handedly defeated all those monsters."

"Well, you did give me the sword."

Tom puts his hands on his sides. "Well, it is a much more suitable weapon than that stick that you were carrying." He rubs his chin. "Although you weren't doing all too badly...."

"Anything can be used as a weapon. Or more fundamentally, the nature of an object is as we perceive it to be. So perception shapes reality."

Tom grins widely and claps Chase on the shoulder. "My boy, I don't think I could have said it better myself." He shakes his head in amazement. "With that keen sense of yours and your innate ability with weapons, I sure would hate to be your enemy."

Chase smiles inwardly. "No, I don't guess that I would like to be my own enemy either." Laughing, he puts out his hand. "Friends, then."

Tom takes it in his own and replies. "Friends." He chuckles. "Well, in honor of our friendship, I would like to give you this." He reaches into his pocket and pulls out a small box. "I've had this for eleven years. I intended to give it to someone but ... well, perhaps you can find a better use for it than collecting dust in a box in my shirt pocket."

Chase takes the box and unceremoniously opens it. Inside lays a ring wrought in white gold bearing a sapphire blue stone. A design resembling that of waves is sculpted into the slender band and encircles the smooth, spherical stone. He places it on the tip of his little finger, smiling. "I think it's a little too small."

Tom shakes his head in amusement. "I guess that you will just have to find some small finger to put it on." He winks conspiratorially. "It is a promise ring."

Chase puts the ring back in the box and looks up. "Promise...."

• •

Maria sips a cup of coffee as she curls up in a couch in the barely used living room. Kae sits across from her in another chair, idly watching the fire blaze in the hearth. She sighs and Maria is brought out of her reverie. Maria sets down her cup on the coffee table and shakes her head in bewilderment.

"Seventeen. Where have the years gone to? You have all grown up so quickly." Her expression clouds over for an instant. "I still remember the day you all were brought here. And now you are a fine young woman."

The fire dances in Kae's soft lavender eyes as she replies absently, "Everything has changed in so little time. I've hardly realized that tomorrow is my birthday. I guess it doesn't hold the same significance it did when I was younger. And the prospect of another birthday seems to spell disaster. Right now, the future in general seems … hopeless. I don't know—ever since Chase left, I've been doing a lot of thinking. These past two weeks have changed me. His leaving was just so … sudden…."

Maria succeeds in maintaining a weak smile in spite of her own doubts. Her eyes become overcast. "Surprise is just another one of life's obstacles. It does not always come wrapped up in a nice little box. We are often forced to make sacrifices. Because, no matter how much we may want something, the price of obtaining it is just too high."

Kae studies her. "Maria—I need to thank you, and I need to apologize."

"For what?"

Controlling the emotion in her voice but unable to hide it in her face, Kae speaks. "For the sacrifices you made when you took us in."

Maria waves a hand in ambivalence. "That is in the past. I admit that in the beginning it did hurt, it still hurts sometimes, but raising all of you has been a blessing. I love you all as if you were my own. You remind me of myself when I was your age; an age when I was free-spirited and did not have to make any sacrifices. But already you have sacrificed more than I ever have, more than you will ever know. That is why I think you should have this."

She unties the necklace around her neck and silently holds it before Kae. Squinting her eyes, she places the necklace on the table and reaches into her apron pocket. "It is missing something." She pulls out a gold ring whose ruby at first seems to be on fire with the breath escaping from the maws of the twin dragons encircling the stone. She slides the ring onto the necklace and once again holds it before Kae. Nodding in satisfaction, she smiles. "Happy Birthday, Kaela."

Kae is speechless, so she simply takes the necklace with the ring and clasps it around her neck. She admires it for a moment and then looks up at Maria. "So this is what you sacrificed. This promise." She clutches the ring and closes her eyes to hold back her tears. "I will guard it with my life."

Maria shakes her head. "It is just a ring. You must guard the promise that it represents." She smiles tiredly as she gets up and makes for the hallway. "It's getting late. You better get some rest."

Kae stretches and slowly rises to her feet. "For the first time in two weeks, I feel that I will be able to."

CHAPTER FOURTEEN

Chase shades his eyes from the afternoon sun as he steps out from the domains of the forest. He shakes his head and looks back at Tom. "It still amazes me that it took me two weeks to make a half-day-long journey."

Tom grins widely. "I admit that your sense of direction is ... wanting." He slaps Chase on the shoulder. "But look at it this way: that narrows down the possibilities of where you are from."

Chase runs his hand through his unruly black hair and smiles. "Still operating on that whole idea of cultures inheriting the ability to control the elements, are you?"

Tom raises a finger. "Have you forgotten that unlike you, I've actually been off this continent?"

Chase crosses his arms and sighs, "Well, people can believe whatever they want to believe. But I personally don't believe in magic."

Tom straightens his back and raises his brow. "Who said anything about magic? Think of it as a cultural or even physical trait." He looks around and then points to an eagle flying high overhead. "For example, birds can fly, but you and I cannot. Does that necessarily mean that the bird has magic? Just because something or someone can do something that someone else cannot does not mean that it is magic." He adjusts his pack. "We use the word 'magic' because it refers to something of which we have no real knowledge. And people are scared of what they do not know." He looks away, caught up in memory. "People can use your fear against you, to control you. It has been used to fuel wars. Look at the current state of the world. War is upon us. And we are fighting an impossible adversary who possesses no ethical compunctions whatsoever. That battle we fought the other day—that illusion—*that* was magic. It was not natural. It arose from the depths of a realm which I will not name. I fear for the world for in its ignorance it does not possess the necessary protection from it." He looks up at the sun and then stares out onto the fertile plain before them. "We must pray for the salvation as recorded by the prophets of centuries past. Therein lies our only defense against this threat."

"Are you implying that all those forces in the Nesthra Islands, all those people fighting for their freedom, don't even have a chance?" Chase gasps as he thinks of Cole and Ashe on their way to what may be their deaths.

Tom looks back at Chase, insurmountable pain of inevitability stretching across his haggard-seeming features. "Even with the savior from the prophecies, the chance has always been slim. But that's the wonder of the human spirit. It keeps fighting even in the face of defeat. It clings to the hope that if it keeps fighting long enough, it will survive. And if it dies in the process, at least it went out in a blaze of glory."

Chase clenches his fists in determination. "Only when we consign ourselves to defeat do we fail. If what you are saying is true, then you, I, and the Emerald Guard would have been annihilated when we fought those monsters." He rages. "Tell me. Tell me how it is possible that we stand here now? Why are you and I not dead? The human spirit *is* our defense. Our innocence is not a weakness, but a strength. To say otherwise is to accept defeat and allow the evil to consume us in our ignorance."

Tom scratches his chin. "I am just being realistic, but you do pose a good question. Why *are* we still alive? If I recall, you were the one to break the spell. Perhaps you are our savior."

"Frankly, I am tired of your conjectures. First, I am Gaelithian with the power to control the winds, and now I am some mystical redeemer? I hardly find these irrational conclusions realistic." Chase bluntly voices his opinion. "Your words seem to be vehicles by which you hide the fact that you have lost hope."

Tom is surprisingly calm in light of Chase's accusations. "I've lost more than my hope." Clearing his throat, he nods. "This is the southern edge of the Northern Woods. We should part here, unless...."

Chase puts his fists to his sides in conviction. "I'll be fine here."

Tom nods. "Very well. This should not take longer than a week."

"A week?" replies Chase exasperatedly.

Tom queries. "Is there a problem? Provided you ration your provisions you shouldn't starve, and the forest is full of nourishment. So meet me here, at this spot, in a week. Can you handle that? I do not want to have to come find you."

Chase observes his surroundings, noting his position relative to the mountains rising to his right with the sun just beginning its descent behind them. He fidgets. "Don't worry." He can hear a brook bubbling not too far off behind him and reasons that he is still a ways west of the waterfall. As long as he follows the river, he should find where he intends to wait. "Once I have been to a place, I can always find my way back." If he does get lost, he can enlist the help of the dryads. Chase muses at this hindsight which would have proven useful during his two-week trek through the woods. He smiles. "Besides, I am among friends here."

"Friends?"

Chase smiles. "A dryad, a fish, and a sea serpent."

"You keep strange company." Tom cocks his head. "And I thought you didn't believe in magic."

"I understand their nature. There is nothing magical about it; unless you are referring to the feeling."

Tom squints his eyes, and then with a reprimanding tone he reiterates, "Remember, a week. No more and no less." He turns towards the Sylvan cottage.

Chase takes a step forward and places his hand on Tom's shoulder. "This is serious, isn't it?"

Tom looks gravely into Chase's eyes. "You have no idea." Adjusting his pack, he continues down the path leading up a hill to a house that he has not seen in eleven years.

• •

Jessica rushes into the kitchen with Joel not too far behind her. They both seem out of breath, but Jessica is the first to speak.

"Maria! There is a strange man standing outside at the bottom of the hill."

Joel chimes in, "I think he has urgent news, but is afraid to come in."

Maria walks over to the window. A small intake of breath is heard as her hands fly to her chest. "Tom." She turns to look inquisitively between Jessica and Joel, her expression full of hope and, at the same time, despair. Biting her lip, she pulls up her skirts and runs out of the house, rushing down the hill at an almost frantic and breakneck speed. Jessica and Joel chase after her, breathlessly watching as Maria flies into the man's outstretched arms. He twirls her around and then sets her gently upon the ground. Maria puts her arms around his neck as he runs his hand through her long auburn hair. Pulling her close to him, he bends down to softly kiss her. Maria rises onto her toes to meet his lips.

At the top of the hill, Jessica and Joel stand with their mouths gaping open in shock. Blinking, Jessica slowly manages to turn her head to look at Joel. He looks back at her and grins. "It seems that for once, you are speechless."

Jessica punches him in the shoulder but still doesn't say a word. She stares at the scene before her, hardly able to comprehend what in the world is going on. Suddenly, a mystery man emerges from the woods and the stalwart Maria who had shunned such outward displays of emotion throws her cares to the wind to embrace this stranger from her past. Many times Jessica has seen her angry and seen her cry, but not once has she seen Maria truly smile. Maria had always been haunted by some lost dream, ever fading but never forgotten. Now standing here on this hill, Jessica realizes the sacrifice of this woman who had raised these children as her own. Maria and this woodland stranger had been in love; a love which after all this time had not eroded. As selfish as it sounds, Jessica had never considered what Maria's life had been before she had become burdened with all these orphans. She had always focused on her own story and never questioned those told by others. Everything she knows about why they are all here was told by Maria, but she now knows that they were not told everything. What other secrets remain to be revealed? Her proceeding thoughts seem so preposterous to her that the entire situation seems to be illusory. She whispers quietly to Joel, "Either I am dreaming or the world has gone mad." She desperately turns to Joel. "Quick, do something so I know that this is real."

Joel shrugs. "Okay." Without a moment of hesitation, he leans forward and places a kiss on Jessica's lips.

The initial shock of his lips on hers leaves her paralyzed, but then she finds herself drawn into it. She kisses him back, for a moment forgetting where and who she is. As the realization of what she is doing dawns on her, she pulls away. Staring at Joel in disbelief, she tries to speak but her throat constricts with emotion.

Joel smiles dazedly. "Was that real enough for you?"

• •

"And so I am still here, on Smithee," Chase says seemingly to thin air.

A melodious voice answers him. "You couldn't leave things the way you had with her."

Chase sighs, "Nikoi, like I said, my guide has to do some business before we can leave. Why do you think I came here instead of going on to the Sylvan cottage."

"I know what you said, but I also know that that is not the real reason. I also know why you showed her this place before you left."

He puts his hands out in challenge. "Enlighten me." The water silently ripples as he feels the creature's presence come nearer to him.

"You knew that she would need a friend when you left. You thought I would be of much help. Did you not also think that she would come here often? Did you not know that if you waited here, she would come?"

Running his hands through his hair, he laughs a defeated laugh. "That telepathy thing of yours can put others at a great disadvantage, you know that?"

The soft voice laughs knowingly. "I can speak to your mind, but I cannot read your mind. You humans are just so predictable."

Chase rolls his eyes. "Thanks."

"She comes."

Taking a deep breath, Chase climbs up the side of the bank and makes his way towards the top of the ridge. He smiles anxiously when he sees her step from the recesses of the forest and start across the bridge.

Caught up in her own thoughts as she clutches the chain around her neck, Kae does not notice the man standing on the other side of the river until she nearly stumbles unto him. Her heart races at seeing those familiar black boots with a splash of red spilling over the tops. She dare not raise her head to look at his face, holding onto the hope that will be dashed if it is not who she wants it to be. Her fears are immediately shattered by the painfully recognizable voice.

The familiar warmth of the tone, a jest on the verge of something more, floats across the still air. "It seems that we keep on running into each other."

Slowly she turns up her head to be welcomed by those dazzling blue eyes and that radiant smile. Conflicting emotions course through her with the unsteady and erratic force of a torrential rainstorm. She turns away from him and whispers, "Am I dreaming?"

Chase takes a step forward and gently places his hand on her arm, urging her to face him.

With her free hand, she clutches her necklace. "If this is a dream, then I don't ever want to wake up." Quietly pulling away from him, she puts her fists to her sides and takes a deep breath. For an instant she closes her eyes, glistening with tears. "And if this is real, if you are really here, I do not know whether to kiss you ... or slap you."

Chase smiles tenderly and leans forward to kiss her.

The brush of his lips lasts only for a moment, but the effect is enough cause for reaction. Before he has a chance to say a word, she slaps him. Expecting him to storm off now, she turns away in regretful silence.

His lighthearted tone startles her. "It seems that now you have done both."

Kae puts her fingers to her lips. "Now I know this is a dream."

"Why are you so sure?"

Looking down at her hands, she whispers in dismayed conviction, "You are not the Chase I know. The Chase I know would never do what you just did, only in my dreams."

Chase probes teasingly. "So you've dreamt of me kissing you?"

She turns to look at him, her expression serious. "I've dreamt of not being left behind." She blushes. "And of kissing you."

Chase kisses her again.

Kae slaps him again. "I will not let my fantasies control me. I will not let them make me feel this way, no matter how real it may seem."

He caresses her cheek and then pushes her hair away from her face. "You want to be in control of your own dreams. Then you should be able to stop me ... if you can ... if this is indeed a dream." Once more, he kisses her, tenderly and with more passion.

She allows herself to indulge in this kiss, before once again breaking away and slapping him, hard.

Chase rubs his sore cheek. "Why do you insist on slapping me after I kiss you?"

Kae glares at him. "Why do you insist on kissing me?"

"Why do you kiss me back?" he counters.

Realizing her defeat on the matter, Kae breaks down in tears. "Please, do not taunt me so. It is hard enough trying to get through the day without you. I miss you. I miss everything, especially the fighting." She smiles, abashed at her indiscretion, but tears once again fill her eyes. "You made me feel alive. And now you stalk my dreams, a constant reminder of what I did not know I had until I lost it."

Chase wraps his arms protectively around her, caressing her hair and whispering into her ear, "I am here. I am not lost to you."

She hugs him tightly, as if at any moment he is going to drift away. "My senses tell me that you are really here. The warmth and the definitive form of your body ... your eyes that seem to speak to my soul ... your heartbeat resounding through my head ... the bittersweet smell of the forest and your sweat ... and the taste of your lips ... all seem so real. My heart wishes for this to be true, but my mind tells me that you are long gone...."

Chase kisses the top of her head. "I am here now, but I cannot stay...." He holds her closer to him. "I just had to see you again."

She looks up at him. "Where have you been these past two weeks?"

Chase scratches the back of his head. "I never left Smithee."

Kae recalls something. "What did you mean earlier when you said 'It seems that we keep on running into each other'?"

"Do you recall colliding with someone three days ago when you were entering the Green Tavern?" Chase says probingly as he raises a knowing brow.

Kae covers her face and laughs in astonishment. "That was you? Why didn't you say anything?"

Running his hand through his hair, Chase flushes. "Believe me I considered it, but at the time I was still doubtful as to the decision I had made to leave. I realized that until I could accept what I had to do, I wouldn't be able to talk to you with a clear conscience."

"And now?"

His eyes glaze over with purpose. "Just as something keeps you here, something calls me forth." He looks back at her with a sad smile on his face. "I assume it is too much to hope that you will come with me."

Kae smiles. "Assumptions are dangerous. But yes I cannot go with you, at least not yet."

Chase takes her hands in his and looks meaningfully into her lavender eyes. "I can wait for you."

She touches his cheek. "You don't know how much that means to me. But the knowledge that I had a part in denying you this chance to find your parents would destroy us both." She entwines her delicate fingers in his.

He kisses their joined hands. "We will find each other. We will be together."

Kae smiles coyly. "Is that a promise?"

At the mention of the word, Chase lets go of Kae's hands and reaches into his pocket. He pulls out the box that Tom had given him and removes the ring. He slides the sapphire ring wrought in white gold onto the ring finger of Kae's right hand. "A perfect fit." He kisses the finger with the ring on it. "I promise you, Kaela, that we will be together again. Across the distance shall my love find you and keep you until this promise can be fulfilled."

With trembling hands, Kae unclasps the necklace and removes the ruby ring. She places the golden band upon Chase's right hand. "And with this ring shall you remember this promise. Remember the love that this represents and serves to protect."

Kae wraps her arms around Chase's neck and means to kiss him. Chase hesitates, keeping his lips just clear of hers. His eyes twinkle mischievously as he whispers, "You're not going to slap me again, are you?"

Kae laughs in spite of herself. She raises her chin in cheerful defiance. "I haven't decided yet."

Enjoying her eager playfulness, Chase bends down to kiss her. He finds his kiss to be welcome, both reveling in the warmth of each other's tender touch. Waves of absolute exhilaration course through them. The power of a raging sea and the intensity of a blazing fire swirl and dance to an endless cadence of emotion. Their lips part, but the energy still strums between them in an unbreakable bond. Kae takes Chase's hand and places it over her heart. She smiles up at him in wonder, her eyes a brilliant blaze of lilac. "I feel your presence here."

Chase nods. "As do I." He looks around them. "What do you say we get off this bridge and go for a swim?"

Kae links her hand around his and lets him lead her down to the bank. "I'd say that that is an excellent idea."

CHAPTER FIFTEEN

Jessica closes her eyes, inviting the warmth of the sun upon her face. Her golden hair glistens in the radiant light, flowing on a breathless wind with each delicate step she takes. She smiles as she senses his hesitant presence behind her.

"A voice whispers to me. I do not know from whence it comes but what it brings reveals to me truths of which I would have never guessed or admitted to."

Joel takes his place beside her. "What sort of truths?"

Jessica opens her eyes, dazzling amethyst gems through which she sees the world. "In a way I guess I have always known, but after you kissed me, I was certain."

Joel blushes, with a hint of mischief playing across his features. "Certain of what?"

She sighs contentedly. "When you kissed me, it felt so right. But it shouldn't have. And the fact that you did kiss me tells me that you know this to be true as well."

"I don't understand."

Jessica turns to him, but her gaze rests on some distant thought. "There is a destiny, surrounded by a secret that we all share but are unaware of. Part of that secret lies in our pasts; from where we come. We are all orphans. How can we be sure of who is our brother or sister, mother or father? The bonds that have been formed were meant to be, no matter how much we try to ignore them. Lara and Ashe will marry. Kae and Chase are soul mates. And you and I, well ... that would not be a possibility if Ashe is my brother."

Joel looks down at his hands. "And if you and he are brother and sister, then my kissing you was a mistake bordering on incest."

Jessica sighs absently, "Yes. But the idea of Ashe being my brother was something that was instilled within me. There has never been a special bond, like that of you with your brothers. I consider him a confidante as best. I know that sounds heartless, but I can't help but feel that if it had ever been any other way, considering that Ashe is not my brother, then this destiny that involves us all would be but a fading dream." She now looks at Joel, into those piercing blue eyes full of life and an untapped wisdom. "I know that you see the truth in this, not because you want it to be so, but because it simply is."

"Jessy, you talk of destiny, but what of free will? Do we not also have a choice in how we live our lives? I do not understand these visions you see or voices you hear, and perhaps you do not either. All I know is that these conclusions you have made are based on something that may very well be imaginary. I would not put too much credence into these fleeting moments until you have learned their origin. It may be leading you down a path of destruction, cloaked in the illusion of the truth that your heart desires."

Jessica smiles sadly. "I understand your concern and your doubt, Joel. In regards to free will, was it your choice to kiss me, or was some mystical hand guiding you?"

Joel scratches his head. "Frankly I am getting quite dizzy running around in circles and such. I suggest we enlist the knowledge of someone who can give us a definitive answer. We need to confront Maria."

Nodding in agreement, Jessica starts back towards the cottage. Joel follows for a few steps and then stops suddenly as if he had run into some invisible barrier. His brow furrows in concern. "Jessica, what of Cole?"

She turns, fists clenched in anxiety. "What do you mean?"

Joel studies her face for a moment. "Please, don't hold back the truth from me." Setting his jaw, he continues, "You never mentioned him … when you were talking about our destiny."

Jessica struggles to find the right words, eventually giving up the idea of euphemisms to just tell it as it is. "The future is obscure, but somehow I manage to get what I believe to be glimpses of it. But these glimpses are only possibilities because of the existence of free will. I have seen each of us, in one form or another, but when I look to Cole, I see absolutely nothing."

Joel thinks on this, sitting down and crossing his legs. "Well, that means that his future is not yet written, right? I mean, perhaps he has not made a choice yet that will determine the path he is to take and the others have, so their futures would be more definite. That is why you have seen theirs and not his, right? You said yourself that you were only certain after I kissed you. That was a choice that I had made. I don't need some incarnation of fate to tell me how I feel or how to think."

"I hope that you are right, Joel." She crosses her arms and smiles. "So, what were you thinking when you kissed me?"

Joel rises to his feet and shrugs. "That if you punched me for whatever measure I took to show you that what you were seeing was real, at least it would be worth it." He grins widely and then runs the distance back to the cottage before Jessica has a chance to react to his words.

Jessica chases after Joel, admonishing herself for once again being completely caught off guard. In all her life, only Joel had managed to surprise her—or make her laugh. Only he truly understood her, could predict her next move, and be duly prepared for her wrath. She stops before the doorstep of which Joel had sought refuge only moments before. As she catches her breath, her train of thought sends her to a reality of which she had been trying to avoid. Despite all the things that only Joel can do, there is one more that illustrates the impact he has had on her. This particular "only" strengthens her conviction that the visions seen and voices heard are purveyors of truth. If Ashe is indeed her brother, and Joel and herself are not meant to be together, then why is Joel the only one to have ever deeply hurt her?

• •

Maria smiles faintly. "As much as I am glad to see you, I am set with a heavy heart at what this meeting portends."

Tom returns a weak smile that does not reach his blue eyes. "Cara contacted me last night. On her way home she had been confronted by one of Mala's minions, who told her that there is a traitor amongst us. She doesn't know who it is, but she is on her way to Nesthra to inform Chris of the threat. She will impart this information to Old John as she passes through the Southern Woods, and he will in turn inform the rest."

Maria digests this with a complacent face and finally comments, "Can we trust the word of this malevolent messenger?"

Tom nods. "It is true that they do often deal in prevarication but truth is always revealed in the light. The words were simple enough but that in itself can be a form of deception. We must take every precaution necessary and we must not forget our main objective."

"As the seven stars descend from the heavens the seven keepers of the sight must guard them with their holy light," Maria recites with conviction and purpose.

Tom smiles warmly. "It has been long since I have heard that, and I am glad that your lips were the ones to speak it." His eyes twinkle with mischief. "Do you remember what we used to do under the cover of the stars?"

Maria blushes. "You make it sound so scandalous." She smiles. "We were married. There was a time when nothing else mattered. We were the only two people in the world." Her features are once again downcast. "But that time has passed. We have responsibilities now. Our duties require different things of us. I to stay here and you to roam the world in search of answers." She sighs, "It seems that Kae and Chase are doomed to the same fate."

Tom grins knowingly. "Appearances can be deceiving."

Maria laughs. "Well, that's a cliché if ever I heard one, but you are right. I was comparing two very different situations."

Tom agrees. "Not to belittle what we had, but our love was not the forbear to prophecy." He smiles wistfully. "But it did bear a child."

Maria puts her hands over her racing heart. "Oh, dear. Why had I not thought of it before?"

Tom leans forward in concern. "Maria, what's wrong?"

She claps her hands over her mouth in tearful joy. "Through our love we fulfilled part of the prophecy. She was born with the gift that has only just begun to manifest itself." She recites, "As the seven stars descend from the heavens the seven keepers of the sight must guard them with their holy light. What better way to guard one of the stars than with a mother's love?"

Tom shakes his head. "Those were the sentiments of Lady Aurora." He recalls the precursor to a conversation nearly twenty years ago. "You remind me of Lady Aurora."

Realizing this connection to the past, Maria feigns affront. "My lord, one must not speak such blasphemy."

Laughing, Tom once again takes her in his arms. "Only in the presence of a lady such as yourself."

Maria puts her arms around his neck. "You scorn my good reputation. I will not allow you to despoil either my name or that of Lady Aurora with your vile words."

"How will you silence me?"

"Oh, I have a few ideas." Maria kisses him.

After they kiss, Tom bows deeply and receives Maria's hand. He gently places her hand in the crook of his arm and leads her up the hill. Smiling at her, he whispers, "I see you remember well how we first met, although at the time there was much more venom to your words and circumspection in your actions."

Maria rests her head against his arm as she gently admonishes him. "You, however, have not changed one bit."

• •

Jessica quietly sits at the kitchen table with her hands clasped together as she waits for Maria and her friend to come inside. Joel is straddling a nearby chair with his crossed arms resting on the back of it. He looks intently at Jessica.

"Jessy, are you sure you want me to be here?"

She only nods. "This involves you, too." She looks up expectantly as the front door swings open. Maria and the stranger walk in holding hands. The stranger smiles at Jessica with his blue eyes, and for an instant Jessica feels as if she has seen those blue eyes before. Both he and Maria enter the kitchen, but they remain standing. Without pretense, Jessica speaks, "Sir, forgive me for being so forthcoming, but you are stranger to me and yet I seem to know you."

Maria looks at the stranger. "See what I mean?"

The stranger nods. "Manifested gift indeed." He smiles at Jessica and gestures towards a seat, tacitly asking whether or not he could sit down. Receiving permission, he nods to Joel and pulls out a chair for both himself and Maria. He guides her before taking his own seat. His brow furrows as he makes eye contact with Jessica. "It intrigues me that you are so adept at cleverly interjecting straightforward remarks in carefully framed decorum."

Jessica smiles mischievously. "And you, sir, ingeniously frame reprimand in compliment."

Joel laughs at this little game. "Ooh, let me try." He rubs his hands together as he briefly contemplates over the matter. "Will you, sir, choose to reprimand the compliment she made to you upon noticing the subtle interpolation of her opinion or compliment her on reprimanding your deceptively complimentary reprimand?"

Maria puts her hand over her mouth in a futile attempt to stop from laughing. Gathering her composure, she has the final word. "Well, I for one reprimand any compliment regarding this absurd behavior, even if the compliment serves to reprimand the reprimand by way of framing such honest dissertation in propriety." She folds her hands before her. "Now, there are matters that must be addressed. I do not expect the actions we took to be understood, but please bear with us. I had hoped for this confrontation to be delayed until you two were older, but circumstances drive us to act now." She looks over to the stranger.

He continues, "After we are done, please feel free to ask us any questions," he looks at Jessica, "and do not be afraid to be blunt. We want for you to understand the enormity of the situation and the role you play in all of this.

"First, let me introduce myself. My name is Tom Sylvan." He notes the slight intake of breath that both Jessica and Joel make, but each remaining silent so that he could continue, "This is my home, and Maria is my wife. For the past eleven years I have been on a mission whose sole purpose is to locate enemies of the dream of a united Ilia that we are trying to realize. One such enemy is Mala, whose forces tried to invade Smithee just yesterday. Thankfully, the attack was squandered before it could escalate. These are perilous times we are living in, reminiscent of the conditions surrounding the Lion Wars that eventually sundered the united kingdoms of Ilia as we know it. Another war forebodes certain doom."

"But hope rests in the legend of a savior who will rise above the ashes to once again bring peace to Ilia," Maria explains. "In truth, such foretelling has been distorted over the centuries, with the original translation being lost. There is rumor of a sacred cave upon whose walls the prophecy was scribed, but the secret of its location was buried with the ancient kings of Ilia. What we have ascertained with our limited information and insight, however, is that our salvation is not in the form of one person, but of seven. There is also reason to believe that in order for salvation to come, Ilia must first be destroyed, ravaged by flames that consume the world."

Jessica becomes more and more withdrawn, as the recollection of visions of the future that had imprinted themselves in her memory are once again brought to life with Maria's words. She looks to Joel and sees in his eyes that he remembers well what she had told him she had seen.

Tom clears his throat. "Maria and I are members of an organization that calls itself 'Oracle Seven.' There are only seven senior members, but there also exist several others who play key roles in helping us to accomplish our ultimate goal: As the seven stars descend from the heavens, the seven keepers of the sight must guard them with their holy light." He nods to Jessica. "Similar to the visions you have, we are able to see the future, and with prophecy as a guide, can manipulate events as a means to achieve the desired outcome of a united Ilia at peace."

"Our sight is limited, however, and there are some things that have happened that were never planned." Maria takes Jessica's hands in hers. "That is where free will comes in. I fell in love with Tom, and bore a child to him." Tears well in her eyes as voice trembles with regret. "For three years we raised that child, but one dreadful night would serve to not only tear apart our family, but countless families across Ilia." She regains her composure. "Tom had been in service of the Assyrian Royal Navy but what he did that night also served the purpose of Oracle Seven."

Tom puts his hand on Maria's shoulder. "I was the one who brought all the orphans to this place, my own child becoming one of them in light of the need to safeguard them from their pasts. I brought them here, to this cottage that was sheltered by the landscape with the mountains to the east and west and the forests to the north and south. And in this cottage have they lived for the past eleven years, myself being absent from my own home and my own family so the past could be left undisturbed."

"And I stayed here, taking on the responsibility of raising the orphans and the child that I could not call my own. Each of us in Oracle Seven had our specific responsibilities to attend to. My responsibility, however, was never looked upon as such because I was given the chance to share their childhood, and from the shadows watch my own child grow up. It was necessary to hide the truth of their pasts because of the inevitability of their futures. We offered them a chance at a normal childhood, before prophecy would steal even that away from them. Already, you each have encountered your own special abilities, abilities that define the seven orphans that were brought here that night as the saviors of legend." Maria inhales deeply as tears threaten to blur her vision. "Those abilities have manifested themselves in ways that I could never have imagined. Ways that have haunted my conscious for some time now and make me question the decision that we had made in denying our child the right to know their own parentage. Jessica, when you had your first vision, I had nearly lost you." She doesn't bother wiping away her tears as she continues, "The first vision is always the hardest, and although I knew this, seeing what it had put you through nearly killed me. And if Joel hadn't been there, it could have killed you. He had helped you through it, just as Tom had helped me."

Jessica's jaw is set. "So we are all illegitimate children who will one day bring salvation to Ilia through the use of some supernatural ability that has the initial power to kill us? And Tom here is my father who, together with you and the members of Oracle Seven, has seen the future as laid out by an obscure prophecy written on the walls of a cave whose location no one knows, and have manipulated not only events but children in hopes of fulfilling this prophecy?"

Joel adds rather incredulously. "Not to mention, that Mala's minions stalk our borders, and this war that is upon us will most likely bring about the end of the world, only to allow for its salvation by the seven of us stars who have descended from heaven that are to be guarded in the holy light of the seven keepers of the sight."

Maria wrings her hands nervously as she risks a glance at Tom. "We deserve your anger, but please do not let it cloud the task at hand. As difficult as it may be, you must understand that we had your best interests at heart."

Jessica grimaces. "We don't have to understand anything. I have just one question. Am I the only child you have had, either together or with different people?" Joel puts his hand on her shoulder, in part to calm her down, but mostly as reassurance.

Maria and Tom definitively nod their heads then look down in exhaustion, emotionally spent.

Jessica rises from the chair and Joel follows her lead. Without so much as a *Thank you* they leave the room, having found the answer they initially sought but losing so much more.

CHAPTER SIXTEEN

As she looks back at Cole. "You're awfully quiet."

Cole sighs, "Do you think that that Old John fellow was actually calling me a flagrant idiot, or was he warning me of what I will become?"

Ashe puts his hands on his hips and shakes his head. "The vicious cycle he spoke of ignores the fact that even though your parents could very well be flagrant idiots, children are also a product of their environment. We all were raised together in the Sylvan cottage. And in spite of the first twelve years in which we were around our parents, through your actions I have seen that you have made the choice to not be a flagrant idiot."

"How can you be so sure that I have made such a choice? Perhaps the time has not yet come when the choice is to be made." Cole rubs his temples in frustration. "I just don't want to make a mistake that will cost us everything. I mean, we are heading into war for crying out loud." He exhales deeply. "And it doesn't help that I feel we are also heading into a trap."

Ashe takes a drink from his water skin and then passes it onto Cole who then takes a drink. "One can't anticipate everything, so making a mistake is inevitable. Given this, worrying about what might happen only gives rise to undue stress and creates a *very* irritable traveling companion." He slaps Cole on the shoulder in jest. "I am not saying that we should walk blindly into the path of danger or that we should not prepare for possible scenarios, but you should trust in who you are. I believe in you. Do not doubt yourself; then you only create problems where there are none." He smiles and catches the water skin as Cole passes it back to him.

Cole feels something rub against his leg. He looks down to see Shadow staring up at him with her amber eyes. Cole kneels down and scratches her behind the ear. "You believe in me, too?" Shadow grins her wolf smile as her tail enthusiastically wags from side to side. Cole laughs. "I guess you're right."

Ashe smiles. "Of course I am right." He starts off again down the trail and calls behind him. "You're lagging behind. I would hate to leave you here. Especially if Old John or some other character mysteriously shows up and fills your head with nonsense again, then just as mysteriously disappears."

Cole yells as he runs to catch up, Shadow right beside him. "This wouldn't take so long if we had taken the horses."

"And then what, leave them on the shores of Cape Terna? I would rather they stay at the cottage so at least the girls could make use of them. Besides, Lara would kill us if we took her horses away from her."

Cole once again states his doubts. "That is, if we survive this war for her to do so."

Ashe shrugs and instills some lighthearted humor on the matter. "Oh, believe me, even in death she'll find a way to make her revenge."

Cole laughs, presently forgetting his worries. Shadow takes a defensive stance as a low growl resounds from her throat. The laughter is cut short as the hairs on the back of his neck begin to rise. He holds up his hand in a "Halt" gesture and looks cautiously around him.

Ashe silently comes up beside him and observes their surroundings before risking a glance at Cole. He whispers, "What's wrong? I don't sense anything."

Cole whispers back, "That's because whatever is out there is not natural. The air reeks of magic."

Ashe furrows a brow. "What do you know of magic?"

Cole's eyes focus on an area to their right. "I know enough." He cocks his head towards the wolf at his feet but his eyes remain fixed. "And do you doubt her senses?"

Ashe cautiously looks around again. "What do you think it is?"

"I am not sure, but I am going to find out." He leaves the trail, cutting through the forest to the right, in a tacit request for Ashe and Shadow to follow.

Ashe calls after him, "This could be the trap you are so wary of." If Cole had heeded the warning, he gave no indication of doing so. Sighing, he leaves the safety of the path and follows Cole and Shadow into the woods.

Cole stops at the edge of the forest and looks out onto the vast meadow before them. He motions for Ashe to wait as he removes his pack and takes a few tentative steps forward. He lowers to his haunches and presses a palm to an area of trampled grass. Looking back at Ashe, he speaks, "A battle was fought here today."

Ashe frowns. "By whom?"

"Twenty against three thousand."

Ashe takes a step forward. "That was not a battle. That was a slaughter."

Cole nods. "Three thousand bodies were strewn across these meadows. They didn't even have a chance."

Ashe stops dead in his tracks. "Three thou...."

Cole stands up and retrieves his pack from where he had left it at the edge of the forest.

Ashe storms after him. "How is such a thing possible? And where are all the bodies?"

Cole looks blankly into Ashe's troubled green eyes. "Magic."

Cole and Ashe watch quietly as Shadow walks to the center of the meadow. She lowers her tail and howls a lament for the men lost this day.

• •

"Hyah! Hyah!" Cara encourages her horse as she casts nervous looks behind her. She snaps the reins and leans forward farther, her pounding heart threatening to escape her chest. She can hear the labored breathing of the horse as it continues its run on sheer adrenaline. Cara frets in fear of the moment when this reservoir of energy will give way to exhaustion, causing the horse to fall dead beneath her. Tears sting her eyes as the inevitability of it all threatens to consume her. After meeting up with Old John, the vile creatures had appeared out of nowhere. And now they were chasing her on their stumped little legs that should have made it physically impossible for them to even catch up to her, much less gain distance.

In a single moment of desperation, she pulls up on the reins, bringing the horse to a sudden halt. She quickly jumps off and fumbles to remove the harness. Taking the horse's face in her hands, she commands, "Return to Pete. Be swift. Let them know of my failure." She smacks the horse on the rump, sending it north towards Verdana. They will be upon her soon, but as she dies she will look into the hideous face of evil and show no fear. Standing alone facing east on a path through the Southern Woods, she clutches her crystal and sends a silent prayer to the heavens.

A wolf cry reverberates through the forest. The doleful sound seems to have originated just through the line of trees on her left. She looks down at the crystal still held in her hand. She was given this upon initiation into Oracle Seven. They struggle to keep the hope for the human spirit alive, and they keep fighting to the bitter end. Old John had told her that Shadow had found her charge. He had also warned her that the charge was a flagrant idiot. Taking her chances, Cara runs for where she had deemed the wolf cry to originate, admonishing herself for consigning herself to defeat. She is not running from the fight, only evening the odds.

She sees two men up ahead, both tall, one with brown hair and the other black. She calls out, "They are coming!" The two ruggedly handsome men turn in astonishment and Cara immediately singles out the one with black hair as Shadow's charge. She runs to them and screams urgently, "To the center of the meadow. Hurry!" Without hesitation they follow her command. Upon joining up with Shadow, the three stop and face their enemy.

The striking man with wonderfully dark hair yells to his friend, "Protect her. Let me handle this."

As one of the creatures breaks through the line of trees, Cara pulls out her dagger and with a deftly accurate throw, buries the blade in the head of the monster. It bursts into a cloud of black dust as an ear-splitting death wail escapes from its lungs. The dagger drops to the ground. Cara pulls out another dagger and casts a wry grin at the black-haired man. "I don't need protection."

The man's jaw is set but a smile reaches his eyes. "How many are there?"

"I counted twenty as they were chasing me, but there may be more."

The man nods. "Do you think they will try to surround us?"

Cara shakes her head. "No. These are Mala's mindless killing machines; they are deadly but stupid. They are the lowliest of the low."

The one with brown hair smiles. "Are they stupid enough to come through where you had, to where we can just pick them off one by one?"

Cara frets. "It's not as simple as that. Once they are close enough to cast their spells, we are all dead. Long range is the best way to defeat them without getting killed yourself, but unless either of you has sharp throwing implements, we are severely outnumbered because I have only four left, to include the one in my hand."

The brown-haired man frowns. "So, Cole, any bright ideas?"

Cara inwardly smiles now that she knows this dark man's name. Four more creatures emerge from the woods, each bursting into inky clouds as her daggers find their marks. She yells rather unnecessarily, "I'm out!"

Cole takes a step forward and laughs. "Hey, Ashe, do you want to see what a flagrant idiot can do?"

Ashe puts his hand on Cole's chest. "What are you going to do?"

Cole lowers to the ground. "Just distract them for me, will you?" He crawls on his hands and knees towards the enemy-infested tree line, disappearing into the tall grass of the meadow.

Momentarily, three more creatures emerge from the forest and head for the two people standing in the middle of the meadow for all to see. The sun reflects off a blade held by a hidden third party just before the three creatures turn into dust like their friends before them. The same scene repeats itself, each new set of creatures surprised to find a third person lying in ambush, until the enemy is eventually nothing more than dust in the wind.

The assassin stands to reveal his hiding place off to the right of where all the creatures had come forth. Even from this distance, the two people standing in the center of the field could see his grin. Shadow bounds forth to rejoin her charge, signifying the "All clear." Ashe runs to meet up with Cole and Cara takes his lead.

Cara retrieves the various knives littering the ground and straps each into their rightful place. One adorns each of her upper arms, one hangs at her hip, and two more strap around her legs. She looks up to see both men staring at her with unrestricted curiosity. Crossing her arms, she smiles. "Is there a problem?"

Ashe bows his head. "My lady, we only wonder at how one such as you should come to possess such accoutrements to which you are so intimately knowledgeable."

Cara laughs. "There is no need for such formality." She shakes her head. "Honestly, my lady…."

Cole smiles, a smile which nearly brings Cara to her knees. "Excuse my friend Ashe here." He holds out his hand. "I am Cole."

She takes his hand, his touch giving her flesh goose bumps. She looks up, his deeply black eyes staring down at her in expectation. She remembers herself and replies, "I am Cara." Releasing his hand, she smiles. "I believe I owe you my life."

"It was your daggers that saved the day. And you were also the one to warn us of the threat." Cole kneels down to pet Shadow. He looks up at her and smiles. "I owe you mine."

Ashe laughs. "Why don't we just call it even and get out of here before any more of those things come back." He looks to Cara. "Mistress Cara, shall we escort you on your way?"

Cole laughs. "I doubt you need an escort." He smiles at her once more, causing her breath to catch in her throat. "But if you don't mind the company, it would appease my conscience if I found you safely to your destination." He stands. "So, where are you headed?"

Without preamble, she replies, "Nesthra."

Ashe chokes. "Are you joking? You do realize that there is a war going on down there, don't you?"

Cara nods. "And that is precisely why I must go there. I have urgent news that simply cannot wait."

Cole crosses his arms. "You're just full of surprises. Well, Cara," he crooks his arm, "shall we?"

CHAPTER SEVENTEEN

Joel angrily follows an angrier Jessica out the front door into the fresh spring air. She makes it halfway down the hill before falling to her knees in overwhelming grief. Tears unremittingly roll down her cheek onto the green grass beneath her, soaking the earth with her sorrow. She cries into Joel's shoulder as he comes to sit beside her and cradle her in his protective arms. He holds her tightly, assuring her of his presence and sharing in her bitter misery. The truth had been stalking the hallways for eleven long years, never once being admitted or even hinted at. Their entire lives have been lies neatly wrapped up in more lies. The world was crumbling around them and they could do nothing to stop it. All they can rely on is each other because that is the only thing that seems to be real.

Jessica clutches his tear-moistened shirt and sobs. "Please be real. I couldn't stand it if you too were a lie."

Joel holds her ever tighter. He presses his chin to the top of her head, closing his eyes to hold back his own tears. His body trembles with the force of his emotions as he manages to hold back the flood threatening to gush from his eyes. "I will always be a reality for you. And you live in me. You will have to get used to the fact that no matter how hard you might try, you can never be rid of me." He caresses her hair. "When you are ready to stand on your own two feet, we will stand together. Until then, let me be your strength."

Her tears fall faster now as she listens to his words. His body quivers, and she knows that this is tearing him up inside. She stares up into his impossibly blue eyes full of concern that far exceeds obligation or sympathy. Her pain is his own. She whispers, "And when we can again believe that we can fly, we will soar. But until then, we will believe in each other." She reaches up to touch his cheek. "It is not a weakness to cry." He lowers his head as a drop of wetness falls onto her arm.

She moves her hand to the back of his head and draws him into a kiss. Her parched lips sting with the salt of his tears, but she dare not pull away. In a world that has all but abandoned them, this one pure moment of reality is all that they have. With all of the lies that are woven by the tongues of men, only a heart conformed to the truth can be trusted. And from this trust can they build their faith so that they may one day believe again.

• •

Lara rears her horse as a sudden breeze sweeps across the plain, bringing with it a desolate sobbing that strikes the very core of her being. She turns towards the cottage, brushing a strand of hair from her face. Snapping the reins, she turns her horse back towards the cottage. She sees Joel and Jessica huddled together on the hill so she brings her horse to a trot and jumps off. She runs towards them. "What's wrong?"

Joel looks up at her, tears filling his eyes. "Everything."

Lara bites her lip in worry and then runs the rest of the way up the hill. The door to the house swings open in a fury as she rushes in. A startled Maria and a stranger stare at her. She looks to Maria and demands, "What's going on? What happened?"

Maria sighs, "We told them. We told them everything."

Lara glares. "What entails 'everything'?"

Maria weeps into the stranger's shoulder. The man looks at Lara. "Our mission is in jeopardy, so we had no choice but to tell them of their pasts. We told them about the prophecy and their parts in it."

Lara rages. "And now you act so surprised that they should respond in such a way? They are too young for all of this. I am twenty-two years old and even I am not sure if I can handle it. I remember all too well why we are here and who we are, but they were only three at the time."

Maria steps forward. "And we told Jessica who her parents are."

Lara clears her throat. "I thought that you didn't know." She clenches her fist in fury. "What else haven't you told us?"

Maria looks at Tom and then once again turns her gaze upon Lara. "I am Jessica's mother."

The contempt welling up inside Lara sets her golden eyes on fire. "Excuse me?"

Maria repeats. "I am Jessica's mother."

Unable to contain her resentment, Lara slaps Maria with the force and fury of a windstorm. Through gritted teeth she glares down at Maria. "You don't deserve that title." Casting a warning look at the stranger, she storms out of the cottage, breaking free of the confines that were threatening to suffocate her. She takes a deep breath and expels her wrath into the swirling wind around her, forcing it to carry her scream across the land and sea so all the world will know of the anguish brought about today. Breathing heavily, she stalks down the hill to where Joel and Jessica await. She looks down at them.

"For eleven years you have been fed lies. It is time for you to discover the truth." Sitting down before them and crossing her legs, she begins.

"Eleven years ago, the Lion Wars, which have been fought since the death of the High King of Ilia three thousand years ago, officially came to an end with the signing of the Dragon Treaty by King James of Jewel and King Lanacan of Laentus. Any notion of peace, however, was abandoned with the appearance of a threat from Sentra. That threat is in the form of a person you know as Mala. She is the self-proclaimed queen of Sentra, a desert continent to the southwest of us. She has set her sights on ruling all of Ilia and, sad to say, she has the power to do so. For eleven years she has been building her powers and now she is finally ready to wage her war. If she succeeds, she will bring this world to ashes. Her first target is the Nesthra Islands. Only one thing stands in her way: the seven of us." She sighs.

"I have no knowledge of our pasts, only of what ensued the night we all became orphans, but I do know part of the prophecy that has been unceremoniously placed before our feet to fulfill." She recites:

> *"A centuries-old war finally ceased*
> *But danger lurks in a mysterious region*
> *Safeguarded from the threat are six*
> *And they shall inherit the powers that be*
> *One of fire, a skilled warrior*
> *One of water, who shall see the truth*
> *One of wind, hears all and sees all*
> *One of earth, with the power to heal*
> *One of energy, senses true intentions*
> *And one of both day and night, to whom will be told the*
> *   world's secrets*
> *Destined to defeat the evil power*
> *But only two, by their union, shall bring peace*
> *And shall all things be in balance*
> *Until the end of time."*

Joel frowns. "That's only six."

Lara nods. "Only six inherit the 'powers that be,' or the forces of nature. As it should be, because peace is achieved through balance. The seventh entity is the antithesis of balance: Chaos."

Jessica questions. "What are the extents of these powers?"

"They can be boundless," Lara answers, "but limits are set by the wielder's own faith and confidence, not only in God," she smiles at each of them, "but in themselves and in each other."

Jessica remembers one of her visions. "But these abilities also have the power to destroy."

Lara nods. "Yes; if used for the wrong reasons, all can be lost. But the destruction is more than the prospect of a lost cause; it also destroys what the person could have been. You lose your soul."

Joel shivers. "That sounds so … permanent."

"It is," replies Lara. She sighs, "The power can be overwhelming sometimes. And without the maturity necessary to harness it, the very act would mean certain death." She looks at Joel. "We hadn't originally planned on keeping such an enormous secret from you, but our overzealousness nearly got Chase killed."

Joel nods. "You are talking about Chase's fifth birthday when Cole took him into the forest, aren't you?"

Lara smiles. "I sometimes wonder whether your intuitiveness is coincidence, or if it is connected to your abilities."

Jessica punches Joel. "You better not even dare to try to read my mind."

Joel smiles. "I don't have to in order to know what *you're* thinking."

Jessica resists the urge to punch him, her curiosity overriding any other emotion she may have been feeling. "So Lara, if Joel is Energy and I am Day and Night, what are you?"

"I am intrigued that you would use such a definitive tense in describing the abilities you possess." Lara rises and clasps her hands together in joy. "You have cut out all the preamble and gotten right to the source of the matter. Already you understand that these elements are not merely something you can manipulate, but are the basis of who you are. Whether or not you know it, they have shaped the type of person you are."

Joel questions. "So, I am the light. I like the sound of that."

Jessica stands up and twirls around. "Then I am the sun, with the entire universe revolving around me."

Lara shakes her head. "You two are having way too much fun with this, but I am glad to see you smiling."

Joel stands and takes a few steps toward Lara. "We may have been living lies for the past eleven years, but not everything was false. Chase and Cole are my brothers. And far as I am concerned, you are my mother. I am sure my biological mother was heartbroken over the loss of her child, just as Maria is, but you are the one who raised us. You were the one who was always honest with us. I remember you singing us to sleep at night and watching over us when we were sick. Even just now, when you were telling us of our powers, you left out all the empty histrionics and gave the information to us straight. You respect us enough to not frame the truth in excuse. Thank you."

Lara stands staring at him, at a loss of what to say. Her teary eyes smile endearing warmth to match the grin on her face. "You do me much honor with your words and, in seeing this man disguised in a boy's body before me, I should thank you. You truly are the light."

Jessica stops spinning and smiles giddily at Joel. "There are so many of you. So many lights. Too many." She trips over her own feet and falls onto her behind. Rubbing her dizzy head and sore bum simultaneously, she pouts. "I don't think I like being the center of the universe."

Joel gives her a hand and pulls her up. Putting an arm around her waist to steady her, he laughs. "Then I guess the universe makes you its center just to scorn you."

Jessica nods but immediately regrets doing so. "Exactly."

Joel rolls his eyes and laughs. "Believe me. You fit the role well."

Jessica glares at him, and then turns to Lara. "So, you never did tell us which one you are."

"I" ... two streams of fresh mountain air blow past them as Lara brings her arms up before her ... "am" ... the currents begin to dance around each other until forming a circle like a miniature tornado ... "the Wind!"—and she rises a few feet from the ground, floating in midair. The winds subside and Lara slowly descends until her feet once more touch firm ground. She casts a lightheartedly reproachful gaze at Joel and Jessica. "And you should do well to remember that."

CHAPTER EIGHTEEN

Chase wrings out the wetness from his shirt and smiles over at Kae sitting on the bank not too far away.

"That was refreshing." He pulls his shirt back over his head. "But next time we go swimming, would you remind me to remove my shirt?"

Kae giggles as she stares at the damp shirt clinging to the muscles of his chest, herself drenched from head to toe.

"Well, I don't have that luxury. But since you have made the request, I will do my best to fulfill it."

Chase sits down next to her and wraps an arm around her shoulders. He smiles as he whispers into her ear, "You were just checking me out."

Kae turns to him and gasps. "I was not." He stretches his arms over his head and Kae is unable to look away. "Do you want me to slap you?"

"What?" Chase replies innocently. "I was just stretching." He smiles at her. "But if you slap me again, I will just have to kiss you again."

Shaking her head, she laughs. "You're impossible."

He grins. "I know. But that's why you love me." He leans back and supports himself on his elbows. "I make you feel alive, remember?"

Kae leans down to kiss him. She smiles down at him with her lilac eyes. "And how do I make you feel, Chase?"

He jumps up and runs up the slope to the center of the bridge. Holding his arms out to his sides, he looks up and screams, "Like I am the king of all Ilia!" Holding an arm out to her, he smiles warmly. "And you are my queen."

Kae wraps her arms around her knees and laughs delightfully. She watches as Chase bounds back down towards her.

He holds out a hand and bows. "My Lady, may I have this dance?"

Kae takes his hand and slowly stands up. She nods her head in all propriety. "Yes, my Lord, and you may have all the dances hereafter."

Chase twirls her around and flips her, supporting her in his arm. They gaze into each other's eyes for a moment. He pulls her back up and smiles. "You seem surprised."

"I never knew that you could dance," she replies as they part with only his hand holding hers to lead her.

Chase kisses her hand and bows his head. "Neither did I." He takes a deep breath as he looks around them. "There is just something about this place that makes me feel confident."

"You're drawn to this place, aren't you?"

"Yeah, I guess you could say that. I remember one day I had been exploring the woods and I heard this loud thundering as in a storm, but the sky was clear. My curiosity took control and it led me to this place. Seeing the waterfall for the first time, I knew that I was surveying a masterpiece. The sheer beauty of it left me speechless, but I also recognized the raw power of God himself being released. The crystal-clear waters cascading down from the mountainside is stunning to behold, but is deceptive in its strength to pull someone under and then sweep them away." He looks at Kae. "In a way, it reminds me of you."

Kae raises her brow. "So I am a waterfall? That is a rather interesting metaphor." She taps her finger on her chin. "But as a destructive force of awesome elegance, how long will this last before all that is left is a meandering river following a set course to the deep blue sea, where all the tributaries that demarcate the lands lose the individuality of their own identity to become part of the greater whole?"

Chase shakes his head. "You worry too much."

"Only in compensation for your own rash behavior," she counters.

"Your passion drives you to act when your mind tells you to wait. And because of this you're unpredictable, like a firestorm. You burn so brightly for a time, but then are extinguished by your own fury. There has to be something in our lives to provide balance. I feel lost without you. Only when you are near do I feel complete." She smiles. "And only in these past two weeks have I realized this. I believe that every person has a soul mate, another half that is their opposite that serves to reach an equilibrium of sorts. There may be connections with other people, but nothing can ever be as complete and seamless. I believe that we balance each other."

He caresses her hand and whispers, "So of fire and water do we find the balance that is sought." He brings her into his arms, cradling her as they stare at the crystalline falls before them. "Did I mention that I have found some of the answers I have sought?"

Kae turns to look at him. "Seriously? That's wonderful." She looks up expectantly and frowns when he remains silent. "Well, aren't you going to tell me what you have discovered?"

Chase shrugs. "Nah. I was just going to leave you hanging. I want to see you all flustered and angry."

"Well, if you're going to play it that way, I guess that I just won't show you what I found," Kae replies matter-of-factly.

Chase rolls his eyes. "Fine." He kisses her on the forehead and begins, "The symbol on the talisman my mother gave me stands for fire. And apparently, there is another talisman that was crafted from the same rock but bearing a different symbol. But the manner in which I discovered this was rather strange. The jeweler placed the talisman in my hand and asked me what I saw. When I told her, she said that I was "the one," whatever that means. I believe that this talisman is far more than a simple keepsake from my mother." He squints his eyes as if trying to focus on a distant object. "And I ... my dreams ... have become more vivid. I almost saw my mother's face, but then the dream ended. And I had a vision of a flame sword. I was trapped in an illusion at the time, but I think the vision was real."

Kae ponders this. "Do you remember those stories you used to read to me when we were younger? About the Ancient Peoples of Ilia?"

"Not this again." He shakes his head and sighs, "I got the same lecture from Tom, a message-carrying pirate on a secret mission that somehow involves him paying a visit to the Sylvan cottage." Raising a finger, he adds, "And the only person in all of Verdana with a boat, and who was willing to also be my guide."

Kae refrains from commenting on this matter and instead pursues her previous train of thought, "There were essentially four tribes, each capable of manipulating a certain element. The only vestiges of their cultures are various myths regarding legendary weapons and warriors who will fight an evil that will threaten to consume the world. There are rumors that these cultures still thrive in hidden parts of the world, like inside mountains or shrouded in mist, and also of underground passage-ways where they can travel unseen by the world above who has all but forgotten their existence." She frowns slightly as she idly runs her fingers over the wet dirt of the bank. "We choose to turn history into legend in an attempt to ignore the possibility of something more because such an idea threatens the comfort we find in a normal yet mediocre life." She stares back at him. "You feel that something more remains to be found, yet you cast aside any suggestions regarding matters beyond the scope of what you have considered to be your life up to this point."

Chase hugs her to him. "Again, you have managed to upset my opinion by integrating what I believe to be true with something that I believe to be not." He kisses her shoulder. "But my life has been anything but mediocre. I never told you, or anyone else for that matter, what happened on my fifth birthday. And it has haunted me ever since." He looks down at his hands, remembering all too well how he had come so close to dying. "Cole had taken me to the forest. I was captivated by what I saw around me—the trees and its protectors, and the animals, but mostly just the feeling that I was in a different world. I became lost and the forest suddenly became a very scary place. I could hear boop-boops calling to each other in the distance, but I was more concerned by the growl emanating from the bushes only a few feet away. I was being stalked by a lion and as it leapt out from its hiding place, all I could do was stand there. I closed my eyes and held out my arm in a vain attempt to ward off the creature's attack. I envisioned its claws tearing me to shreds over and over again." He looks up at Kae, a profound sadness inherent in his blue eyes. "Then something happened that I still do not understand. I remember this power surging through me and a light that would have been blinding had my eyes been open. The next thing I knew, the lion was dead, smoke billowing from its blackened remains."

Kae brings his hand to her lips and tenderly kisses it. Leaning back against him, she looks up at the crimson clouds languidly floating across the orange sky. "You once told me to stop lying to myself. You said that I had been afraid to admit the truth. Chase, the truth lies before you. Open your eyes."

Chase sighs, "You're right. I have been running from the truth. It all just seems so absurd."

Kae laughs softly. "Absurd relates to what an individual deems normal. But what normal is changes through time. If two weeks ago it would have been normal for us to be fighting, imagine what changes can take place in a century, or three for that matter." She sighs, "And with the addition of war, the change was brought about that much more rapidly. Who knows, we may still have had a High King of Ilia whose steed was a dragon instead of a horse. You are right that we cannot ignore our pasts, and I understand your reasons for your journey, especially given the ghost that has haunted you for the past eleven years, but just remember the promise that the future holds."

The red of the clouds fade to a soft pink as the orange sky gives way to a fast-approaching horizon of deep blue. Chase rests his chin on Kae's shoulder and kisses her on the cheek, his warm breath a sweet caress. "The ceremony should be small. Only our closest of friends shall be there, and well of course, the priest. And at night, under the stars shining brightly from the heavens. But the brightest star will be you, with jewels of ruby and sapphire in your hair falling gracefully over your delicate shoulders. Your sparkling blue gown the color of the ocean waves will wrap around you in a series of ingeniously placed folds that accentuate your frame in a way that will leave me and everyone else breathless."

Kae giggles as she stares up at the stars beginning to burn brightly in the night sky. "And for our wedding, you will be the epitome of a prince, with your dashing smile and overwhelmingly debonair presence that will make me weak in the knees. If not for the look in your eyes and the pain in my heart for being even any small distance from you, I wouldn't make it down the aisle. The red velvet accents of your dark blue suit will give to your dazzling blue eyes a fire to outshine that of the stars."

Chase smiles. "I see you standing by my side, and I am no longer afraid." He laughs. "It truly is unbelievable. But if I am this savior from legend who will receive an equally legendary weapon, I must first learn to harness this power."

Kae turns her entire body to face him and crosses her legs. "We'll learn together."

Chase stares at her. "I don't understand."

She smiles. "Like you said, I am a waterfall."

He shakes his head in amazement. "How long have you known?"

Kae shrugs. "Two weeks. I have been to this waterfall every day since you have left, and on the day that you left, Nikoi helped me to realize a truth which I too had been trying to avoid." She leans forward and smiles coyly. "I am glad that this is one secret we can share. That way, we can fight the ghosts of our pasts together."

Chase leans forward and kisses her. Kae smiles at him before rising to her feet. She holds out a hand and he takes it, standing up himself. Occasionally looking backwards, she leads him closer to the waterfall. "I want to show you what else I have discovered." Letting go of his hand, Kae scrambles along the mossy rocks of the wall which the cascade tumbles over.

Chase follows her lead, but not nearly as sure-footed as Kae on such a perilous climb. Kae disappears behind the waterfall and he frantically calls out to her. "Kae!"

She pops her head out. "Come on, slow poke." Seeing the deathly white cast to his features, she frowns. "Are you all right?"

Vehemently shaking his head, he yells over the roar of the falling water. "No!"

Kae shakes her head and laughs, helping him the rest of the way up. "Sorry, I didn't mean to scare you."

Risking a look over the edge, Chase looks at Kae and raises an eyebrow. "A rather precipitous descent, don't you think?"

Kae shrugs. "If we climbed it, yes, but I find it much easier and quicker to just jump." She reads the question on his face and answers it. "Do you forget so quickly? I am the waterfall. I will not let it pull you under and sweep you away." Laughing, she takes his hand and leads him to a niche behind the waterfall. "Isn't this great?" Taking a deep breath, she closes her eyes. "It can be our own little hiding place within our own little hiding place." She smiles at the superfluousness of the statement as she sits down and leans against the back wall.

Chase surveys the relatively large size of the space, at least enough for five people to sleep, albeit not comfortably but nonetheless secure from the elements and creatures that may lurk below. He stares through the sheet of water rushing past them, spraying a soothing mist into the makeshift cave. He gasps. "I can still see the stars!"

Kae giggles. "I know. We can see what goes on outside of this little window to the world without the world even knowing we are here, much less the very existence of this alcove."

Chase peers intently through the waterfall as he holds up a hand to signify a warning. "There's something moving across the bridge."

Kae springs forward to get a better look. "It seems to be men. A lot of them."

Chase nods his agreement. "Soldiers. I wonder where they are headed." He squints his eyes. "What's that on their armor?"

The moonlight reflects off a white chestplate set into the black metal of their armor. Kae clutches Chase's sleeve as she gasps, "Those are Sentran ranks!"

Chase sets his jaw as he places a hand on Kae's shoulder. "The Sylvan cottage. We must warn them." He rises to leave.

Kae stands but holds him back. "We'll never be able to get in front of them." Tears fill her eyes. "What are we going to do?"

"We can go to Verdana, or to the castle. We can warn the king...," he replies reassuringly.

Kae cuts him off. "They are most likely burning as we speak. And even if all these troops somehow miraculously bypassed the castle and Verdana, we would still be too late to help our friends."

Chase runs his hand through his hair in contemplation. "We have these abilities. We should be able to use them."

"But to what extent? Take out the rear guard while the front is busy annihilating our friends, and then be killed ourselves?" She goes to her knees and puts her palms together. "Dear Lord, we need a miracle tonight. Please guide our hand as we venture into what very well may be our deaths." She abruptly rises and races out from under the safety of the waterfall.

Chase runs after her. "What are you doing?"

She smiles at him and then places a kiss on his mouth as if it is the last time their lips would meet. "You were right. We should be able to use our abilities. And if we aren't successful, at least I found you." She kisses him again and smiles. "Take off your shirt." She jumps off the ledge into the pristinely cerulean lake that serves as the reservoir of the waterfall.

Chase quickly removes his shirt and plunges feet first into the icy chill of the waters below.

CHAPTER NINETEEN

The white waters churn violently, threatening to drown him, but some force buoys him. The force swirls in flashes of periwinkle light that counteract the gravitational pull of the waterfall as it plummets into the lake. A hand pushes softly against his back, driving him forward and reassuring him that he is safe. His lungs strain with the effort of holding his breath, but Kae's voice whispers gently in his ear, "Breathe." Putting his faith in her presence, he exhales deeply. The pressure that had been building in his lungs dissipates and he finds that he truly can breathe underwater. Inhaling the artificial air, he laughs in amazement of such an exhilarating experience. Kae is in her element and she is sharing with him all the wonders of her powers. He can feel her hands on either side of him now, steadying him as they break free of the rapidly swirling current. The storm is suddenly behind them with only calm waters lying ahead. With her hands still on his sides Kae pulls him upward, their heads momentarily breaching the surface.

Kae releases him and swims on ahead. She turns to him before diving once more. "I trust you can handle the rest by yourself."

Chase shakes the moisture from his hair and lunges forward, swimming towards the southern bank. He pulls himself ashore and makes for the foot of the bridge upon which the Sentran ranks are crossing.

Kae is waiting for him, hiding in the shadow of the bridge. Standing there drenched and dripping, she still manages to look beautiful. The moonlight reflects off the water, casting a blue glow upon her wet hair. Her smile is mirrored in her lilac eyes as she whispers softly, "In spite of the situation, I cannot help but smile in considering what just happened. I was swimming through the water, but it was so much more than that. I was the water. And I was able to bend it to my will."

Chase stares at her as he runs his fingers through his damp hair. "I could breathe it as if it were air. But it was so much purer. Untainted." He touches his index finger to the tip of her nose. "Just like my Kaela." His brow furrows and he closely examines her hair. He leans his forehead against hers and whispers, "Your hair is blue." Kae smiles as he twirls a strand around his finger. "I kinda like it."

Tears unexpectedly well in her eyes. "I am scared, Chase."

Putting his hands on her shoulders, he lowers his gaze to match hers. "I love you, Kaela. Remember that. If we don't make it through this, at least we were granted this day to spend with each other." He squeezes her shoulders before removing his hands. Nodding resolutely, he clenches his jaw. "What's the plan?"

Kae stares thoughtfully at the wooden bridge above them that is trembling with the footsteps of the Sentran troops. Without averting her gaze, she whispers vehemently, "Burn it."

With one last kiss, Chase nods and climbs the rocks, positioning himself in the corner between the bridge and the slope. Placing a hand on the wooden platform, he closes his eyes and calls forth the anger, calls forth the fury that burns just beneath the surface. He summons the pain of knowing what their failure would mean. He takes the fear that he has harbored these past eleven years and uses it to fuel the fury. Opening his blue eyes, he releases the power surging through him, erupting forth like a volcano. The bridge bursts into flames, the angry tongues trapping those soldiers on the bridge and burning them alive. Flaming embers pour down upon the river as the bridge collapses, the sizzling cinders hissing snakes as they reach the water. He can hear the cries of alarm turn into agonizing screams of pain. Their burning bodies plunge into the stream, some already dead and others seeking respite from the flames.

Kae acts quickly, calling forth her powers of water to trap the fallen soldiers beneath the tumultuous waves, drowning them and crashing their fragile bodies against the sharp rocks. Soldiers at the ends of the bridge see the watery death waiting to swallow them, so they desperately cling to the cliff, all the while their skin burning. Yet they too are swept away by the torrent as a pale blue arm reaches out from the depths and claims them for its own.

The soldiers standing on either cliff look on gravely as they watch their companions die. The voice of their commander bellows and the men who have crossed the bridge turn their backs on the scene without so much as a word. Those trapped on the other side of the river continue to stare helplessly, unable to heed the command of their leader to march on and unable to help their friends.

An arrow of flame shoots into the sky, bursting at its apogee high above the trees and raining fire down onto the trapped remainder of the black hordes below. Their black leather uniforms go up in flames, and they drop to the ground trying to extinguish it but to no avail. The angry fire has a life of its own, clinging to its victims like a hungry lion to its fallen prey. The fire goes out, leaving behind a charcoaled mass of steel and bone. Others cower behind their shields, only to be swept away by a bone-crushing wave that hammers the life out of them and carries their broken bodies into the raging river of which their comrades have already met their fate.

Chase stares at the waters rising high above him, himself unharmed by the wave that parts to either side of him. Black blurs rush past him, the roaring of the river muffling their cries. He can muster no sorrow for these men. His gaze continues upward until he can once again see the brilliance of the stars. Floating high above him on the rushing waters, arms outstretched and eyes closed, is Kae. Her shimmering blue dress clings to the back of her legs and her turquoise hair whips across her face as she stands motionless and unaffected by the waters streaming beneath her. The last of the bodies are carried into the river and out to sea. Kae drifts to the ground as the waters gradually recede. Touching land right in front of Chase, she opens her eyes. Taking a step forward, she moans and collapses into Chase's arms. Falling to his knees, it takes most of his strength just to lay her carefully upon the ground.

Breathing heavily, he leans forward on his hands and hangs his head in weariness. He raises his eyes to see the remainder of the Sentran forces on the other side of the river marching stalwartly onward towards the Sylvan cottage, ever intent on their mission. The strength of his arms leaves him and he hits the hard-packed dirt, lying motionless beneath the stars above as he closes his eyes and drifts into a dreamless sleep.

• •

"The stars are restless," Jessica whispers as she stares up at the night sky. She hugs her knees and shivers involuntarily. "Something stirs in the night."

Joel stands with his arms crossed as he looks warily into the trees. "My skin tingles in anticipation. Some evil marches this way."

Lara takes a few tentative steps forward as she closes her eyes. "The wood whispers a warning."

Maria clutches the sleeve of Tom's shirt as she clears her throat. "She has found us. Mala is here." Upon voicing the deepest of her fears, an orange ball of fire shoots into the distant sky, shattering into thousands of fiery arrows that rain down upon the earth. Everyone stands facing the forest now, their breath caught in their throats as they can now discern a direction from which their fears have arisen and have been confirmed.

Putting aside her fears and rising to the occasion, Lara commands. "Make ready. Mala has set her army upon us. We will stand and meet it."

Jessica closes her eyes and bows her head, awaiting the approach of the Sentran forces.

Maria grabs Lara's arm and pleads, "They are not ready."

Yanking her arm away, Lara glares. "Have you so little faith?" Sparing no more time, she runs for the stables and mounts her horse. Galloping back to the others, she paces her horse in front of them and addresses them. "Our strategy is a simple one. Be patient. We must bide our time and build our powers. If we respond too strongly, too quickly, we will exhaust our resources to the point of putting our very lives at risk. Wait for my command." She pauses to allow time for her words to sink in. Clearing her throat, she continues, "I see the black hordes of the Sentran army marching through the forest towards where we stand now. I hear the clanging of their armor amidst the pounding of their feet upon the forest trail. Their weapons are of steel, their armor of leather, and their resolve is of stone. I see Verdana burning and the castle under siege. But no matter the monstrosity of their deeds, thoughts, or appearances, they are men.

"And each one of you is a weapon. A power lies within you. Release it. Your inner strength is your armor. Your confidence your shield. And who can deny the resolve of those with right on their side? Tonight we do not defend ourselves. We defend the life which is at risk of being destroyed. We make our stand here. And we stand together. These powers were invested within us by God. So trust in Him." Lara halts her horse and looks at each one standing before her in turn. "Believe."

Joel steps forward and stares solemnly into the twisted blackness of the forest beyond. "I believe."

The pale moonlight dances across Jessica's features, giving a ghostly pallor to her smiling face. Her eyes open with a start and she declares evenly. "They are here."

A black army breaks free from the demesnes of the forest, their numbers swelling the countryside by the hundreds. Their curved blades glisten in the moonlight, raised over their heads by arms heavily clad in black armor. A great battle shout goes out from their leader and as each man lends their voice to the cry, the hills are sent reverberating with their charge.

Jessica chants, "When darkness falls...." An inky cloud descends upon the soldiers. Some halt their charge as their vision is clouded, but the stronger of spirit fight through their loss of sight, breaking free of the blinding blackness.

Joel continues, "…the unenlightened stumble upon Grace and are blinded by the light." The soldiers who escaped the spell are greeted with a paralyzing white light that brings them to their knees. The skin around their eyes swells, a red tinge encircling them as they strain to see again.

Lara calls forth the winds and sets them upon the hundreds of men still charging from the forest. The soldiers are thrown backwards onto the ground, gasping as the air is knocked out of them. The force of the gust had crushed the torsos of many, leaving them dead where they had fallen. Seeing that no more soldiers lurk in the forest, she calls out to Jessica and Joel, "Now!"

Lara turns her attention to the fallen men before her. Flicking her wrist, she closes her fingers around some invisible force, snatching the breath of life from the Sentran soldiers. Their bodies convulse, seize, and then lay motionless as they die of asphyxiation. A simultaneous whistling escapes from their slightly parted blue lips as the air rushes out of them, a decrescendo as their life becomes nothing more than breath in the wind.

One by one the stars blink out as Joel gathers their energy and transfers it to the air, charging it enough to call forth a thunderstorm. His eyes spark blue and electrical currents race through his black hair as he acts as the conductor for the amassing energy. Lightning dances across his fingertips. Raising his arm towards the soldiers, he releases the power in an array of blue charges that pierce their bodies, leaving gaping holes through their chests. They fall where they stand, their faces forever frozen in masks of bloodthirsty intent. They had not been given the time to realize their fate, nor had their blood been given the chance to flow before congealing into a swollen mass of hardened redness.

Jessica attacks her portion of the army with a fear that seizes their hearts. She latches onto the inner recesses of their minds, pounding their memory with the combined frenzied thoughts and cries of all the people they had murdered. She takes these fears and multiplies it with the force of her own anger, an anger fueled by eleven years of not knowing and of betrayal. Some retch as others pant hysterically. She watches as the blood leaves their veins, their hearts eventually slowing to a stop with each moment that passes.

Hundreds of black-armored bodies lay before them, twisted in various scenes of death. None were held in the cusp between life and death. Not one of the enemy stirred. The hills that had resounded with their charge now lay silent. The victors survey the carnage, their breathing slow and steady. The realization of the feat that they had just accomplished, that the three of them had just annihilated an entire army, slowly creeps up on them like some nocturnal predator.

A raspy whisper escapes Maria's throat as she rests her hand upon her chest, "My God.... There are so many of them."

White clouds of breath billow from their mouths as a sudden chill passes over them. The shadow of a man on a black steed appears before them. The air rings with his sinister laughter. Rearing his horse, he gallops off into the distance and disappears into the cloak of midnight.

Joel speaks. "How did they find us? Who was that?"

Tom answers. "The traitor."

CHAPTER TWENTY

Nikoi arches her long neck over the cliff, peering down at the two youths lying on the hard earth. The girl rests peacefully on her back, like a fragile flower whose petals would wilt at the slightest touch. Traces of deep blue highlight her brown hair, fanning out beneath her. The boy, however, paints a different picture with his limbs sprawled about him and his head turned to the side. His black hair is tousled more than usual, with the ends red as if dipped in paint, or blood. The clear water flowing around the sea serpent's body ripples slightly as she sighs. A little orange fish swims beside her, his tail slowly swishing from side to side.

Twiggy's voice pipes solemnly. "Are they going to make it?"

Nikoi sadly shakes her head. "It is too early to tell. Their breathing is rather shallow. With the way they rushed in last night, and that being the first real use of their powers, I am surprised that they have lasted to morning." She stares up at the red sun lazily rising in the rosy dawn sky. "But their will is strong and they have much to hold on to."

Twiggy swims to the other side of Nikoi. "We will not let them die." Twiggy looks up at her hopefully "We will watch over them."

Nikoi looks once again upon the boy and girl. "Yes. We will watch over them."

• •

Lara kneels beside Joel and nudges him awake. "How well have you rested?"

Joel rolls onto his stomach and uses his arms to push himself up. Squinting in the red light of morning, he scratches the back of his neck and yawns. He stretches, immediately regretting it upon discovering that he had slept on a rock. Putting a hand over the sore spot in his side, he mumbles, "Is that a rhetorical question, or does it really matter?" He blankly stares at her. "Given that you have taken the liberty of interrupting my much needed sleep, I warrant that whatever this is about is important. Because I know that you wouldn't have woken me if it was otherwise, right?"

Lara stands and gives him a hand to do the same, although she pulls him up rather abruptly. She briskly walks off towards the stables, a tacit command for Joel to follow. She mounts her horse and watches Joel clamber onto his. Gritting her teeth, she fumes, "Your sharp retort answers my question. And if it we were not so pressed for time, I would use that time to teach you a lesson about speaking to me in such a disrespectful manner." She spurs her horse and quickly adds, "You may be the light, but as you said yourself, I am your mother." Her horse bounds from the stables and out into the open field.

Joel charges after her, calling out, "Hey, where are we headed?" Receiving no answer from Lara, he resigns himself to finding out once they get there. Suddenly unnerved, he pulls up on the reins and stares out at the countryside before him. More hesitantly he calls out to Lara, something in his voice possessing her to halt her steed and turn to face him. Licking his lips, he starts. "Lara, we killed all those men last night, didn't we?"

She nods. "Yes. What's the problem, Joel?"

"Where are all the bodies?"

Scanning the field for any sign of the battle that had taken place the previous night and finding none, she frets. "I ... I don't know." Rearing her horse, she urges, "Come on. We are running out of time." Once more she sets out in a mounting gallop that leaves Joel hard-pressed just to keep up, her black stallion skirting the edge of the forest.

For an instant he loses sight of her as her horse breaks left into the forest. His own horse, however, gallops along the invisible path that Lara had taken through the woods. He can once again see her up ahead, a dot of white on black as she barrels through the forest as if the trees weren't even there. Then even this smudge on the horizon disappears as Lara rides on, multiplying the distance between them.

The leaves whip past him as his steed darts past trees, dodging them moments before Joel even has a chance to react. He realizes that although he holds the reins, the horse is guiding him. Joel is somewhat freaked out by this, but as long as he isn't running into trees or being hit by their low boughs, he cannot complain. A thundering sound rips through the air, startling Joel enough to make him almost lose his seat. Regaining his balance, he pats the horse's neck in gratitude that it had not faltered. "I have no idea what your name was before, or even if you had a name, but from here on out, I will call you Thunder."

The thundering noise is louder now, but it no longer frightens him. He is more scared of the cliff ahead and the fact that Thunder exhibits no signs of stopping. He pulls up on the reins but the stupid creature ignores him. Digging his heels into the sides of the beast, he screams hysterically, "Stupid. Blind. Dumb beast!" Closing his eyes, he holds his breath in preparation for the fatal plummet he knows awaits him. He feels the muscles of the horse move beneath him as the stupid, blind, dumb beast continues its deadly gallop into oblivion. When the weightlessness that should have already come fails to arrive, he shuts his eyes tighter, fearing that this is some malevolent trick to get him to open his eyes and see the nothing below him as he falls to his doom.

He lurches forward as the horse comes to a sudden stop. Confused, Joel chances to take a peek. Lara sits on her horse before him, her features a mixture of amusement and frustration. Joel looks behind him to discover that he has safely crossed the rift. And to his right rises a magnificent waterfall. He looks back at Lara, flustered and fuming, "Why didn't you tell me that the stupid horse could fly?"

Lara sets her jaw. "It can't. You forget so quickly that I control the wind. And the horse is not stupid." She sniffs. "Considering your attitude earlier, it only serves you right. Now, I need your help. Or rather," she motions towards the ground, "they do."

Joel peers around the horse's head which had been blocking his view. He scrambles off the horse when he sees Kae and Chase frozen in the epitome of death. His heaving frame towers over them, casting a long, dark shadow upon the ground. The sight of his brother lying there makes his stomach heave, but he finds himself unable to look away. He stares for a long while and an emptiness begins to consume him, driving away the pain and the regret that he had felt numerous times before. He ponders why this is so and comes to the conclusion that whereas there previously was the possibility of seeing his brother again, death is a journey from which he, or anyone else for that matter, cannot return home. At least, home in the sense of the earthly place we are eager to leave and upon leaving it yearn to return to through the course of our mortal lives.

He feels that his mind should be racing in a desperate search for answers as to why his brother is still here, what had happened, and what he can do to help, but is not surprised that he has been so analytical up to this point. Somewhere deep inside, he feels a twinge of sadness but he shuns the feeling. Too many tears have been wept already. And his grief will not save his brother.

Joel looks at the waterfall before him. "With all its power and majesty, we have no way to harness it. If only I could take that energy and transfer it to them, just as I had drawn the energy from the stars last night." He looks at Lara, the skeleton of an idea forming in his mind. "Can you build a fire?" Remembering his manners, he quickly adds. "Please."

Lara nods and sets about collecting the needed materials.

He turns his eyes upon Kaela. She looks so peaceful. The sadness slowly creeps upon him again, cutting through the numbness and finally breaking his trance. He swallows the remorse building up in his throat, but it is there again and he must swallow once more, and once more. His vision clouds as the well-springs of his eyes are replenished, threatening to overflow and fall forever upon the pallid statue of the angel in blue.

His tears fall upon Kae's body, but instead of rolling off her skin in thin rivulets, they dissolve upon contact with her flesh as the dry earth would hungrily drink the drops of an infrequent rain. His eyes burn with the salt of his tears and all he can say is "Of course." Joel catches a teardrop on the tip of his finger and carefully places it upon Kae's partially open lips. He watches hopefully, leaning over her so the remainder of his tears would not be wasted on the earth. When he can cry no longer, he tells Lara, "I have done all I can. Take her into the water. Let her breathe its air."

Lara follows his instructions, taking her sister in her arms and floating into the mists over the river. Joel watches until they disappear and then turns his attention to his brother. The fire Lara had built is a strong one, and he is glad for it. He needs all the help he can get. Taking a deep breath, he focuses on the task at hand until that is all that exists. All other thoughts are driven away and his emotions are forced into the deepest chambers of his heart. Placing the palm of his right hand on his brother's neck and holding his other hand palm up out towards the fire, he closes his eyes. At first, there is only darkness with the morning light creeping in at the edges. Letting go of the physical boundaries of the world, the darkness consumes the light and is complete. He can feel a warmth on his left that is accompanied by a dancing red light and he invites it into himself, drawing the energy of heat and light and transferring it into the receptacle that is Chase's body.

The source of energy dwindles and the link is broken. Joel opens his eyes and his senses are bombarded with the life thrumming around him. Through the gray tendrils issuing forth from the charred kindling of the fire, he can clearly see the array of blues, reds, and yellows that color his surroundings, blending wonderfully into the purples, oranges, and greens that are its derivatives. The smoke from the newly extinguished fire invades his nostrils but the piney smell of the forest holds rein here.

He can hear the water thundering over the cliff as if he were directly below it, and he could taste the sweet honey air. When he pushes his left hand against the earth for balance, he can feel the earth pushing back. And so each atom, each fiber of his being, was intrinsically connected to the rest of the universe and the rest of the universe to him. He is able to perceive the tiniest speck of dust and ascertain the smallest trace of a thought. For each leaves their own signature, a message floating in the sea of oblivion waiting to be deciphered, and only he has the key.

He senses Lara approaching and turns to face her. He smiles inwardly at the surprise registering on her face, catching her despite her extensive measures to be stealthy. She clears her throat. "I did not want to disturb you, but it seems you have finished here." She kneels beside Joel but stares at Chase. "I knew that if they had any chance at all, you would be the one to give it to them. Now all we can do is wait and pray that our hopes are not unfounded and our efforts are not in vain." She clasps her hands before her and frets. "I understand how you transferred the energy from the fire to Chase, but what energy is there to be had in a tear? And how come you only had me build one fire instead of two?"

Joel stretches his cramped legs out before him and ponders the questions before answering, "To answer your second question, I had to take into account their respective abilities. And these abilities I had discerned through a heightened intuition that seems to accompany the powers of energy. So, in considering their ties to fire and water, and their contrary natures, I logically came to the conclusion that while fire would save one, it would be the death of the other. Here, my deeper intuition also played a role, for if I had given in to the sadness I felt at the prospective death of my brother, that too would have killed him. In truth, I was not even aware of such a consequence and so my actions were a very real manifestation of my hidden powers."

Joel scratches his head. "Now, as to your first question, the answer is a little more complex." He pauses as he gathers his thoughts. "Pure water, like that of the waterfall, is a molecule. And because it is a molecule, its components do not possess a charge. Sure, pure water is an excellent conductor of electricity, but that charge must be introduced. Tears, however, contain a compound of salt. And salt is the most ionic of forms one can achieve in nature, an ion itself being a charged particle. Therein lies the difference. And because of this intrinsic property, and with the added fact that the tears were my own, myself being the essence of energy, that energy was transferred into the electrolytes to provide the current necessary to revive Kae. And after this introduction of energy into her system, the pure water would be enough to sustain her while at the same time cleansing her system of the ions that would have, in time, led to a deterioration of her abilities...."

Lara stands and looks down at Kae, resting on the bank where she had left her. "Because the electrolytes would just keep flowing through her body, and with the energy that had been required to save her no longer needed, it would have sent a shock through her system."

Joel nods suspiciously. "That is correct, but I wonder as to how reading romance novels can lead to a greater understanding of chemistry."

Crossing her arms, Lara shrugs nonchalantly. "And I wonder how you convinced Maria to let you keep your pet squirrel in the house."

Joel opens his mouth in protest and then just as quickly closes it, sighing, "Just please return my science books to my library when you are done with them."

Lara smiles her victory. "And I will not tell Maria about Sparky." She sighs, "I slapped her, you know."

Joel looks up. "Do you regret it?"

"Not at the moment ... but in time I must forgive her trespasses and she must forgive mine."

Joel nods contemplatively. "Yes, in time."

CHAPTER TWENTY-ONE

Her world was shrouded in darkness, a palpable presence threatening to draw her away from a light of which she can only remember, and with that memory suffocate her. The dense air clung to her like a second skin, drawing tighter around her body with each straining breath. Something like sand sifted between her fingers and toes as she desperately crawled forward, strangling the hopelessness that coaxes her to give in and rest. She thought to herself that she must be in some ethereal desert, highly conscious of the oppressive heat seemingly magnified by the bleak blackness of her surroundings. She felt as if she were trapped in a sphere of ebony nothingness that absorbed all the heat of some unknown source while simultaneously banishing the light which is her distant destination, her only hope of salvation. Unable to stand and too determined to rest, she continued her crawl through oblivion.

Pants of excruciating effort escaped from her dry throat, the futile licking of the deep and flaky crevices that had been her lips only amplifying their sharp sting. Her arms trembled with exhaustion and her chapped skin began to prickle in the heat. The last vestiges of her strength stripped from her, she collapses onto the swell of sand and rolls onto her back as she gasps for the air that refused to come. The sweltering red blisters covering her hands burst, the bubbling blood mixing with the scorching sand in a cacophony of absolute anguish, irritation, and pain. She would have cried out had she a voice to do so.

And then she saw it. It was faint at first, a spot of gray in the infinite night. It seemed to be a star, struggling to shine and only growing brighter as she focused on it. Then, one by one, more points of light broke through the darkness. The radiance showered down on her like a heavenly rain, its droplets soaking into her body and extinguishing the perilous heat that had consumed her. The wetness seemed to course through her like blood, herself feeling the energy that slowly replenished her strength. A drop of light landed on the corner of her mouth and her thirst was forgotten. She lay there breathing in the air of effused light that continued to rain down upon her, driving away the oblivion that had been her sphere of existence. The starlit rain dwindles, the black clouds receding from her mind until they too fade, leaving behind a colorful arch of promise that she is safe.

Kae can feel the wet but solid earth beneath her and the gentle mist of a waterfall wrapping around her like a comforting blanket. She opens her lilac eyes to see the crystal-blue waters rushing down from the mountainside and the emerald-green leaves of the trees framing the azure sky soaring above her. A rainbow dances amongst the clouds of mists and she smiles. Remembering the events that had brought her to the place of forever night, she scrambles to her feet. She ignores the lightheadedness that plagues her and endeavors to keep focused. Her heart races frantically as her eyes scan the riverbanks, looking for some sign of Chase. Finding nothing, she closes her eyes and whispers a distraught prayer, calling out his name.

She can feel the bond between them but it is weak, as if his very soul was drowning in some liquid opaqueness. She reaches out and can see him now, his arms flailing as he frantically swims for that unattainable light. She cries out in despair, unable to help him. He seems to hear her plea, for his eyes open and he struggles harder for the surface. His mouth moves, and although she cannot hear the words, she senses that he is calling her name.

The scene expands to encompass a sphere of watery bleakness, an oblivion much like her own. She sees him struggling but making no progress. Her heart leaps fiercely one last time against her chest and experiences a paralysis of sorts as she comes to realize the inevitability of his efforts. She is reminded of her own futile struggle, thinking that if some watcher had looked upon her they would have observed the scene of which she now beholds. She takes a deep breath, holding onto the hope that whatever gift had been granted her would also be bestowed upon Chase.

She watches helplessly as his movements become more labored, eventually becoming more spasmodic until slowing to a heart-wrenching stop. She cries out once more, a desperate sob more than anything. His lips part ever so slightly and this time she can hear him as he calls her name. A sadness pervades the fading blueness of his eyes as an even sadder smile spreads across his serenely calm face.

Her heart lurches and she feels the urge to vomit, but she cannot tear her eyes away from this specter of death. Her love had drowned in the inky waters of nothingness and all she could do was watch. She can still feel the bond between them that had not broken even in death, but looking upon his unmoving body denies her any consolation.

A light surrounds the ebony globe. The waters of its surface evaporate in the white heat of a steady temperature that is careful to not boil the liquid in fear of cooking the body floating lifelessly in it. The waters recede as a white cloud forms around the outer surface of the sphere, but Kae wearily opens her eyes in the knowledge that the holy light had been too late.

Kae stares solemnly up at the cruel clarity of the blue skies. A gray cloud of smoke enters her vision, drawing her gaze towards the cliff. Two figures are silhouetted in the smoky screen, one standing and the other crouched. She can hear their voices over the roar of the river but the words are indecipherable. Taking action not borne out of curiosity but rather an overwhelming need to not be alone, she climbs the hill. She reaches the crest and makes her way for the cliff, the voices becoming clearer as she approaches and the smoke settling to a thin film. The two figures were making some sort of agreement, the tone of their voices shifting from analytical, to sarcasm, to a severity that sends chills through her body.

She recognizes the voices now, Lara being the one standing, and Joel, now reclined upon the rocky ground, had been the crouched figure. Their backs are towards her and she means to make her presence known, but the body lying on the ground brings her movements to a halt. The two people blocking her view only provided her with a small portal to see through, but what she saw was enough. Gathering her courage, Kae takes a tentative step forward.

Joel turns his head in alert of her presence, abruptly standing up and smiling his obvious delight. Lara turns as well, letting out a deep sigh upon seeing her sister alive and well. Kae ignores them, her eyes focused on Chase sprawled so haphazardly upon the hard earth before her. His black hair seems to shine red in the sunlight, and she remembers the comment he had made about her own hair. Slowly she kneels down beside his body, her features a pristine mask of calm to hide the torrent of emotion raging just beneath the surface. She stares at his bare back, the sweat upon it glistening in the sunlight....

Kae quickly rises to her feet, biting her lip with a hesitant hope. She looks over her shoulder at Joel. "I saw him die, yet he sweats."

Joel nods. "He did die, but I reached him in time." His expression is a mixture of pride and sorrow as he holds Kae's gaze. "He lives." As if to accentuate his words, Chase moans feebly.

Kae rushes to his side, helping him in his effort to sit up. Caressing his face with her hand, she stares gladly into his bright blue eyes. "Hello you."

Placing his hand over her hand resting on his cheek, he smiles. "Hello."

• •

Jessica stares unblinkingly at the untouched scrambled eggs and half-eaten bacon on her plate. She notices Tom sitting across the kitchen table from her, inhaling his breakfast and occasionally passing a furtive glance her way. Maria bustles about the kitchen, more for her own distraction than a necessity for the room to be clean. Jessica can feel Maria's eyes upon her as well, trying to bore a hole in her mind in order to decipher the thoughts and emotions that she may be feeling. Annoyed by their uneasiness, Jessica rises abruptly from her chair and dumps the lukewarm food, including the dish, in the trash receptacle. She glares at Maria, daring her to voice a reproof. Storming through the threshold, she strides to her room and slams the door shut, making clear her wish to not be bothered.

Maria wrings her hands as she looks to Tom for reassurance. Setting her resolve, she stalks out of the kitchen and into the corridor. She gently knocks on the door to the room that Jessica shares with Kaela, whispering a feeble, "May I come in?" She receives no answer so she tries the doorknob, finding it to be locked. Sighing, Maria pulls out the crystal in her apron pocket and transports herself to the other side of the door.

Not even startled by the uncanny intrusion, Jessica speaks evenly, "Nice trick, but that doesn't impress me much. And it only proves that you have absolutely no regard for my privacy." She stares harshly at Maria, her eyes glimmering with meaningful contempt. "Now do that shimmery thing once more and disappear into thin air. Who knows, you may be trapped in that between state of not here and not there and I will never have to see or speak to you again. I would like that very much, Maria."

"So this is the type of person you choose to become: resentful and cruel? You may not choose to recognize me as your mother and that is something I will just have to live with, but nonetheless I will not let you give up. I will not stand by and watch you waste away to become a bitter old hag who scorns her life."

Jessica smiles disdainfully. "I do not scorn my life. I scorn you. And I have not given up. You have." She gestures wildly. "You see me as some weak, little, ignorant child. You are so afraid of saying the wrong thing, the word that might tip the balance against you. In case you haven't noticed, the word has been said. The balance has been tipped. And if I were some weak, little, ignorant child, you wouldn't have said the word in the first place. You knew what the repercussions would be, yet you confessed the truths you had hidden. And if I were some weak, little, ignorant child, that fact alone would have allowed me to forgive you, but I can't." She huffs. "And as far as I am concerned, all you have done is watched, so how would this be any different? Because you have finally acknowledged me as your daughter? No, I will not accept that nor will I accept that your heart had acknowledged what your words could not."

"Scorn begins with but one seed, and that seed will continue to grow until it consumes you. If you continue on this path, let me forewarn you that it shall be your downfall."

Jessica sighs in frustration, "Is that one of your visions, or is that some philosophical garbage one recites when they can find no words of their own?"

Maria stares blankly at her. "Experience is the best teacher. I have seen resentment turn the most noble of ladies into a power-hungry witch. She had fallen in love with a man whose heart belonged to another, and in her resentment was seduced by a power that promised her everything but would inevitably not only destroy her but those around her. Her name was Mala."

Sighing, Jessica sits down upon the edge of her bed. "You draw comparisons where there are none. I am a fourteen-year-old peasant girl who has visions. And with these powers bestowed upon me, I can have everything, but I do not want it. I am only human and I cannot ignore my emotions but nor will I let them cloud my judgment. You cannot expect me to be happy and polite all the time, for what is happiness and politeness without sadness and rudeness to counter it? As the world seeks balance so must I, but I must first come to terms with myself and what I must do. But you must understand that lying to me does not help, nor do excuses help to find a solution to the problem."

Maria sighs and sits down next to her. "You are far more mature at fourteen than I was at that age. There is much expected of you and you have only just recently discovered your powers. Please, let me help you. If you will not let me be your mother, let me be a friend. But you must also understand that you must discover your past for yourself, as part of the learning process and to better understand your power. The same goes for the others. I am bound to an oath to let you discover the right path for yourself, but I may serve as a guide. My roles as a mother and as a member of Oracle Seven are founded on this." She smiles slightly. "Yesterday you had essentially asked whether or not Ashe is your brother. He may not be by blood, but his mother and I raised you two together as if you were. He knows you as his little sister and he loves you dearly. Do you not love him as your brother?"

Jessica closes her eyes. "I do. But in acknowledging this love, I must deny another."

Maria clutches her hand. "If denial is the path you have chosen, remember that your mind can be fooled but true love never lies. You will look coldly upon him and speak harsh words but as you do, your heart will only be torn. Will you be able to look into his eyes, seeing the love he bears for you, and not falter in this resolve? And if you can, will you then run to your room and cry, keeping a stern face during the day but weeping throughout the night? And when you find this balance you are looking for, will you be so indifferent to your surroundings that you will simply no longer care?" Her brow creases in concern. "Jessica, in the strength of your resolve, this pride shall be your undoing. The line is not where you have defined it. Day and night coexist in an interval of time that we designate as twilight and that ambiguity is the bane of the human condition. Our vision is only clear when it is predicated on truth."

Setting her jaw, Jessica whispers tersely, "Thank you for the advice, but I have made my decision. For a time I had indulged in the fantasy, but I must return to reality. Ashe is my brother and that bond transcends all else."

Maria is obviously torn between her duty and her conscience. "If that is your decision," she rises and proceeds towards the door, "just know that what you have called fantasy is reality. You have believed the lie."

Unlocking the door, she turns the knob and leaves, closing the door softly behind her.

Jessica stares gravely out the window, her back straight in the epitome of composure and resolve mirroring that of a cold sculpture of stone. A tear threatens to escape from the corner of her eye but she brushes it away. She stands and closes the heavy curtains, blocking the light that had pervaded the room and leaving her in utter darkness.

CHAPTER TWENTY-TWO

Two travelers stare across the valley littered with the white tents of the camp. Tendrils of smoke rise lazily from abandoned campfires and banners wave despondently in the subtle breeze. A few dogs search absentmindedly through the field but there are no other signs of life. Even in the sunlight of midday the eerily tranquil waters of Cape Terna that lie beyond seem a sadder shade of aquamarine.

Cole shrugs uncomfortably as he passes a glance towards Ashe, raising his brow in sarcasm. "This looks rather promising."

Ashe shoulders his pack and sighs, "We have come this far. And who knows, the occupants of those tents may still be in them or out on some expedition." He starts down the hill and Shadow follows him.

Cara emerges from the forest, whistling upon seeing the desolation spread out before her. "For all those tents, one would imagine that the camp would be more... sprawling." She looks at Cole. "Well, we will know more once we reach the camp." She paces down the hill, catching up with Ashe and leaving Cole alone with his doubts.

Presently Cole joins his companions, walking briskly down the hill into the valley of solitude. He marches on ahead of them towards the command tent as designated by the multicolored pennants adorning the threshold.

The flap of canvas is rolled to the side and he can see a rather young gentleman leaning over a table perusing several maps and marking various points upon them with a red pen. Cole remains standing outside and clears his throat, indicating his presence. The man looks up at the sound, his calculating brown eyes peering intently at the guests. Sticking the red pencil behind his ear, he rolls up the maps and stands up straight. Clearing his throat, the man speaks with reservation. "May I help you?"

Cara pushes her way between the two men. "Hello, Chris."

A light dances across his eyes for an instant but no smile reaches his lips. "Mistress Cara, what a surprise it is to see you here, although I wish it were under better circumstances. I trust you bring news of the utmost urgency."

Cara nods and indicates her companions in turn. "This is Cole Blader and this is Ashe Sylvan. They are new recruits bound for the Nesthra Islands. Our paths crossed on our journey here. You can trust them."

Humor plays across his features. "That I will decide for myself." He looks at the two men. "I am Lieutenant Christopher Atkins and when on the mainland I am your commanding officer. You will address me as 'sir' and I expect no less than the utmost regard for myself, your own persons, and your peers. We are fighting a war. Squabbling amidst the ranks will not be tolerated. Save your rage for the enemy. Is that understood?"

Cole and Ashe reply in unison. "Sir, yes sir." Cole shifts his balance from one foot to the other and ventures. "Sir, may I ask as to where are all the men?"

Lt. Atkins clasps his hands behind his back. "That, Private Blader, is exactly what I would like to know. A week ago three thousand men set out to secure the area. The last reports brought by a rider indicated that they should have returned yesterday morning. We are scheduled to ship out on the morrow with six-thousand men, but half of them are missing." He runs a hand through his short, thick brown hair. "I have sent out twelve scouts and all have returned empty-handed."

Cole and Ashe look at each other in a silent understanding. Cole speaks. "Sir, we believe we know what has become of your three thousand men. On our way here, we encountered a score of monsters. They had been chasing Cara here but beforehand they slaughtered an army of three-thousand men."

Lt. Atkins sits in the leather chair behind him. "What proof can you offer of such an outrageous testimony? For I find it difficult to believe that only twenty creatures of the dark could defeat three thousand men. And what is more intriguing is that, if your tale is true, you encountered the same number and live to tell the tale."

Cole replies, "I am offended by the implication that we are somehow in league with these foul beasts, and you should do well to thank us for providing the information that others have failed to obtain. And not only do we live to tell the tale, I can assure you, as can Cara, that the dark minions which have plagued this camp are no more. As for proof of our testimony as to the fate of your men, I can offer none for their bodies are in the hands of the enemy. We arrived at the battle site after the fact, but the stench of blood and magic still hung oppressively in the air."

Lt. Atkins scoffs, "If there were no bodies, how can you be sure there were three thousand, much less one?"

Cara asserts herself, "For one who preaches of unity, Chris, you seem rather eager to instigate a fight. You are the officer here, so command your behavior."

Chris accuses her, "And you seem rather eager to defend this man whom you have just met, Cara."

Rather calmly she retorts, "He doesn't need me to defend him. I am merely warning you that you are crossing the line and that you have passed a rather unfair judgment upon someone whom you have not even made an effort to know. And your cruel insinuation indicates to me that you still harbor the grudges of your past. I could very well be equally cruel and state that your change in character is suspect."

Speaking as if Cole was not even present, Chris glowers, "Why do I have the feeling that you trust this stranger more than you trust me at the moment?"

Cara leans down to rub the fur behind Shadow's ears, looking mean-ingfully into Chris's cold eyes. "Perhaps, because I do. There is a traitor in Oracle Seven. This message serves as a warning, and however you construe this warning is entirely up to you." Weary of the tense transaction, she exits the tent with Shadow loping alongside her.

Cole watches her leave, his mind trying to piece together the jumble of information he had just received, and Chris watches Cole, trying to discern the manner of the man whose very presence disturbs him. Cole runs after Cara, oblivious to the attention being paid him.

Ashe clears his throat, speaking for the very first time, "Sir, do you believe in God?"

Unperturbed by the question, Chris answers resolutely, "He has always been there for me, guiding me and revealing to me who He is. And knowing who He is, I trust Him completely. He gives my life purpose and offers a hope in a world that would otherwise be meaningless. So yes, I believe in God. How could I not?"

Visibly relaxed, Ashe smiles. "Then by the strength of your conviction I see that you are no traitor. Now, let me confide in you something that may prove to be enlightening." He leans forward as if in conspiracy. "If you have faith in God, and man was created in His likeness, would it not also be prudent to have faith that He is at work in the life of your fellow man?"

Staring at Ashe as if seeing him for the first time, the lines stretched across the lieutenant's brow become less pronounced and his eyes dance with some thought akin to kindness. This silent moment of appraisal passes and he once again focuses on his duties, placing before Ashe a crisp piece of parchment accompanied by a quill and ink pot. With a command to his voice inherent of his position, Lt. Atkins speaks, "The paper reads: *This is a contract for military service. A consignment of three years serving under the banner of the Golden Bear of the Emerald Army is to be initiated upon day of receipt. Be informed that desertion will be considered an act of treason, and the punishment is death. The conscripted person shall exhibit conduct becoming a soldier with the utmost regard for all persons involved with an emphasis on the citizens of the enemy state. Any case of an atrocity committed against members who pose no evident* means of harm shall be prosecuted by a court of law, and in the case of a guilty party those involved shall be dishonorably discharged from the military.

For participation in the military, the enlisted member is warranted a starting monthly salary of five hundred Gems. This amount is subject to change. Weekly allowances ranging between ten and one hundred Gems may be awarded for merit, leadership, contribution, and/or physical achievement. Each soldier shall be supplied with uniform, boots, sword, knife, and blanket. Those serving as medical personnel shall also receive these accoutrements along with the supplies necessary of the profession. When in camp only, daily meals shall be served and fresh linen may be furnished upon request.

Early termination of military service will only be granted for reasons of the medical nature. If the soldier is severely wounded in battle in such a manner as to be unable to perform the tasks required of him/her, he/she shall be honorably discharged. Should the wounded soldier choose to remain in the army, he/she shall be evaluated and, if seen fit to serve, shall be assigned to a stationary position at headquarters. Afflictions of the mental or emotional nature that interfere with the performance of the soldier are to be considered case by case, and if severe enough may warrant discharge in a manner as seen fit by a court of law.

Temporary leave, however, may be granted by special request taken to the commanding officer in charge of the specific unit of which the soldier is assigned. Such a request must be written and must be authorized in order to be official. Be informed that this is only a request and the granting of it is not guaranteed. In times of war, absence without leave will be handled as a desertion.

Upon completion of term of service, the soldier must turn in sword and knife as supplied by the Emerald crown as well as any medical supplies but may keep uniform, boots, and blanket. A monthly salary in accordance with the amount earned in the final month of service shall be awarded for a full year after completion of consignment requirement, provided that the *person remains an exemplary model of behavior and holds allegiance to the crowned king of Smithee.*

This contract is lawfully binding and any breach will be considered a crime. If you understand and agree to the terms as described above, sign your full name in the space provided." Lt. Atkins clasps his hands behind his back as he concludes his reading, patient and reserved as he lets Ashe read the contract for himself.

Humor plays across Ashe's features as he reads the last line. "This makes it sound as if I really have a choice." Dabbing the quill in the ink, and somewhat amused by the attention to tradition, he signs his name and pushes the document across the table towards Lt. Atkins, who signs it as well. Ashe stands at attention. "Sir, it shall be an honor to serve my kingdom under the command of an officer such as you."

Lt. Atkins nods. "Yes, but I doubt your friend will share the same sentiments. Have him report back to me as soon as possible."

Ashe salutes and turns to leave, but Chris beckons him, "On second thought, stay. I make it a point to get to know all who are under my command." He motions to the chair and smiles warmly. "So, Private.... Pardon me, I seem to have forgotten your name."

Ashe takes the seat proffered, clearing his throat uneasily. "Sylvan, sir."

Recognition dances across his features for an instant, before settling into the stern repose becoming an officer. Lt. Atkins shifts slightly in his seat, however, and his smile seems to be more forced. He continues, "Ah, yes, you must be from the Sylvan cottage nestled between the two great woods that cover this continent."

"I was not aware that the cottage was so famous, sir," Ashe replies warily, contemplating the manner of this man of which he had been so certain only a moment ago. He peers around the small tent, noting the various maps and books. They are mostly books on strategy, history, and geography, but a few on mythology caught his eye. Jessica had always loved reading the mythos of Ilia, having always been fascinated by the unusual and mystical realms as created by these fantasies. He himself had always thought them to be exaggerated, but he could not deny their basis on truth considering the circumstances. In truth, he had only been considering the circumstances without focusing on what they meant. From the day he received the summons, his goal had been to get to Cape Terna; and now that he is here, he finds himself pondering a simple question—why?

Lt. Atkins speaks. "Is there a particular volume you are searching for? I must apologize that my collection is not as extensive as I would like, but feel free to borrow anything that may seem of interest."

Ashe scratches the back of his neck, somewhat abashed. "Sorry, sir, you were saying?"

Lt. Atkins shrugs. "It was of no consequence. In your silence I have learned more about you than a simple question could have discerned. Sylvan, hold onto that little cottage of yours if it will help you survive the war, but hold no illusions that when you return it will remain as you had left it. Three years is a long time, and things, people, change rapidly in times of war. Do not forget where you come from, but do not let that memory strangle you."

Ashe stares solemnly at the lieutenant. "Wise words, sir, but save them for the weak. My memories are bittersweet and lack the substance to perform such a task as you have described. The only strangling will be done by my hands to those black Sentran hordes who dare to terrorize our borders."

Lt. Atkins nods. "Well spoken, but soon we shall see if you have the mettle to match your claim." He leans forward. "Now, tell me more about these creatures you encountered."

"Sir, I mean no disrespect, but you have heard my story and only a fool will repeat words that the listener will only choose to ignore. If I may ask, sir, how is it that six thousand men have been rallied for this cause? I was unaware that Smithee had even half this population."

Lt. Atkins shakes his head. "Your words lie, for they in themselves are disrespectful, but I will disregard them and will answer your question." Leaning back in his chair, he continues, "What most people see of Smithee are farmers who work the land, but the heart of Smithee lies within the land itself. High in the mountains, deep within caves, and low in the tunnels that demarcate the land below where the wind blows, thrive the "Peoples of the Earth," and from whence do we obtain the men of whom you speak. And in the earth do many men still wait, wait for the summons for which they were born to answer."

Ashe laughs. "That was lovely, sir. Real poetic. And strangely reminiscent of a legend I once read; but if what you say is true, then the time of judgment is upon us and this war is the spark to the fire that will consume the world."

Lt. Atkins sighs as he places his chin on his hand. "A crazy notion, isn't it? But one thing does concern me: why are you here?"

Ashe clears his throat. "There was a letter. I was summoned. I am to protect the people of the Nesthra Islands, guarding them from persecution and repression."

He taps his finger upon his lips. "But why?"

Ashe opens his mouth but his throat is dry. He finally answers in a hoarse whisper, "The circumstances…," his voice trails off as he finds himself unable to finish.

Lt. Atkins leans forward, vehemently pressing his point, "Ashe, I know who you are. Do you?"

He stands angrily. "Just because my last name is Sylvan…."

Lt. Atkins stands as well, interrupting him, "That is only a name. True I recognized it, but I should have recognized you for who you are immediately. Cara had been trying to tell me, but I was too… suspicious… to notice." He clears his throat and walks around the table to stand before Ashe. "You are a Chosen One."

Ashe takes a step backward. "No. I am a guide to the Chosen One. That is my task. I should never have come here. I have strayed from my duty."

"You have signed the contract. Your duty is here." He sits upon the edge of the table. "Desertion in times of war is paramount to treason."

Taking an offensive stance now, Ashe glares at the lieutenant. "Is that a threat ... from a traitor?"

Lt. Atkins stares back at him, but his look is of pity. "It is a warning, from a friend. I mean you no harm. As you, I too am a guide, and like your own duty, mine also rests on more than one man. Those who are Chosen are chosen for a reason and they each have their own task to perform. Circumstance may have brought you here, but to this end is where your destiny lies."

"And what if I shun this destiny you speak of?"

Lt. Atkins smiles sympathetically. "Then again I ask you—why are you here?"

• •

Cara shivers as a shrill wind races through the desolate camp. The wolf pants heavily at her side, its breath curling in the unusual cold of late spring. She has always hated springtime for its indecision. Warm one day, cold the next, or warm but windy, or rainy. Frustrated, she crosses her arms and squeezes her eyes shut. The wolf nudges its nose against her leg, as if reminding her of its presence. Shaking her head, she kneels down and scratches the wolf behind its ears, still contemplating on what she should do. It would seem that spring is not the only one that has trouble making a decision.

One of them would surely ask her questions, so her options were to tell the truth, lie, or expect them to respect her wishes of remaining silent on the subject. But they had saved her life, and for that she owes them an explanation. Whether to be candid or open is yet to be determined, her discretion or lack thereof depending on them.

Shadow leaves her side and she knows that one or both of them approaches. Slowly she stands and turns to face him who would be either her savior or her executioner. Somewhat embarrassed by the sudden surge of emotion at the sight of Cole, with his mysteriously dark features and penetrating gaze, she looks down at her hands folded before her.

His approach was silent as ever, yet she could sense his presence and feel those gorgeously dark eyes of his staring at her, boring a tunnel to the very core of her being. Gathering her courage she lifts her head to look at him, and upon seeing the concern drawn across his face, she realizes that no matter how hard she may try, she will never be able to lie to this man. They have only just met, but such a condition seems trivial to her now. A knot forms in her stomach, and she knows that this is guilt; guilt for even considering keeping her secrets from him.

Preparing herself for his interrogation, she takes a deep breath and waits. And she continues to wait, wondering what is keeping him. All he does is stand there, not even seeming to contemplate how to begin. And then he does something of which she had never expected. He smiles. Not a coy or a sympathetic smile, but he smiles in such a way as to light up his face and make his eyes dance with some ethereal flame. All of her apprehension melts away and she finds herself laughing. Why, she could not say, but she was laughing all the same.

Putting his hands on his hips, Cole laughs with her. "That was great. It seems that your confidence and willfulness are not to be strangled by a sense of propriety. You remind me a lot of someone I know."

Cara teases, "I have never met anyone like you before." She pokes him in the chest. "So, who is this person that I remind you of?"

He shrugs. "A girl back from where I came from. Two, actually." He laughs at the look of affront on Cara's face, smiling in the realization of how she had taken his words. Shaking his head, he clarifies, "They are like sisters to me, and I love them both as sisters."

Detecting the hesitation in his voice, Cara ventures, "Perhaps, you love one more than as a sister?"

Cole stares at the dreary gray fog rolling in from the bay. Squinting his eyes as if shielding them from a blazing red sun whose presence at the moment was best described as questionable, he takes a deep breath. "I thought I did, for a time. But it's like the wind. You can feel its gentle kiss upon your neck, its fingers rustling your hair, hear the whispering of its words, taste the sweet fruit of its being, and smell its enticing fragrance all its own, but the moment you reach out your hand or try to embrace it, it drifts away as if it had never been there to begin with. That is the essence of my love for this woman—unrequited and unspoken, yet perhaps only existing because we always yearn for that which is beyond our grasp."

"And if things were not as you say they are?"

Cole laughs bitterly. "It is useless to try to change what is, so why should I ponder on what could have been?"

The sour tone in his voice makes her regret broaching the subject. And as he spoke of his hopeless love, the more she felt she could relate. How could she ever hope to compete with this woman whom he has, in not so many words, deemed as perfect? She can now admit her foolishness. She had blamed Chris for her own ignorance. The futility of her puerile infatuation would have crushed her spirit had it not been for the sudden recollection of her duty. Her duty transcends all else, even love, and it is the means to her survival.

Sitting down on one of the log benches crudely placed around the remains of a campfire, he clasps his hands together before him with his elbows resting on his knees and questions politely, "Cara, may I ask you a personal question without you taking offense?"

Cara sits down across from him, her posture involuntarily mimicking his. "You may ask the question but, as to my offense, that depends on the question." She hangs her head and whispers, "But even if I were to take offense, you at least had the propriety to warn me, unlike myself."

Noting her discomfort, but uncertain as to the source of it, he continues, "Cara, why did you defend me, or rather, why did you feel the need to address Lt. Atkins' behavior, and in front of us for that matter?"

She had been expecting a *What is Oracle Seven?* or *Were you and Chris a couple?* but this, this she had not been prepared for. She had been ready to give facts and reasons, but this question puts into play her feelings and, given her feelings, any reasons she may have given to hide those feelings would be transparent. Her mind struggles to form some excuse, some lie, but the effort is in vain. She could not lie to him. This much she had already admitted to herself. Sighing, she looks up at him, avoiding the deep black wells of his eyes in fear of getting lost in them forever.

"I wanted Chris to see that I was no longer the frightened girl he had once known. I once thought that I loved him. But I was young and it was convenient because I knew that he loved me. From the way he was treating you I knew that he was jealous, and I played on that. He had been cruel and deserved the shame. I want you to trust me." She dares to look straight into his eyes now. "But those are only excuses. True, it is what I did and it is what has happened and it is what I thought, but they do not answer your question. The why is this: I felt that I owed it to you. I felt that I had to prove something to you. And by you, I do not mean you and Ashe. I mean only you." She studies his reaction, disappointed by his apparent indifference. Sighing, she tears her eyes away from his, suddenly flushed and becoming annoyed by his interminable silence. She shakes her head, admonishing herself. What had she expected? Him to rush to her side and comfort her? Profess his undying love for her?

Cole stares at her, even after she looks away, seeing the weakness she obviously felt. But the sight of her has never invoked in him a sense of pity. She possesses this inner strength and confidence; a fiery determination that flares just beneath the surface. He could see it in her eyes whenever she dared to look at him. And when she did look at him, there was a connection. He could not explain it; himself unsure whether it was mere curiosity or something more. She was a mystery to him; infusing him with a desire to unlock her secrets.

And, more importantly, she is here, a reality unclouded by the fantasy borne from years harboring thoughts of what could have been. He had been foolish before. And now he is scared. Lara had been safe, convenient, because he knew that she would never see him as anything more than a brother. With Cara, he is in danger of having the walls he had so carefully built around his heart come crashing down. Of course, all these feelings he kept hidden behind a mask of indifference. It hadn't been hard. He has been wearing one for most of his life. In seeing the despair wrought on Cara's face, though, he knew it was time to put the mask aside. He wanted to comfort her, tell her what he has come to understand his own weakness, but the words simply wouldn't come. He found his mouth opening and closing, and his hand twitching, but his thoughts escaped from the confines of his mind as if someone had thrown open a door.

She rises to leave and he sees his chance slipping through his fingers. Cara is not the inconstant and intangible wind, but in the next moment she would be gone just the same. Her back is to him now and he feels more than sees the ends of a rope fraying and its separate threads spreading out to live their independent lives in the obscurity of an unknown yet decidedly harsh world. Some feeling stirs deep within him, agonizing in its sudden intensity. A slight breeze ruffles his clothing, seeming to calm him and allow him to gather his thoughts as if it had pushed the door to the cell of his mind closed. Standing, he speaks softly. "The wind whispers to my soul...."

Cara stops at the sound of his voice, its softness melting her and nearly bringing her to tears. She can feel him looking at her and she is immediately regretful. She should never have stopped. She is only torturing herself. She cries under her breath. "Please, don't speak...." Biting her lip, she takes a few steps forward.

Cole clears his throat. "The wind whispers to my soul, igniting the fires of my heart and rescuing me from this sea of despair...."

She finds her feet stopping once more. Her mind wills them to keep moving but they refuse to listen. Her heart pounds as his words echo through her head and fill her soul with longing.

Stepping forward, he whispers, "To the earth my body is bound, but my spirit wanders the boundless horizons of the heavens. The current of your love sparks new hope...."

Cara clenches her fists at her sides as she finishes the poem, "Yet from the arms of love I flee, falling from Grace to the dark depths of eternity." Turning her head only very slightly, she whispers, "The Song of the Forsaken."

Cole moves behind her, his breath warm against the back of her neck. "Yes. It's strange really. I had always done my best to avoid the fantasy realms of myth and magic, but it seems that the past few years of my life have been spent in a daydream." He laughs at the irony. "And now the reality that I finally face seems to lie in the words of a poem straight from legend."

Cara looks down at the ground, painfully conscious of his proximity and the unexpected turn their encounter had taken. "So, are you forsaken as well? Do you fear to love?"

He laughs uneasily. "Why is it that I can face twenty creatures of the dark without even breaking a sweat, but the moment I face you, I can barely even breathe?" Wiping his sleeve against his damp brow, he is somehow not surprised that his hands are shaking. His entire body tingles and he passes into a hysterical stage of unexplained euphoria. "Your presence does something to me, and I can no longer hide behind the apathetic walls that serve to both protect and imprison." He places a hand on her shoulder, forcing her to face him. "Cara, will you help me break free? Or will you leave me forsaken?"

Looking into his eyes and for once seeing the emotion that he had tried so hard to conceal, her resolve shatters. This man before her is broken, asking her to mend the wounds he has ignored for so long. She can see him being suffocated by his own doubt, dragging her down with him. She lifts her chin in sudden confidence. "No. I cannot help you."

He desperately searches her features for an answer, confused. "You will not help me? You will forsake me?"

Cara smiles sadly. "I said that I cannot help you. There is a difference. And you have forsaken yourself."

She turns to leave but Cole gently grabs her arm. His mouth drops open, but then he closes it in defeat. Releasing her arm, he whispers hoarsely, "Will you return to Verdana now?"

She nods. "My duty here is done. But another task awaits me." She hesitates and then finally looks at him again. "Cole, I...take care of yourself." She holds her breath for a moment, fighting her urge to resist and losing, but the inertia of reason keeps her moving forward. She dare not look back. She has made the first step. She must see this through. She can be of no help to him if he has already admitted defeat.

He watches her slender form walk steadily away from him, her soft brown hair loosely swaying in the gentle breeze. He remembers now that he had forgotten to tell her how beautiful it was, not all constrained and twisted up into a bun. She is a woman with a character to match his own, and now she dons the mask he had finally laid aside. A drop of wetness falls upon his cheek and he furiously wipes it away. He can feel the walls he had torn down being rebuilt. He had taken a chance and had been denied. This time, he would fortify his walls with the regret of a love that was refused the chance to blossom. Each brick would serve as a reminder of a longing, and now, a painful truth.

With each step she took his wall grew higher and thicker, but her words laced with some harrowing prescience stayed with him and halted him in his task. He pants heavily as the new barriers of his existence bulge with uncertainty. Cupping his hands around his mouth, he calls out. "Cara!"

Seeing her falter, he runs towards her, Shadow sprinting alongside him. He stops in front of her, blocking her path, breathing heavily and smiling. "Cara, will you fly with me?"

A light dances in her eyes as she opens her mouth in unrestrained delight. But an overwhelming sadness paints her features with its hopeless hues and her mouth closes, setting into a frown. "How can you fly with broken wings?"

CHAPTER TWENTY-THREE

The dark knight kneels before a regal woman dressed in a low-cut gown shimmering white with the light of the artificial moon. "It is done, my queen." He turns up his head as the corner of his mouth twists into a sinister smile. "The wheels of war have been set in motion, and the Chosen have taken up the cause."

Mala leans forward in her throne of twisted metal gleaming black and white, her long hair falling before her in rivulets of a black stream. "You find this amusing, my lord?"

The man rises to his feet, clearly unafraid of this powerful woman sitting before him. "I find it pathetic, Your Grace, and none less than we had expected. They have been secluded and now the world will come rushing in at their feet, asking them to save it. They have only just learned of their powers and are but children, in all senses of the word. Their power may be great someday, but that day has not yet come; nor will they ever surpass your own power, which has been strong for the better part of thirteen years and growing stronger with each day that passes. Pardon my forthrightness, my queen, but they have no chance." He snickers as a sly smile stretches across his face. "Humanity gets in the way of human ideals."

Leaning back in her chair, she sighs in frustration, "You underestimate them. Just as you had underestimated me. You forget there had been a time when I was the pupil and you the master." She motions to the luxury around them. "And now, look at what we have become. Look at what I have accomplished. I am not ready to lose all I have gained just because I was too blind to see my own weaknesses. They may be children, but they are not without their seven stupid guides." She smiles at the discrepancy. "Six."

The man smiles with her. "However, I still think you put too much faith in them. After all, what is faith to one such as you? What is loyalty? Love?"

She rubs her temple. "I tire of your games. Make your point and then leave me to my solitude."

He bows deeply. "As you wish, my queen. The point is that there is no point. The war gives you something to do, an outlet of the power surging through you. In the end you will gain nothing, and you know this. All you have is this waste of a continent, your power waiting to be unleashed, an army of the dead and magical, and me. You may gain the world, but what will you do with it? Everyone will be dead, everything will be scorched, and as for the one you seek... well, what love can you possibly bear for him? You tried to kill him. And when everything is said and done, when the world is nothing more than ashen remains, only I will stand beside you."

Mala scoffs, but her lips curl in amusement. "You presume far beyond what suits your station. You are a resource, that is all, and you know this. And in knowing this, I am left wondering why you stay. Why do you remain as my most loyal of pets? Or is that a deception? Do you plan to betray me, just as you have betrayed your friends and your duty? Or do you hope to gain something from this arrangement? Oh, yes, you only wish to serve, as you have repeatedly stated; that, and stand beside me as I look upon the ruin of the world." She yawns meaningfully. "You are beginning to bore me. And you do realize what I do to pets in which I have lost interest, don't you?"

The knight strides towards the platform, the black curls atop his head bouncing in rhythm with his step. He stops short of the throne and presents himself with the utmost confidence as he spreads his hands palms up before him in mock supplication. "This choice is my own, and as long as you will have me I am yours. But know this: I am not your minion, Mala. I come to you as a man. I am no more and no less. True, I have witnessed countless lifetimes and have been endowed with certain knowledge, but I am still a man. And you, my queen, to whom I have imparted my knowledge, are still a woman. And you speak of my betrayal as if it were only yesterday. I have come too far, come too close to achieving my goal, to turn back now. And if I remember correctly, it was you who came to me, the jaded princess who wanted revenge. Through me shall you have your vengeance, but only if you let go of the light and step deeper into darkness. You continue to cling to your life line formed of hope, faith, and loyalty ... and love, but these are nothing compared to the power that I can give you." He holds out his hand, offering it to her as if it were the most priceless of gifts.

Mala smiles as she rises from her throne to accept the proffered hand, to accept the darkness. "And what is your goal, my sweet?"

The dark knight chuckles. "Now that you want something from me, I am no longer your pet? Even if I was of a mind to divulge my plans to you it would make no difference, for then I would have to kill you." He waves his hand before him and a dark portal opens menacingly, a supernatural rend in the fabric of time and space.

Her eyes glitter with avarice as the purple abyss contracts and convulses, the rhythm of its pulsation a sourceless call beckoning to her from oblivion and charging the air around it with its undeniable power. Taking his arm in her hand, the corner of her mouth twisting ever so slightly, she lets her black knight lead her into the darkness.

Leaving behind the world of the living and entering into the shadow realm, the couple steps through the gaping maw swirling with the rage of some malevolent storm and the portal disappears behind them, blinking out of existence. Mala releases her companion's hand and takes a step forward. Peering over the precipitous ledge, she smiles and beckons for her knight to join her.

He does not warrant the chasm with even the smallest of glimpses, himself already knowing what rests therein. Instead he closes his eyes and listens, listens to the moans of the dead as they mumble their eternal agony. He could sense them standing, swaying to some unseen and sinister melody, awaiting the redemption that will never come. These thousands of dead men are forsaken, for in their stubbornness they shunned the light. So when the time of their death was upon them, they had no power to escape the darkness. He opens his eyes and smiles, relishing in his victory. Turning towards Mala, he bows deeply and calls forth in exultation to the heaving mass below them. "Bow before your queen, oh minions of the dark, and you shall rise up once more as stayers of the light."

A cry issues forth from the dead and rotting as they uniformly lower to their knees, as if such a simple act held within it the gift of rebirth. Their unintelligible moans now a chorus of expectant voices, calling out the name of their queen. "Mala! Mala! Mala!" Allegiance was a small price to pay compared to the prospect of an eternity in Hell.

Mala spreads open her arms in a gesture of invitation. "Rise, my army of the dead, and be welcome, for you are home."

• •

Jessica lies motionless upon the wooden floor of her room, her fingers still clutching the blanket which she had pulled off the bed when she had fallen. Her eyes stare unblinkingly at the dusty rafters of the ceiling, but then she squeezes them shut and a rasping breath escapes from her slightly parted lips as she desperately tries to drive away the nightmare displaying itself before her. Her breathing settles and she lets out a moan in accordance with the soreness pervading her every muscle.

Slowly, and with the aid of the bedpost, she pulls herself up. A few moments pass and she is finally able to stand on her own two feet, albeit rather unsteady at first. Plodding her way towards the door, her leaden feet threatening to drag her down with each step, she painstakingly obtains her goal and upon reaching it leans her weary forehead against the warm wood of the door.

She can hear voices, strange voices, originating from the other side of the barricade. They are strange in that she does not recognize them and one of them she simply does not understand why she is hearing it. Is she still dreaming? Or is she hallucinating? She puts her ear against the door in order to hear the conversation better.

The masculine voice that is not supposed to be there is speaking now.

"Were there any other survivors? What news of the Emerald Castle?" His voice is almost accusatory. "Was there no warning? Were the stone walls and iron gate of no protection? How dare they? What are they looking for?"

She hears Kae's voice, trying to soothe the angry man. "Chase, you're frightening them. I know that you're angry, we all are, but you must calm down. We all seek the same answers, but we must first attend to the survivors. You have to realize that this is war and innocents will be caught in the middle of it. You can't save everyone and you cannot change what has already happened. Verdana is gone." She speaks to the strangers. "Come, rest. When you are ready, we will talk. Joel, will you please get some extra blankets from my room? Thank you."

There is a gentle knock on the door and reluctantly Jessica opens it to admit Joel. She recedes into the corner, watching him as he retrieves the blankets from the closet. He turns and makes for the door, never once looking at her, but he stops suddenly and squints his eyes as he turns his head to look at her. Smiling, he speaks, "I'll be back shortly. We need to talk." With that he leaves the room and treads down the hallway to the vacant one that had previously been occupied by Cole and Ashe and now serves to accommodate the refugees.

Keeping his promise, he returns and closes the door behind him. He takes a seat in the chair in front of the desk and stares at Jessica for the longest time before finally beginning.

"So much has happened today, and its barely even noon. I am exhausted, running on this sense of duty and obligation. This morning

I was up with the sun. Lara had said it was urgent, that we may already be too late. We took the horses into the forest and she led me to a waterfall. We found Kae and Chase there, dying. I saved Kae. I saved her with my tears. But Chase died. He died, Jessica." He rubs his eyes, irritated. "And then he was alive again. He's here now. He never even left Smithee. Apparently he had gotten lost, met some guy named Old John who told him the way to Verdana and about a guy with a boat named Tom. He said—Chase said—that Tom had business at this cottage, but he didn't know what it was." He looks searchingly at Jessica but receives no response from her. He continues, "Tom gave him a ring and he gave the ring to Kae. They're together now. But Chase says that he cannot stay here, that he must continue his journey.

"Kae says that last night they had fought some Sentran soldiers. They destroyed the bridge by the waterfall, decimating a good portion of the dark forces, but they had overexerted their powers and it nearly killed them. That rain of fire we had seen was Chase's power. Kae has the power of water. It seems that we all are Chosen. I still wonder what exactly that means." He sighs, "All this and I still have not had breakfast.

"And when we rode out this morning, all of the bodies were gone. Disappeared. I don't like it. When we were coming back we came across some weary villagers. It was then we learned that Verdana had been destroyed. The Sentran soldiers had burned it when they made their way here. It is uncertain as to how many were able to escape. Lara is searching the area for survivors as we speak. According to the refugees, there had been no warning. It had all happened so quickly. They said that the streets were filled with smoke when they stumbled from their homes. The villagers were crowding at the portcullis gate in order to escape, but it was closed. It was then they realized that the enemy still remained outside the gate and that the walls themselves, stone walls, Jessy, were burning. Can you believe that, Jessy? These men were not human."

Jessica whispers, "They had been, once. But you're right. They are not human. They are not even of the living. This was an army of the dead, revived by magic. The battle last night only delayed the inevitable.

The bodies did not disappear nor did we kill them. They merely returned to the darkness and will rise again. I have seen this."

Joel runs his hand through his hair. "So there is no end to this. They'll just keep coming. What are our options? Keep them here, somehow, until we can find a way to defeat Mala?"

"We'll do whatever we have to. We have to keep in mind that Mala is our prime target, her army a mere distraction, and she is, without a doubt, the most vulnerable. She hides behind power and throws her minions upon us because she herself is powerless. Her magic is not her own. It is not who she is, unlike our own powers which define us. Her ability is to change what is natural to unnatural. What has been created is utterly destroyed and warped to suit her own purposes." She moves towards the window, momentarily looking out of it before turning her gaze upon Joel. "We must focus on the task at hand. I ... we cannot be distracted. Everything is too complicated now."

Joel bites his lip. "You have made your choice. I will respect your decision."

Jessica stares at him, almost viciously. "I told you not to read my mind. Does no one respect my privacy?" She sighs as she sits down upon the bed. "But at least you understand."

Joel rises abruptly, pushing the chair aside as if it had somehow scorned him. "No, I do not understand. Am I not real enough for you? Or is it that I am too real? No, don't answer. Like I said before, I do not need to read your mind to know what you are thinking. I see it in your eyes, and if I wasn't so exhausted I would feel sorry for you. You confuse what is real and cloud reality with assumptions and obligations based on half-truths. And because of your indecision, things become complicated. Only when you adjust your vision, your perception, will you find the peace necessary to fully embrace your power and who you are. And until you do, until you can be comfortable with yourself, I will always be a challenge to you. We are only fourteen. We have time. But I cannot wait forever."

Jessica rubs her temples. "What are you saying, Joel?"

He throws his arms out to his sides, frustrated. "Isn't it obvious, Jessica? There can be no 'us.' At least not until you have worked through whatever issues you have. I will always be there for you, as a friend, and I will be your strength if you need me to be, and I will always believe in you, but I should never have kissed you. You weren't ready." He sighs and walks towards the door, his back to her. "Let me know when you are. But know that I am making no promises." He opens the door and in the next flurry of a moment he is gone.

Jessica jumps out of bed and slams the door shut, panting heavily in anger and regret. She makes her way back to her bed, huddling beneath the covers and drawing from them whatever comfort they could provide. Wiping away an angry tear, she grits her teeth. "I hate you, Joel Blader. You can have your pity, your friendship, your strength, your stupid faith. I don't need any of it. I don't need any of them. All I need is my power." She cries despondently, frightened, as those dark words and darker visions dance through her head. "Is this how Mala feels? Am I ... like her?"

• •

Maria stands atop the hill with her arms crossed, as if in physical imitation of the inner struggle to keep herself calm and collected. She speaks as Tom exits the cottage and walks towards her. "I've sent the birds. One should reach Cape Terna by nightfall but it will take a few days for the other messenger birds to reach the outlying kingdoms."

Tom clears his throat. "Do you think they'll reply?"

Maria shakes her head. "No, but at least they will know of the situation. Mayhaps we can save other towns from the fate that was visited upon Verdana. At least they will have warning." She turns to face him. "Has there been any word of survivors?"

"Lara isn't back yet." He sighs as he puts his hands in his pockets, "That could mean anything."

She smiles weakly. "Let's be hopeful for once, all right? I don't think

I can stand to worry anymore. I'm exhausted." She sighs, "I just wish that things were … different. I want her to be happy."

Tom smiles, noting the turn the conversation had taken. "She's just like her mother, you know. Stubborn, willful, proud…."

Maria punches him lightheartedly. "I just wish I could be the mother to her that she needs. She's drifting… and I'm frightened. I guess I always had this picture in my mind of her throwing her arms around me—accepting me for who I am—and us having long talks in the middle of the night, sharing our thoughts and secrets." She turns her head towards the heavens. "Is it too much to ask for my own daughter to call me 'mother'?"

Tom wraps his arms around her, bringing her hand up to his lips and kissing it. "Give her time. Her entire world, her entire life up to this point, has been shaken and she is confused. She needs to regain her balance, doubly so considering her abilities, and she will. We all need time to adjust to these rapid changes that are occurring."

Maria looks back at him. "Do you ever tire of running? Do you regret the responsibility and sacrifices expected of you and for you to make?"

Tom inhales deeply and clenches his jaw. "This is our duty, and even though at times I stop along the trail and wonder what other possibilities lie hidden deep within the forest around me, I have promises to keep. I cannot be selfish. The future of the world as we know it is at stake. Such a responsibility is a burden that we all share, we inhabitants of the world. We do not need to be part of some prophecy to make a difference. The future is a construct of individual lives, each person a brick contributing their share to create a firm foundation infused with the perseverance and strength of the human spirit. I have traveled the world many times over and have witnessed many miracles. I have seen an old man who could barely walk rescue a child from a burning building. I have seen battle-hardened generals of two warring nations put aside their swords so that they may shake each other's hand, all at the bequest of one woman. I have seen children grow into adults. And I have seen mothers who have given their children better lives then they could ever have wished for them-selves. These are all miracles.

"There are times, however, when there is a crack in the foundation. It is infinitesimal at first, but stress factors enable the crack to grow and spread its influence to the other bricks and eventually the foundation upon which the future was built begins to crumble. Now is one of these times and the condition of the world will continue to worsen lest the few strong bricks remaining join their individual strengths and relieve the stress placed upon the world.

"These bricks serve a purpose, yes, but they by themselves can only see the world through their own eyes. They do not possess the ability to see the whole picture. Thus, they must seek aid from the Builder of the world, who laid the very first bricks of the foundation. The Builder, being merciful and not wishing to see his creation destroyed and saddened by the taint ravaging His world, shines His light upon the world so that He may guide the Chosen. That is our duty. We are His guiding light. And in remembering this, I continue along the trail upon which I had been walking, gladly sacrificing my own selfish desires to tackle the responsi-bility bestowed upon me."

Maria steps away from him as she remarks rather coldly due to her guilt. "A simple no would have sufficed. Please excuse my moment of selfishness."

Tom puts his hands on his hips. "I must say your egotism astounds me. First, you accept your role as a member of Oracle Seven, therein giv-ing up your entire life to be infused with the light of wisdom; then you seclude yourself in this little cottage so you can raise seven orphans all by yourself, thus relinquishing your freedom, your marriage, and your ticket to see the world which you so love; and ... and you even have the nerve to give your memento of me to some seventeen-year-old girl so that she could be one day be reunited with her true love. I am amazed. Simply amazed."

"You mock me with your words," Maria nearly cries. "What about the fact that I am trying to convince you to stay or that I am more concerned about my daughter acknowledging me for who I am than about the refugees slumbering in our house or that, no matter how futile, protecting the children from the pain effected by their ignorance is more important to me right now than guarding this knowledge that we had sworn to keep hidden until the time for revelation is come?" She sighs, "I know my duty and I will not endanger our mission, but that does not make this any less hard to deal with." She fumes, "All of a sudden you are back in my life and just as quickly you will be gone. Do you have any idea what this will do to Jessica? And me? You are allowed to walk away from your problems but I, I am the one left to deal with them. Do you realize what it takes to raise seven kids, all different and unique but still with the penchant to drive you crazy at the end of a long day? Did you know that Joel had a rat for a pet and even brought this thing into the house, our house? I found it in his laundry of all places. And after the day is done, when I am alone in my bed, I think of you, wondering where you are, if you are even still alive, and if you ever loved me. Do you still have my ring, or did you give it to the first pretty girl that looked at you with shy eyes? Are you married, Tom, and have you come here for a good time because you were in the area?"

He interrupts her raving, "I am married, Maria."

Maria nearly chokes on her own words. "What!?"

Tom laughs and draws her into his arms. "I am married to you, or have you forgotten? But you are right. I no longer have your ring. I gave it to Chase."

Maria hugs him in merriment, forgetting her anger of only moments before. "You did? Seriously? How did you know? Did you have a vision too?"

Tom smiles. "Yes, seriously. But no, I did not have a vision. Although ... there was something in the air.... It just seemed the right thing to do."

She sighs happily as she turns in his arms and stares out at the western horizon, "I am glad." She looks back up into his blue eyes, darker than normal in this receding light of the afternoon. "For eleven years I have harbored this fear that my life before Oracle Seven was just some dream, forever fading into fantasy as the harsh reality of the present takes precedence. For eleven years I have been perpetuating this fate that is my duty to protect but at the same time have run from my own destiny. For so long I had looked at my youth as something that I had sacrificed, but I see now that it was something that I had been given, just like the prophecy-free childhood we had given to the Chosen, to our daughter. But whether a sacrifice or a gift, this is my life now and I will live it." She turns her gaze upon the orange sky beyond framed by the rugged mountains of the west. She smiles and whispers a prayer, "I am ready to receive the light, O Lord. Light the way so that I may guide your lambs through the encroaching darkness."

Tom lowers his head to be level with Maria's, resting his chin on her shoulder. "Hmm? What did you say?"

Shaking her head, she continues to stare out at the horizon. "Nothing. I was just staring at the sunset. You know, it is one of those many things that we take for granted. What if tomorrow the sun did not rise? What if the world was to be forever shrouded in darkness? What would we do? And if we knew of such a phenomenon prior to its happening, how would we spend our last days of sunlight? How many people would accept the inevitability—or worse, perpetuate it—and how many would choose to do something about it?"

Tom laughs as he hugs Maria closer to him. "You worry too much. The Lord Himself fights for us, and as for Mala, well, she has not realized the propensity of the situation she has gotten herself into. With only seven people privy to the most possible of futures for Ilia, the world is already in darkness and its people will continue on in their daily lives strolling down the streets of blissful ignorance. And we who are not ignorant are tasked with letting our light shine in hopes of guiding them onto the one true path that leads to life. Here on Smithee, the war in Nesthra is viewed as far away and separate. People believe this war will never consume them but beneath this false sense of security something terrible and unidentifiable haunts them. Evil will feed on this unspoken fear and, in the end, it will destroy them. Unfortunately, despite our best efforts, some will still choose to live the remainder of their sun-soaked days in the darkness that so blinds them with the radiance of the lie."

"And this makes you cheerful?" Maria asks incredulously.

Tom smiles. "No, but the fact that there is still hope for humanity does. God has given us His light so we can defeat the darkness. He has called forth the Chosen to preserve that light and to teach others how they can do the same. Even the physically feeble or impaired are not spiritually defenseless if they possess this hope. It is when we let the darkness rule our hearts that all hope is lost. There will come a day when there will be no more second chances and the sun will not rise for those that have refused the light. But for now, even for the lost, all the yesterdays and todays have been graced by the presence of the sun. So, yes," he breathes deeply and closes his eyes for a moment before resuming, "for the benefit of those forsaken souls, it makes me happy that Tomorrow is not Today and that when Tomorrow finally does come they will at least have the memory of the sun as it had shone Yesterday."

Maria wraps his arms around her and together they face the setting sun. With a solemn smile a single tear rolls down her cheek and she speaks softly yet resolutely, "That same dark day will be one of glory for the children of the light."

CHAPTER TWENTY-FOUR

The sun was setting and still there was no sign of any survivors. When she had set out early this morning, it only seemed logical that she was the best choice for this seek-and-rescue mission, but as the day waned her hopes died with it. Flying high above the forest and the surrounding area, she could see each little ant scurrying along the ground and even hear them munching on the spoils of their hard labor, but any shred of evidence of human activity was gone. And not gone like it had a mind of its own to get up and leave, but gone as if it were missing—snatched up from this world as it had aimlessly wandered through the turmoil that had become its life.

Some wisp of a whisper had been thrumming through her head all day, but it was always beyond her grasp, beyond her recognition. She would listen carefully, focusing on it just to get some idea of its source, but it seemed to be everywhere and nowhere all at once. Several times the murmur seemed louder in certain places and she would hover there, always trying to tune into it, but then she would be thrown backwards as if she had run into a wall and a sickness akin to how she felt when she had been indoors for too long would overcome her. Once she regained her equilibrium, she would return to the same spot and find it disquietingly empty—as if the nameless whisper had moved on. It was during these moments that she felt utterly shut out from the world, not as the only one left, but the only one left behind. Wherever the human race had gone to, or been taken, she alone had been excluded. She alone had been denied on account of something that she had no control over. She is the Wind.

And then it dawned on her. Hopeful that her epiphany would prove fruitful, she cannot resist laughing away her uneasiness as she makes her way back home to the Sylvan cottage.

Like a breath of fresh air Lara was home again and they all knew that any news she had would be welcome. The waiting was the most unbearable part and in knowing this, Lara began her briefing of the situation as soon as she touched firm ground. Everyone had been outside on the hill, awaiting her arrival as no doubt predicted by Jessica. Letting her arms fall to their place of natural rest at her sides from the slightly extended position that helped her to control her landing, she speaks softly yet loud enough for everyone to hear.

"This land is Smithée, a land of mountains and forests, lakes and rivers. The land itself is alive and it is the season in which the land has been renewed. Its hills sing of the people who have traversed here and toiled here. At no other time is its song so strong.

"Yet, even now, this song is but a vibration upon the strings of my heart. I know it exists, but that is all. I cannot hear it. Its words are beyond my understanding." She sighs and then looks straight ahead, her vision focused on something beyond even her sight. "I am the Wind. The Sky is my Home. The Earth is apart from me and I from it."

She turns to Joel and Jessica and, as if by the strength of her gaze, they step forward in unison as the others simultaneously melt into the background. Smiling her encouragement, she continues, "I reassign this mission to you. This will test your abilities and push them to the limits, and even perhaps beyond them, but through your combined skills, I know that you can accomplish the task for which my abilities were a hindrance. As is always the case, I fear that we do not have much time. Go now. And Godspeed."

• •

"So," Joel whistles, "any ideas on where to begin?"

Jessica ignores him, confidently walking forward through the brush as if she intimately knew each branch and leaf and pebble and their positions relative to herself.

Joel follows her closely, the darkness hiding his smirk but his tone giving away his amusement. "Do you have any idea where you're going?"

Jessica turns. "No, but you're following me and that has to count for something."

Joel shrugs. "Just making sure that you stay out of trouble."

Jessica resumes her path, sniffing in feigned contempt as she does so. "Who appointed you as my keeper?"

"Keeper?" Joel replies in mock offense. "Since when did I become the lackey? You will not catch me bowing and saying, 'Yesth Masther'. Nuh-uh. No sirree. I prefer the term 'guardian angel.'"

"Whatever."

Joel stops and slowly turns his head to look around and above him. A slight smile crosses his lips as he breathes in the wonder he is feeling. "Can you hear it?"

"Hear what?" Jessica calls back to him from a few yards away.

"The spirit of the land is singing. " Raising his arms with his palms towards the starry heavens, he speaks in a voice full of power and wisdom, "The vibrations of its song reverberate through everything that is part of the land; and the land is connected to all things, except the air over which it holds no sway nor bears allegiance."

Jessica turns to stare at him, her lavender eyes sparkling with longing but her voice as melancholy and monotone as the voice in her dreams. "Yes, I hear it, among other things."

Joel breaks away from his reverie to look at her. "Other things?"

The power and wisdom that had been infused in Joel's words just moments ago now lends themselves to that of Jessica's. It is now Joel's turn to listen. She speaks, "I hear the cry of an ancient civilization, first as a rising up of unparalleled victory, and then as one of sorrow as their glory fades into memory and later, as is the fate of all great things, transformed into a legend whose history is considered myth. I hear the story of the past told as something current by those who lived it, and for the sake of nostalgic dreams by those who were born an age too late."

"Well," Joel begins, "it seems to me that the age we live in is not the one that we believe we belong in. There will always be something better. Days of adventure yearn for peace, and tranquil times manifest wanderlust. Why is it that we dream of things that are, given the state of the world, beyond our grasp? Don't you think it to be somewhat hopeless?"

"If they weren't beyond our grasp, then they wouldn't be dreams," Jessica replies matter-of-factly. "And no, for in these dreams do we find hope."

"But dreams fade, just like the starry night as the new day dawns."

"The old dreams are replaced by new dreams." She rubs her hands together, clasps them, and rests her chin on them as if in prayer. "As we change, and as the world changes, so do our innermost desires. Dreams are inconstant, like the moon. But no matter in what form they may come, they still exist. For without dreams we simply have given up, and life becomes meaningless."

"So," Joel theorizes, "the only thing giving our lives meaning is our dreams, which in themselves are empty and inconstant?"

Jessica punches him. "No. We place value on our dreams and, in turn, our lives become worth living. We value life, friendship and love. All these things are desires that makes our dreams that much more substantial. Dreams are only empty if we accept the impossibility of them."

"But they're still impossible, right?"

"You're impossible."

"Haven't we already discussed this?"

Jessica seethes. "Impossible is nothing. It doesn't make a difference."

Joel rubs his chin. "I am glad to hear you say that."

Jessica turns, frustrated. "So then, what was all that about impossibilities?"

Joel shrugs. "Just wanted to see which 'Jessica' I am speaking with."

"You make me sound like I am schizophrenic or something."

"Well," Joel teases her, "you do hear voices."

"I know there is at least one voice that I don't want to hear right now," she retorts meaningfully.

Joel remains silent throughout the rest of the night, moving as quietly as humanly possible through the dry leaves that litter the ground, speaking minimally and only to give advice on which direction they should head. Finally, he speaks, "I know what you want to hear, but I cannot... I cannot... an apology will not mend this."

Jessica stops suddenly, her emotions boiling just beneath the surface of her skin. "Are you blaming me?"

"NO!" Joel loses his composure for an instant but then regains it momentarily. "No. I do not blame you. But neither am I at fault. It is just the situation. It is the way things are. What I ... what you ... what we want ... it's a...," he lowers his shoulders in defeat and sighs, "... it's a dream."

"Right," she sighs, "a dream...." Clearing her throat, she nods her chin towards the east. "The sun is coming up."

They both stand still, watching the golden fingers stretch through the forest towards them, silent, as if witnessing a funeral. The vigil lasts for but a moment before they continue their trek, but it is enough. It will have to be enough.

• •

"You're still here."

Cara turns at the sound of Cole's voice. She looks up at him for a moment before returning her gaze to the rosy skies that herald the dawn. Sitting there perched atop the cliffs with the waves thundering below her, she looks like a bird ready to spread its wings and fly away. But the sadness that consumes her weighs her down and keeps her here, clipping her wings and denying her her freedom. She speaks softly but the wind carries her words to their intended listener. "A bird came in the night. A messenger."

Cole sits down next to her, crossing his legs. "What news did it bring?"

"Verdana is gone. Burned to the ground. No sign of survivors."

"Burned?"

"Yes."

"Mala?"

"Yes."

Cole sighs, "So what are you going to do now?"

Standing, she breathes deeply. "I will go where there is need of me. I will fight. The Sentran shores are calling my name...."

"Cara...," Cole interrupts, "I know you feel that this is your duty, your mission—and I am not telling you to not go—but your wings are not broken. They are merely bruised. In time they will heal." He tries to hold her hands but she brushes his away. He sighs, "I know you cannot help me ... but I promise you that one day I will be ready to fly. I hope that when we are on equal footing that you will fly with me."

Closing her eyes and clenching her fists firmly to her sides, she turns away and speaks forcefully, "I will be on that boat to Nesthra."

Standing, he concedes, "I understand." He starts back down towards the camp below but he stops as he is reminded of something. "Shadow, she likes you. And even considering the circumstances, I know she is glad that you are going to stay with us for a while longer. She will miss you very much when it is time for you to part ways. Perhaps you might consider taking her with you. I know she will make sure you are safe and will not let anything bad happen to you."

Cara turns back to him and smiles through her sad eyes. "Tell Shadow that I like her too, and I too am glad I am going to stay for a while longer. I will miss her very much when it is time for me to leave, so I accept your offer of companionship. I will very much like having her by my side. She will be a kind reminder of the friend that I am leaving behind."

Cole nods and then continues on his way, leaving Cara to her solitude that now seems just a little less lonely. Returning to her lonesome perch, she is once again overwhelmed by the questions that continue to plague her. For the first time in her life, she is uncertain and finds the feeling rather disagreeable. She is daunted by the sense that she has somehow been excluded from the realization of the dream of the future that she is trying to preserve. For the first time in her life, she must look to someone else for the answers. But in order to do so, she must first admit to her inadequacy. Such a submission, however, is not made without the admonition in accordance with one's innate instinct of self-preservation. She must be careful of who she turns to. There is a traitor amongst them. For the first time in her life, Oracle Seven is not the divine council from which she will regain her focus or clarity. No. An outsider is who she needs. She needs Cole.

"Well, if you're coming with us, the boat is almost ready to depart."

Cara turns and stands at the distant sound of Cole's voice. "Yes, I am coming." She looks back at the dark blue vastness and replaces a strand of hair that the wind had blown from behind her ear.

Cole waits for her and takes her hand in his when she reaches him so he can steady her in their descent. "Come on." With a wary look to the skies that had suddenly turned dark and in response to the drastic increase of wind velocity, he adds, "Getting to Nesthra will be half the battle it would seem." She slips slightly on the rocky hillside and his arms instinctively wrap around her waist.

Highly conscious of his proximity, she blushes. "It won't be the only battle."

He looks upon her and laughs. "No. I guess not."

By the time they reach the docks, the water is turbulent and the salt spray washes violently over the barnacled boards. The gray skies are overcast, blocking the brilliance of the sun that is now a hazy orb in the distance. Lt. Atkins pops his head above the side of one of the twelve ships and, upon seeing his men waiting in the relative safety of the shoreline, jumps over the edge onto the creaking port below. He runs a short distance before stopping and cupping his hands over his mouth.

"It is now or never."

Motioning for them to follow, he runs up the gangway, inspiring his men to do the same. The three thousand troops board the ships relatively quickly, motivated to begin with but now apprehensive of the wooden hulls that would carry them across the rough whale-road that led to the enemy's dark shores.

Cara, Cole, and Ashe had wound their way to the front of the crowd, undaunted by the stormy seas that awaited them. Joining Lt. Atkins on the flagship, they were prepared for the worst and had prayed for the best. It would be a bittersweet moment for them all.

As the sails unfurl and the ship exits the harbor, Lt. Atkins gazes upon the shore of his homeland and inhales. "We leave behind peace and come into war." He smiles. "From this moment on we are no longer men of Smithee. We are Ilian."

Chapter Twenty-Five

"There," Jessica points, "do you see it?"

Joel squints his eyes and stares intensely at the spot to which Jessica is pointing. Shaking his head and putting his hands on his hips, he sighs, "Nope. I don't see a thing."

"It's right there."

He turns his head to her, a look of complete helpless confusion on his face. "Right where?"

She taps her foot, contemplating. She claps her hands together as an idea begins to form in her mind. "Okay." Biting her lips, she continues, "Okay, Joel. Close your eyes." She turns his head towards the area and takes a deep breath. "Now do you see it?"

Joel laughs as he reaches out his hand, his eyes still closed. "Yeah. Is it really a … a….?"

Jessica laughs. "What else could it be?"

Joel shakes his head in bewilderment, smiling. "A datrymia." He opens his eyes. "Even now that I know it is there, I still don't see it. I can't even sense it now."

Jessica kneels and summons the bird towards her. "It's such an amazing creature. I wish you could see it how I do. But I think … I think it's a self-defense mechanism. Some sort of invisibility technique."

"Then how can you see it?"

She shrugs. "Perhaps it has to do something with my connection to shadow and light. This bird survives on its elusiveness. It likes to remain a mystery. Extremely intelligent. Highly cautious."

Joel closes his eyes and smiles. "What I see is light taking the shape of the creature. I see its aura." Clearing his throat, he adds, "I see you."

She turns to him. "I know you do. That's why you know me so well."

Kneeling, Joel whispers, "I think it is intrigued by us."

She whispers back, "Why do you say that?"

"Well, it isn't running away."

She considers this. "Or maybe he doesn't see us."

"But it's looking straight at us."

Jessica wonders. "Is it? You didn't see it before and you were looking straight at it."

He opens his eyes as a thought darts through his head. "Jessy, do you think you can turn invisible?"

"I guess it's worth a try." She smiles. "I'll be seeing you."

Joel watches intently as she tries to disappear, incredulous, but not too overtly surprised when her image flickers for a moment and then stabilizes. He claps and nods his head in modest approval but is stricken by the look on Jessica's face.

She wraps her arms around herself and stares at Joel, scared. "Where did I go?"

Joel cocks his head. "What do you mean where?"

She shakes her head vehemently. "I went somewhere. Someplace I have never been before. It wasn't a bad place, but it wasn't here."

"Do you think you can go back there?"

"I'm not sure if I want to."

He nods his understanding. "Okay. Let me try. Tell me what you did."

"I just blinked."

"That's it?"

She looks exasperatedly at him. "I don't know. All I know is what I did and what happened."

He blinks. Looking around, he sighs, "Okay, I guess that didn't work." Something rams into his back, sending him to his knees. He looks behind him to see the datrymia staring belligerently at him. Getting up and dusting off his pants, he questions, "Why did you do that for?"

The datrymia lowers its head and prepares to attack again.

Joel stares directly into its eyes and suddenly the revelation hits him. He can see the bird. The real bird and not just its aura. Putting up his hands in self-defense, he shouts, "Look, birdy, I don't want to hurt you, but if you hit me again, every action has an equal and opposite reaction."

The datrymia raises its head, takes a step back, and stares inquisitively at the intruder.

Joel slightly lowers his fists. Slightly. Keeping a wary eye on the bird, he speaks, "You see me now. Don't you? You didn't see me before. But now that you do see me, you think I am a threat. I was . . . invisible . . . to you before but now that I have made myself invisible—or I believe that to be the case—we exist in the same plane and therefore I am visible to you." He cracks his neck to his right and then to his left. "So the only question I have left is this: you see Jessica. You saw her before. So why attack me and not her? Not that I am telling you to attack her now, of course."

The datrymia looks past Joel and at Jessica. It looks back at Joel and in its silent stare speaks volumes.

Joel nods. "She is not like you. But I am. You are supposed to be unique. You are light. As I am. She is different. And that intrigues you." He smiles as he sees the surprise register in the bird's eyes. "Yeah. I know exactly how you feel."

The bird seems to remember something and lowers its head again.

Joel lowers his fists completely. "But there is something else, isn't there? Are you protecting her?" Sitting down and crossing his legs, he whispers, "So am I."

The bird raises its head, contemplating.

"Will you let me help you protect her?"

The bird shakes its green feathers and the crystal inset into its forehead glows citrine.

"Strange," Joel exclaims, "I hadn't noticed your color before."

The bird lowers its eyes as if ashamed.

He nods. "Ahh. This is your true self. You kept it hidden until now. Do you trust me then?"

The datrymia blinks its eyes and Joel does the same. Upon doing so, he finds that the datrymia is gone and Jessica is sitting on the ground. She smiles. "I could still see you, but for some reason I think it worked."

Joel laughs as he scratches his forehead. "The datrymia running me down gave it away, didn't it?"

She smiles conspiratorially. "So what did you say to it?"

"Oh, that's right. You wouldn't have been able to hear us, would you? Good thing."

She sulks. "You say that like it's so obvious."

"Well, light and shadow is one thing, but sound is a completely different animal. You may hear voices but you are not immune to all forms of camouflage."

She stands. "Fine. But you do realize what this means, right?"

"What?"

"It means," she pokes him in the chest, "Mr. Know-It-All, that you could turn invisible to the world but I will still see you. More fundamentally, I am blind to nothing. And I may not hear everything, but I hear what others cannot."

Joel taunts her. "Are you saying that you are better than me? Because if you are, I would have to say that you're crazy, Mrs. I-Hear-Dead-People."

"No," she shakes her head, "just that we are different you and I." She smiles as she looks past Joel. "It's glowing green now. Do you think it means something?"

Joel rubs his sore behind. "Yeah—jealousy." Carefully sitting down on the dew wet grass beneath him, he lets out a long sigh. "You know, the thing about pain is that the initial shock always seems to be the worst but then there is a period of numbness—which is fine—but it later gives way to a persistent throbbing that only serves to remind you of that initial shock over and over and over again, multiplying it into a million little knives stabbing you at random but stabbing you constantly and ceaselessly."

Jessica laughs at the exaggeration of his condition. "Get over it already." Giving him a hand to help him pull himself up, she sighs, "You'll be fine."

He looks incredulously at her. "Say that tomorrow morning when I wake up and won't be able to move because all of my nerves have been stunned into paralysis. You'll have to carry me over your shoulder for the rest of the journey and I will be of utterly no use to you."

Mischievous as ever, she smiles impishly. "Well, if you will be of utterly no use to me, then I will just leave you behind."

"Touché."

"I ... I...," she stutters, "I was just joking, Joel."

He nods. "I know you were."

She stares at him, seriously and almost as if hurt. "I would never leave you behind."

He nods his head once more. "I know you wouldn't."

She sighs, relieved, "I am glad you trust in me so much. You believe in me more than I have the right to be believed in."

"I wish you could see what I do."

"But I don't."

"Not yet."

She nods. "Not yet."

• •

Through the stories of adventure told by the occasional traveler stopping in for a drink and the dusty old books thrown haphazardly into dustier, older shelves of her father's establishment, Rachel knew that the world—that Ilia—was a large and exciting place. It had to be. But up to this point in time, her life, her world, was very small. It had been defined by four dreary walls with four shadowy corners to hide in. The Green Tavern had been her life, and now it was gone. The fires of oblivion had ravaged her welcome prison and the process was made complete when its ashes were swept away by the winds of inevitability.

Oblivion was her destination. Inevitability was her truth. What else could she—a former barmaid whose lessons were in etiquette and self-debasement and with a natural tendency to blush at the slightest embarrassment—expect? She had no right to entertain this idea that she had this "potential" that everyone speaks so fondly of. But, nevertheless, she did.

Behind the doe eyes and nervous smile awaited a restless spirit eager to be set free. Standing here upon this hill, for the first time in her life she felt alive. She wasn't sure if it was just this place or the people she met here, but something deep inside her was unleashed and she was curious to see to where it would take her. She wanted to be able to tell her own stories. She wanted to see the world for herself.

She knew that her journey had been preempted by the fire—that much she could not change—but she could control where she went from here. She had to be methodical, approach this scientifically, because she knew she had much to learn before she was ready to start out on her own. As eager as she was to set out, she had weighed the consequences of such rash actions and determined that it would be more prudent for her to wait. So prudent as ever, wait is what she would do.

Perhaps what drew her so undeniably to the Sylvan cottage was its centrality in her cause. As heir to her father's place in Oracle Seven, she had been brought up in an environment in which she was always aware of the state of the world. Though only four when she was first introduced to the concept of securing the future of the Ilian peoples, she had understood, to the degree permitted by her age, just how important such a task was. As she grew older, she became more attuned to exactly what would be expected of her when her time would come to inherit her father's position, not because of their relationship but due to her own fervor in resisting the temptations of a cruel promise masked in pleasantry. She knew well the face of evil, though hidden it may be. Its very nature motivated her in her commitment to the fight for good.

And now, removed from the life she had known, she was forced to confront the fate that, though expected, came much sooner than she would ever had imagined. She was eighteen, and though older than the majority of her charges, she felt as unprepared for this challenge as they were ready to meet it. Having just two days ago learned of their abilities, they already seemed as if they had been controlling its powers for years. This fact did not surprise her, for she knew of its integral contribution to their individuality, but she was admittedly amazed at the breadth to which they grasped the gifts bestowed upon them. But there was still much that they needed to learn about the nature of the war in Nesthra. It would fall on her to prepare them for battle and guide them in their respective journeys of self-discovery.

She herself did not possess any great abilities, but she would one day harness the knowledge stored within her father's crystal and that will provide her with the tools necessary to successfully complete her mission. Much like a computer that she had read about in ancient texts, the knowledge contained within could be downloaded, accessed, and retained for future use. And like that ancient device, the information could also be encrypted so only a designated user had access. These computers came before the Great Flood, though and, much like most everything else that existed in the antediluvian era, were destroyed. The High King Donovan and his queen the Lady Gwendolyn chose not to resurrect this technology and it was therefore left buried with the ancients. They did, however, commission the design of seven crystals that had similar capabilities and were powered by interfacing with the user's nervous system and were unlocked with a biometric encryption key.

Many safeguards had been put in place so that these crystals could not be misused should they fall into the wrong hands. So the news that they had been betrayed was very troublesome indeed. How could such a betrayal even be possible? Something malevolent was indeed at work here. Whether this information was given to simply sow the seeds of doubt or it truly identified a grievance that persisted within Oracle Seven remained to be seen. And if the latter, how deep does this darkness dwell? Did a member of Oracle Seven simply entrust sensitive information to someone undeserving of that trust or was one of their own a traitor?

Worse yet, if there is a traitor, had they never been of them to begin with? Had they all been fooled by a demon disguised as an angel of light?

Her father had warned her that in the wrong hands, the crystal had the power to destroy. With all that is at stake and with all the doubts and questions coursing through her mind, she decides it is best to just watch and wait. And pray. She must always pray. Rachel knew that in time, the iniquity would reveal itself.

Pete emerges from the stables and steadily walks over to where his daughter stands. "Rachel." He pauses for a moment to collect his thoughts before he continues, "Rachel, do you remember when I first told ya 'bout Oracle Seven?"

She nods.

"Methinks da time 'as come for me to pass dis burden to ya."

She looks back at him in surprise but otherwise remains silent.

Rubbing his temples, he sighs deeply, "I cannae begin ta illustrate jus 'ow much of a burden dis will be. Mah only advice is dat you trust in God and believe in da power of 'is Spirit dat convicts you. Doubt is a seed dat once planted, only continues ta grow and becomes dat much more difficult ta remove." He falters, as if seeming to catch his breath. He looks intently at his daughter's face as if tracing her image into his memory forever. "You 'ave been such a blessin' in mah life. Mah only regret is dat mah mission 'as left you secluded from da world of which ya're so curious." Taking her hands, he smiles and a single tear escapes the corner of his eye. "Promise me," he coughs vehemently, "promise me dat after yer mission is done, you will visit da land of our forefathers. But make dis journey to Phyrre as much for yahself as 'tis for me and as 'twill be fer future generations. In da meantime, enjoy yer life. Do not waste yer days in regret. Seize yer moments of 'appiness when dey come, fer dere will be plenty dark days when ya're waitin' fer da sun." He hugs her deeply, ignoring the tears streaming down his face.

Rachel lays her head on her father's shoulder. "Why do you cry, Papa? In all my years I have not known you to cry." Pulling away from his embrace, she looks at him straight in the eye. "Why do you act as if you are saying goodbye? And why must I relieve you of this burden so early in this fight? Is this not your mission?"

He sadly shakes his head. "No. Da mission is yers ta undertake. Now, mah darlin' daughter, please. Do ya promise to travel to Phyrre?"

She nods. "Yes, but you still have not answered my question. What is the matter, Papa?"

He smiles broadly though the light in his eyes is faded. "I am glad. And things are as dey should be, mah dear. It seems da Creator is eager ta 'ave me by 'is side. I knew dat sooner or later may time would come, but da smoke from da fires 'ave taken their toll and I find it 'arder ta breathe wit' each passin' moment."

She cradles him as he slumps to the ground. "No, Papa. You cannot die. I am not ready for you to leave me."

"But 'tis mah time, and 'tis yers to fulfill da mission dat I began. Do not fear. Do not worry. Da Lord will always be wit' ya." He rises to his feet. "Come. You 'ave much ta learn in da little time we 'ave left."

She stands as well, wiping away her tears. Closing her eyes and taking a deep breath, she manages a smile. "Yes. There is still some time left. I want to spend it wisely." With that, she takes her father's arm in her hand and guides him down the hill to the path that meanders deep into the Northern Woods and onto where Verdana used to be. The forest was one world which both she and her father had duly enjoyed.

CHAPTER TWENTY-SIX

Rachel emerges from the forest alone. Her eyes are clear and lubricated, so only tiny trails down her cheeks give evidence to the no longer present wetness that had caused them. Around her neck hangs a delicate piece of yellow ribbon from which dangles the crystal that only hours ago had been her father's. She takes a deep breath, strengthening her resolve in preparation for the encounter with her mother and the two members of Oracle Seven. They would want to hear all that her father had told her in his last hours, and her mother would be comforted to know that he had gone peacefully. A light had broken through the canopy to shine upon her father before absorbing him in its radiance. It flashed once and they both were gone, but not before he smiled at her with a youth that belied his joy and wonderment. She would speak of his passing as it had been, but their conversation prior to the event she felt it best to leave partially undisclosed. She was uncertain how much of what he had told her they already knew, but that wasn't justification enough to share with them a secret that her father had left for her to keep.

Much of what he said she already knew. He told her about their mission and their responsibilities. He reiterated the importance of acting only as a guide, not as a diviner. He expressed the dangers of being involved in such a crucial prophecy, of which then he recited the prophetic words that led them all to form Oracle Seven to begin with. He also noted that the prophecy was incomplete, so one must be wary in interpreting the meaning of such passages. For this reason, they must always be aware of the condition of the world and the state which the seven Chosen find themselves in. He explained that there was one guide for each of the Chosen, but that they all worked in unison to effect the salvation of Ilia. Her charge, as had been her father's, was Kaela.

She was told that there would be a meeting to serve as her formal induction to Oracle Seven, but for all intents and purposes she already held the status accorded a member of this secret society. At the time she wondered just how secret it was, given how so many people close to her knew of its existence, but then she realized that Ilia is large with a population many times that which comprised her circle of friends. In understanding this, she was immediately humbled by the notion that so many people, whether or not they knew it, were counting on her to do her job. Her father also told her that when they were all to be summoned for the ceremony, the traitor would be the one who would not shake her hand. Evil cannot touch purity, lest that innocence was proffered as a prize. He could touch the clothing on her body, but to touch her skin would be his death. He may also wear gloves to avoid the contact. These things should she look for in identifying the traitor, and these signs are what she will keep to herself when speaking with the others. It was somewhat unnerving to not even be an hour into the acceptance of her calling and already she is hiding information from the group. These are certainly dark times when one does not know whom to trust.

• •

Jessica kneels down and places her hand on the hard-packed brown earth. "There was a castle here." She turns to face Joel. "But it is gone now ... not destroyed ... just gone. It is as if something just lifted it from its place and relocated it somewhere else ... somewhere near ... yet distant."

Joel scratches his head. "Wasn't Lara saying something about her powers being hindered by the earth?" Scratching his chin now, a smile slowly reaches across his face as an idea forms in his head. "What if the castle sank, along with all its inhabitants?"

Jessica stands. "Don't' be ridiculous. This is firm land, not a quagmire. And even if it did sink, what would be the point? They would be that much closer to the world of the dead."

"Not necessarily. If someone had the power to move earth, or at least manipulate it to one's end, wouldn't they do so to save the people inhabiting it who would otherwise have been ravaged by the fires the Sentran army ignited?"

Sighing, Jessica puts her hand on her hip. "Say I believe your premise. Who, then, would have such a power? I mean, we are talking about a complete concealment from the outside world of not only the building but also of the population. And then these people would need to have some way of breathing as well as some form of sustenance beyond grassroots and bulbs." She raises her finger. "Not to mention, a large enough space underground to hold such an institution without the displacement of the earth being so obvious. Because, as I am very well sure that you know, matter just can't simply poof out of existence."

"Nothing 'poofed out of existence' as you say. Do you not wonder why the ground is indeed so hard? It is not soft as one might expect fertile soil to be or for, say, a forested area like this is."

Jessica shrugs. "So what? All the earth was just packed together? If that is the case, that still leaves the question of how the population would be able to breathe underground."

Joel looks above him at the treetops, putting his fists on his hips. "This is just speculation, but what if the trees acted as conduits for the air? I mean, their roots run deep and their branches stretch high into the sky. Would it be too much of an assumption to argue that if one had the power to move earth, they would also possess the power to manipulate it?"

"Again," Jessica argues, "who could have such power? I am not saying it is impossible, especially given our own abilities, but I am curious...."

Joel smiles, one corner of his mouth slightly higher than the other in an uninhibited display of his satisfaction. "I think that if anyone should know that answer, it would be the trees themselves. Or, at least, their dryads."

Jessica nods, ignoring the silly expression on his face. "Yes, they do know. But they are unwilling to tell me. They say it is enough to know that the people are safe."

Joel looks at her, his senses quieted by the magnitude of her own. She truly is an amazing creature, if only he could put that through her thick head. He smiles. "Yes, I guess that is all we need to know." Rubbing his stomach, he groans. "How does heading back home sound? I think I could use a good meal right about now."

Jessica punches him in the shoulder. "When are you not hungry?" Smiling, she takes his hand in hers and heads back through the forest. "But yes, I think we have found the answers we were looking for and it is time we headed home."

Joel inwardly rejoices at the warmth in her tone and the softness in her touch, but he only nods and sets his jaw. This was definitely a start, but he could not push her lest he lose her forever.

• •

Kae follows Chase into the kitchen and crosses her arms as she takes a deep breath. "So, you are leaving again?"

Chase smiles halfheartedly, his blue eyes belying the sad sentiment he feels at forcing her to go through this again but knowing all the same that there is some purpose to his journey beyond the desire to know who his parents are. He takes a few steps toward her, but then stops and scratches his head as if uncertain how to proceed. "I've never been good with good-byes. I am afraid that if I let myself be close to you, I will not be able to go. But at the same time, if I don't let myself be close to you before I go, I know that I will regret it." Instinctively, he closes the distance between them and wraps Kae in his arms. "No matter what happens, know that I am here with you. And you will always have a place in my heart. I love you, Kaela Lee." He arcs his neck down to kiss her, her lips receiving his with great enthusiasm.

Chase hugs her tighter and kisses her forehead. "You are everything that I am not, and everything that I want to become. You inspire me to do great things, and still I wonder how I am humbled in your presence." Gazing into her eyes he smiles, forgetting for a moment that he is saying goodbye. "Many times I have thought that my pride was the answer, but you have shown me that dignity and honesty are what persevere in times of direst need."

Kae looks questioningly at him. "I do not understand."

Chase laughs and shakes his head, realizing his admission. "I have dreams. I have dreamt of many things, none of them good, and each time you have come to me. On countless occasions have you been my savior, dissolving the blackness that engulfs me with the blue radiance of your healing aura." Running his fingers through her blue hair, his eyes begin to glisten with tears. "Sometimes it seems so real, as if a portent of something yet to come. I wake up and am relieved because of the hope that the dreams offer, but I am also wary of what conditions may lead to me needing rescuing in the first place. The darkness just seems to be so absolute and complete...." He shudders.

Kae smiles warmly, seemingly unfazed by his concern. "I think you worry too much."

Lifting her up into the air, he twirls her around and laughs. "Perhaps you are just wearing off on me." Gently letting her down, he sighs, "But I guess that it would do me good to have a modicum of reservation. It might just keep me out of trouble."

Kae wraps her arms around his neck. "For some strange reason, I highly doubt that. But at least you'll have sense enough to get out of it yourself before I have to trek halfway across the globe just to save you." She smiles. "But before you do leave, there is something that I must tell you." She maneuvers her head closer to his and whispers quietly in his ear, "Adrian is the ruler of the sea."

Chase listens attentively, unsure of what he is really hearing. "What is that supposed to mean?"

Kae shrugs. "I do not know. It is just something that the river whispered to me before you returned from Verdana. I do know, however, that it is something very important even though I do not know why or how I even know this."

Lara stops in the doorway, her face ash-white. "I overheard you talking." She walks into the room and places her hands on Kae's arms. "Kae, I believe that part of a prophecy has been revealed to you."

Kae nods, understanding beginning to stretch across her features. "Yes. I sense that it has. So the question remains, is it of any use to us?"

"Of course it is," Chase answers. "We just need to figure out who Adrian is, where he is, which prophecy is being referenced, and what the context is for that prophecy first." He throws up his arms in obvious sarcasm. "Then after that, it shouldn't be too hard to use this bit of information to our advantage."

Lara sighs, avoiding Chase and instead directing her response to Kae. "He is right."

"I am?" he retorts.

Still speaking with Kae, Lara continues, "He must find Adrian."

"I do?"

"I think it would be best to start the search in Laentus because of the reference to the sea," Lara pauses, "but he would need to go to Gaelith first to find any viable means of transportation. It would not do to go chasing a ghost in some dinghy that is liable to capsize with the slightest chance of a storm...."

Tom enters. "I agree. The waters can get pretty rough. And the sooner we leave the better. I had planned on taking two weeks of reprieve before I attempted the waves again, but it seems that plans change with the tides." He slaps Chase on the shoulder. "Don't you worry, I will get you to Gaelith safe and sound. We head out in the morning." Just as abruptly as he had entered, he leaves.

Lara wrings her hands, sensing the sudden tension in the air. "I should leave you two. Jessica and Joel are on their way home and I want to make sure they do not encounter any problems on the return journey." She turns to leave, but hesitates. Looking over her shoulder at Chase, she regains the resolve that had faltered a moment ago. "Promise me you will say goodbye to him before you go this time."

Chase nods. "Yes, I will say goodbye. And Lara, I am sorry for not having done so the first time. I had been foolish."

Lara smiles. "You always were headstrong. But I think that your premature departure was something that you needed in order to figure some things out. I am not saying that it was not foolish, but you had your reasons of which I think you have resolved. Just be careful that you do not walk blindly onto a path of destruction. You have so much potential, but you also have so much passion. I have faith that you will inevitably make the right decision, but not before being lured by empty promises." She leaves.

"And forsaking the ones that really matter," he adds.

Kae hugs him, her head resting on his chest and her fingers prying open the fist that he had inadvertently clenched. "No." She kisses him. "Remember, in your dreams we overcame the darkness together. For a time you may be consumed by it, but you will not lose me, nor I you. I promise."